HIDDEN COURT

THE GATEKEEPER'S TRIALS: BOOK TWO

EMMA L. ADAMS

To be notified when Emma L. Adams's next novel is released, sign up to her author newsletter.

PREFACE

It was mirk, mirk night, there was no starlight;
They waded through red blood to the knee,
For all the blood that's shed on earth
Runs through the springs of that country.

Thomas the Rhymer

If there was one activity faeries loved more than they loved waging war, it was revelry, especially with free elf wine by the barrel.

Half the Court had turned out for my official crowning as the Summer Gatekeeper, and from the number of noble Sidhe gathered under the roses crowning the ceiling of the main hall in the ambassadors' palace, you wouldn't think they thought humans were less worthy of regard than pond scum. Even the Sidhe were capable of pretending to show me a little respect if they got a free party out of it.

I stood on a raised platform flanked with midnight-blue curtains, wearing a dress of deep green edged with gold that billowed around my ankles. My eyes blazed with green Summer magic, the sun had tinted my hair with blond highlights, and the silver circlet moulded to my scalp. The Gatekeeper's mark, a swirling symbol on my forehead, shone with arresting light, the closest I'd ever come to having the mesmerising ability to enchant the senses the Sidhe took for granted.

Lord Raivan, a Sidhe noble wearing a long green cloak and a hat decorated with bright red-and-orange leaves, called the room to attention. "The Sidhe council recognises Hazel Lynn as the official Gatekeeper of the Summer Court. Do you accept your position, Hazel?"

It's not like I'm going to say no at this point.

My voice rang through the hall. "I accept."

Magic streamed outward from the circlet, bathing the stage in green and gold light. To the watching nobles, I looked like I belonged among their finery, but everyone knew it was as much a lie as the glamour they wore to make their perfect features even more stunning. The instant the Gatekeeper's mark had appeared on my forehead when I was twelve and the magic of Summer had roared to life in my veins, I'd been bound to the Court by a curse so powerful the Sidhe would rather pretend I belonged here than kick me out and risk said curse backfiring on them.

"That is all," said Lady Aiten, a Sidhe with olive skin, a waterfall of dark hair, and long, flowing green robes. "Let the celebrations commence."

Everyone turned away from the stage—those who'd actually been paying attention in the first place, that is—as the hall came to life with noise. Vats of elf wine occupied each corner, while buffet tables lined the walls. Plates were piled high with brightly coloured eggs, slabs of meat and jewelled insects, heaps of bright fruits arranged in patterns, loaves of freshly baked bread.

As I stepped around the midnight-blue curtains flanking the stage, a band took my place and began to play, filling the room with an eerie tune that sounded more like a funeral dirge than a celebratory jig. Some of the Sidhe paired off to dance, while others gathered in finely dressed groups, filling every available space between the creeping vines growing on the stone walls. The hall seemed vast by human standards, but with their dazzling magic, the Sidhe appeared to take up twice as much space as they should.

Walking among the Sidhe were smaller fae—piskies, hobgoblins, wood elves, dryads. I watched a deer bound past into the bushes, never quite sure whether it was a regular woodland creature or an unlucky human who'd fallen afoul of the fae. The mark on my forehead and the magical shield in my family's bloodline curse were all that kept me safe from a similar fate, and while I'd survived to become Summer Gatekeeper, it didn't mean I was under any illusions about the average lifespan of a human who stepped into Faerie. Everything about them—from the music to the food, to their lilting voices and eerie beauty —was toxic and irresistible all at once.

Seeing Lady Aiten heading my way, I ducked into the bushes to avoid another awkward conversation. Ever since I'd caught the Erlking's killer—and discovered Lady Aiten had conspired with my own mother to hide his crown while the conspirators were at large—she and Lord Raivan had sought to ingratiate themselves with my family. I highly doubted she felt any guilt for showering me with accusations and having my mother arrested, so it was likely for appearances alone. I had half a mind to disappear back to the Lynn house before one of the drunken Sidhe wandered through my family's gate, because if anyone in this room found out the Erlking's talisman was hidden in my back garden, I'd get a hell of a lot worse than a jail sentence. My entire family would face execution.

"You traitorous reprobate," a melodic voice purred from behind me.

I whipped around, feeling the sting of magic on my back as bolts of vivid green Summer magic collided in mid-air. Everyone backed away from two Sidhe who circled one another on the palace floor, their eyes alight with passion and hate. One, who wore the skin of a large white stag complete with antlers, shucked off his coat and transformed into a giant furred beast with clawed hands like a bear's. His adversary's lopsided green hat fell to the floor as he turned into a grey wolf the size of a car. With a roar, he lunged at the bear-creature, claws raking at fur, teeth tearing into flesh.

"That's enough!" I shouted.

Magic ignited in the Gatekeeper's circlet, spreading to my fingertips. Vines shot from my hands, curling around the beasts, and with a firm tug, I yanked the brawling Sidhe apart. Their fur retracted, and an instant later, I held two struggling warriors in my grasp.

"What exactly are you two fighting over?" I let the vines drop to the ground, releasing my two captives. "Hey —don't turn into a bear again. This is my party you're interrupting."

The Sidhe who'd turned into a bear spat out blood. "This fool claims to be the Erlking's successor."

I glanced at the other guy, who was bleeding from a vicious scratch on his cheek. The room had gone quiet, the band's music pausing to allow everyone to gawk at the fight. *So much for sneaking out of here.* It'd been a long shot to even consider leaving, considering the Sidhe couldn't get through a five-minute meeting without someone drawing a blade or turning into a beast.

"I am the rightful ruler of the Summer Court," rasped the wolf shapeshifter.

"That's not for you to decide." Nor was it mine, though my real test as Gatekeeper would come when I oversaw the crowning of a new monarch. Assuming the Sidhe ever figured out who the Erlking had nominated as heir, that is.

Evidently, some of them had other ideas about who was fit for leadership. What the hell was I supposed to do, kick the guy out? It was technically my party, after all, but getting into a fistfight with a giant wolf was not my idea of a good time.

"None of us knows who the Erlking chose to be his heir, but I would prefer not to begin my stint as Gate-keeper with any of you murdering one another," I told the two Sidhe. "If you try it again, I'll be forced to shut down the party, and everyone else is having a good time here, right?"

Lady Aiten stepped forward, her deep green cloak parting to reveal a dress of shimmering gold. "If you two are seen near one another again, you will be asked to leave. Is that understood?"

Glaring daggers at one another, the Sidhe gave murmurs of acquiescence and dispersed among the crowd to lick their wounds. Lady Aiten remained standing in the centre of the room.

"Nobody else is to bring up the subject of the Erlking tonight," she added. "The next person to start a fight will spend the remainder of the night locked in the dungeon."

A disinterested murmur went through the surrounding Sidhe, whose attention was already back on the band and the elf wine. I ducked into the bushes again, glad to be out of the spotlight. I'd be lying if I said I'd expected tonight to go ahead without a hitch, given my track record. I mean, the Erlking had been murdered before my Trials had even started, my family had been accused of his murder, and the Erlking himself had sent me a posthumous note with a few cryptic clues about his killers. Add in a mentor with his own mysterious loyalties, a best friend whose own brother had been drawn into the killers' plot and my own accidental acquisition of the Erlking's talisman and it was no wonder I was in dire need of a holiday.

Not that I'd be getting one. The Erlking had left no note of his preferred successor, leaving the question of Summer's leadership up in the air. Wolf shapeshifters with delusions of grandeur were the least of the possible threats to the Erlking's throne, since I had little doubt more of his jailed wife's allies would pop up and try to weasel their way into power. On top of that, it was starting to look like my family's collection of old books might contain a more complete record of the Erlking's family tree than the Courts did.

I passed a fountain occupied by giggling nereids and selkies, skirted a group of gnomes doing some bizarre kind of dance which involved tossing one another around, and found an alcove away from the crowds. There, my mother, the former Gatekeeper, watched me with a mixture of pride and sorrow in her expression, her gaze lingering on the circlet on my head. "I should offer my congratulations."

"Please don't." Mum knew I'd spent most of my teenage years resisting the Gatekeeper's role, and. even as an adult, I'd searched for every possible route to break the curse. I'd been counting on the Erlking being alive, though, and now I'd need to ensure the Courts didn't go to war before I even considered resuming my attempt to remove the Sidhe's hold over my family.

Oh, and do something about the world-destroying talisman hidden in my back garden. Relinquishing the Erlking's staff meant leaving it open for someone else to claim, and I wouldn't trust a single faerie in this room with an electric kettle, let alone a dangerous magical artefact which possessed a consciousness of its own. Even I'd never truly grasped its potency until I'd felt its magic slithering over my skin, but damn if I didn't resent the hell out of it for forcing me to lie to everyone in this room.

"One of us should go home," Mum said in a low voice, "but I don't like leaving you and your siblings alone in here."

"If anyone else starts a fight, I've got it covered." I tapped the circlet with my fingertip. "I'd feel more at ease if someone was at the Lynn house at all times."

I'd prefer that person to be me, but it was my party, and I couldn't keep one eye on the talisman and the other on the Court in the same moment.

"I bet that Sidhe won't be the last to make an open challenge for the throne," she said. "It likely won't stop even when a successor is selected, for that matter."

"Yes, I know, but I'd rather deal with that when the Sidhe aren't all in the same room as several large vats of elf wine," I said. "Anyway, River and Ilsa are here, too. Not to mention my self-appointed bodyguards from the Trials. I'll be fine."

The one person missing was Darrow, but he wasn't part of the Summer Court. It was ridiculous to feel slightly miffed at my former mentor for missing my big event, though he'd never promised to show up. He'd fulfilled his duty and removed the mark binding us, yet he'd been at least partly responsible for me surviving my Trials, and his absence dampened my mood even further.

"All right." Mum's gaze panned across the gathered Sidhe, suspicion lingering in her eyes. "I'll see you later."

Poor Mum. Someone had to volunteer to keep an eye on the Erlking's talisman, but the Sidhe were more likely to notice my absence than hers. As she left, Ilsa, my twin sister, waved me over to the corner where she stood with River, her half-Sidhe boyfriend. Her deep green dress billowed to knee-length, while her hair was a darker shade of brown than mine, a side effect of living under Scotland's clouds rather than the Summer Court's perpetual sunshine. She and Morgan—and now Mum— shared the same dark brown eyes, making me the odd one out among the other Lynns.

"Nice job back there," Ilsa told me. "Breaking up the fight, I mean."

"Not being crowned as Gatekeeper." A smile curled my lip. "That's about as much of an achievement as being born. Zero effort required on my part."

"I don't know about that, those Trials were no joke," Ilsa said. "And going into the Vale... confronting the outcasts..."

"Exactly," said River. "Don't sell yourself short."

"That's supposed to be my line." Ilsa squeezed her boyfriend's hand and smiled.

While River dressed the same as one of the Sidhe, his human heritage was evident in the way he kept his curly blond hair cut short, there were faint traces of stubble on his face, and his body was corded with muscle that most Sidhe hadn't a hope of achieving. His worshipful gaze rarely left my sister's face, and I found myself fighting an inexplicable surge of jealousy.

What's wrong with you, Hazel? Ilsa had probably felt the same envy towards me for years, because being a Lynn who wasn't a Gatekeeper meant suffering the faeries' cruel pranks without the Sidhe's magic to back it up. There was nothing Ilsa had that I didn't... except for a steady relationship, a job that didn't involve answering to the Sidhe, and no destructive talisman whispering dark promises in her ear.

My brother, Morgan, walked towards us, holding a glass of crimson elf wine. I reached and yanked it out of his hand. "None of that."

"I'm not here to cause trouble," he said indignantly.

"You never are, that's the problem." Whenever I took my eyes off Morgan in Faerie, he ended up getting totally wasted and doing stupid shit like chasing mermen around fountains and letting his pet faerie dog chew on the Sidhe's tapestries. Okay, he'd mellowed a little since he'd started full-time employment at Edinburgh's necromancer guild and found himself a nice human boyfriend, but that was the problem with my family. We didn't really do 'normal', and I'd prefer not to have to break up another incident.

"Is Mum gone?" asked Ilsa.

"Yep," I said. "The gate's right outside the doors to the palace. I asked Coral to keep an eye out and make sure no Sidhe go wandering that way, but I'd rather someone was there in person."

My sister's expression shadowed, knowing my thoughts were on the talisman. Both of us had mixed feelings on our decision to hide it from the Court, but the brawl I'd just witnessed was proof we'd made the right call. The Inner Garden's healing waters kept the talisman's destructive power contained—for now, at least. I suspected Etaina, the leader of the Aes Sidhe, might know how to get rid of it in a more permanent manner, but making another bargain with her would be risky on multiple levels. Etaina had been no friend of the Erlking's before her people had split from the Summer Court, and I'd be a fool to assume she wanted his talisman for altruistic reasons.

Morgan swiped the glass of elf wine from my hand again. "Why do you two look so miserable? This is supposed to be your party, Hazel."

"I'm tired," said Ilsa. Judging by the dark circles under her eyes, she'd been awake half the night again helping Mum work on assembling the Erlking's family tree while also holding down a full-time job at Edinburgh's necromancer guild and applying for a PhD. If you asked me, that was a more impressive endeavour than being chosen as the Summer Gatekeeper.

River squeezed her arm. "We can leave, if you like."

"You aren't leaving me alone in here," Morgan said. "Not if Miss Gatekeeper won't let me take one sip of elf wine."

"The last time you did, you tried to mimic the Sidhe's

dancing and ended up breaking both of your ankles," I pointed out. "It's bad enough that my guests keep turning into bears and attacking one another."

Morgan snorted. "That's pretty normal for a faerie event. Just wait for the orgy to start."

"It already has." Ilsa pointed to a room through an open door on the left, in which everyone seemed to have misplaced all their clothes.

"It's not a faerie revel without everyone getting naked and banging in the bushes." I rolled my eyes. "You two are both taken, so you don't get to have any fun here."

From the way Ilsa and River were acting around one another, they wouldn't object to getting naked in the bushes without any magic being involved. I averted my gaze from the door, trying unsuccessfully to forget the last time I'd been to a similar event, in which Darrow and I had ended up having an unplanned, incredibly hot make-out session.

I wouldn't lie, I'd been interested to see where those feelings led. But to say our relationship was complicated was an understatement. We worked for different Courts, he wanted to take the Erlking's talisman and hand it over to his own leader... yeah, complicated was an understatement, really.

There was also the clause in my Gatekeeper's contract forbidding me from dating faeries and decreeing that the next Gatekeeper would be chosen from among the children of the previous generation. That day had seemed miles off when I'd been heir and Mum had been Gatekeeper, but now...

"Gatekeeper!" said a frantic voice. A semi-transparent sprite dressed in a miniature version of a lime-green suit fluttered over my shoulder to hover in front of me. "Gate-keeper… Lady Aiten wishes to speak with you, urgently."

I suppressed a groan. "I told her four times this week already—we haven't found the heir. What's this about?"

"It's an urgent matter,'" said the sprite, eyeing my siblings. "Gatekeepers only."

Great. Shooting Ilsa an apologetic look, I made my way through the hall, dodging groups of finely-dressed Sidhe and hooved satyrs, white-haired nereids and bark-skinned dryads. No other humans were present, but groups of half-faeries clustered near the Sidhe nobles, as though hoping to catch their attention. I recognised one dark-haired half-faerie practically tripping over the cloak of a tall elven warrior clad in armour in an effort to stay within his line of sight. It seemed Aila had found someone new to stalk, in Darrow's absence. She shot me a sour look as I passed, and I gave her a smile in return.

Beside the oak doors, Lady Aiten stood in conversation with several Sidhe dressed in armoured clothing. *They're prison guards. Oh, bugger.*

I dodged a waltzing pair of female selkies in shimmering sealskin dresses and went to meet them. "Hey, Lady Aiten. What is it?"

"We've recently found that there's been a breakout from the Summer Court's jail," said Lady Aiten. "During the events when the outcasts attacked the Court."

"That was days ago." A chill ran through my blood. "Who broke out?"

"Lord Daival, former assistant to the Seelie Queen."

2

I looked between Lady Aiten and the armoured guards. "How did you not notice the breakout until now? I get that the Court was in a complete shambles at the time, but it should have taken a day at most to notice a missing prisoner."

"Lord Daival spun a glamour," said one of the guards, an armoured male with long blue-black hair. "He stole a talisman and used its illusory magic to create the impression he was still in his cell. We don't closely inspect every cell each day, especially our long-term prisoners."

"Sounds like your system needs updating." Sure, glamour had the power to make illusions that seemed realer than reality, but the Sidhe were meant to be able to see through such trickery. "Wasn't he in the part of the jail where magic is suppressed, anyway?"

"He was," said the guard. "He broke into our weapons hold to steal a talisman which functioned even in the high-security area."

The sneaky bastard. "Has Lord Daival been seen since? Wait, you don't think he's at the party, do you?"

I looked over at my family members, my heart sinking in my chest. Not only were they the only humans present, the gate leading to the Lynn house lay nearby, with the Erlking's talisman a mere breath away. As the Seelie Queen's former assistant, Lord Daival's first objective would be to free his queen at the next opportunity, but that didn't mean his grudge against my family for imprisoning her would disappear.

"Unlikely," said the guard, casting a look around the room. "However, we will send a team to search for any potential intruders."

"Might be easier to send everyone home," I said. "If Lord Daival *is* here, he might do far worse than start a brawl. Not to mention the mortal realm is on the other side of our family's gate. If Lord Daival sneaks through, the consequences will rebound back on your Court."

"If you end the revel now, the other Sidhe will protest," said Lady Aiten. "I would advise you to let the event proceed so as not to raise any panic. We will conduct a thorough search of the palace and ensure nobody enters the gate."

"In that case," I said, "I'd like to come and look around the jail myself. Think of it as my first request as Gatekeeper."

The guard shook his head. "This is not usual."

"There is no harm in allowing her to go," Lady Aiten said. "The guests will not notice her leave."

"Because they've already forgotten what they're celebrating." Gotta love the Sidhe for their brutal honesty. "Just let me tell my family first."

I made my way back across the room to the others, swatting away a drunken piskie who tried to pull my hair. It should come as no surprise that the Sidhe would carry on partying even with a war knocking on their doors, but if Lord Daival had broken out of jail days ago, he would already have paid me a visit if he wanted to threaten my family. The prison, on the other hand, was a far more likely target.

"What did Lady Aiten want?" asked Ilsa.

I lowered my voice. "Lord Daival broke out of jail. Can you and River keep an eye on things here? Lady Aiten doesn't want to ruin the fun and shut the party down, but I really do need to go and deal with this."

Her eyes flew wide. "Do the Sidhe think he might be at the party?"

"I'd assume he has more sense than to gate-crash, but I recommend someone goes to tell Mum so she can up the defences around our family's gate."

"I will," said Morgan. "The party is shit and I'm bored with being the third wheel."

"Okay. I'll see you guys in a bit." I crossed the palace floor to the oak doors and headed out into the night. Warm air wafted over me, bringing the fragrant smells of Summer's night-blooming flowers, but my skin remained clammy and chilled. *Lord Daival is loose in Faerie.* And if he had his way, the former Seelie Queen would be the next to taste freedom.

"Hazel, wait!" Coral, my half-selkie friend, hurried to catch up with me. Her blond hair bounced in waves to her shoulders, while she wore a mottled cloak which became her skin when she shifted into a seal. Beneath, she wore the dark clothing of a bodyguard rather than party-appropriate clothing, though her stint as my self-appointed watcher should have ended when I became Gatekeeper.

"Sorry, Coral," I said. "I have to go to the jail. There's been—"

"A breakout," she said. "I was visiting my brother at the jail when they found out. I'll come with you."

"Are you sure?" I wouldn't say no to company, so I gave her a grateful smile and addressed the two guards. "Coral will be coming with me."

Neither of them objected, so I let the Sidhe overtake us, moving closer to Coral. "How's your mother?"

She grimaced. "Devastated, but better than before. As her clarity of thought has returned, she has resumed her position as queen. My brother was poisoning her, as I feared."

My chest tightened. "I'm sorry."

"It's okay," she said. "Now she's recovering, I'm free to stay here in Summer. I'm not required to stay in the Sea Court, and I want to visit my brother before…"

Before the Sidhe executed him for treason. I wasn't the only one who'd had to face some major life changes lately. When Coral had come to the Summer Court in search of employment, she'd never expected to end up becoming the next in line for the Sea Kingdom's throne after her brother had been arrested for shooting the Erlking using their mother's talisman. I was sure the Seelie Queen had been the one to lure him over to her side, as she'd done to her other followers, and she'd do much worse if she was allowed to see daylight again.

The path veered sharply to the left, leading us to a large sprawling building grown from the forest itself.

Ancient oaks stood at each corner, while their branches and roots interlocked to form the walls of a forbidding structure. The guard tapped the side of the wall with the point of his spear, causing the branches to retract around a door-sized area to let us in. Dim light filtered in from the narrow gaps between interlocking branches, and the gloom put me in mind of tunnels too deep below the earth for natural light to penetrate. I heard Coral's teeth chattering at my side as we walked.

"Was Lord Daival imprisoned near the former Seelie Queen?" I asked the guard.

"No, but they were in the same high-security area of the jail." He led the way through identical corridors lined with cells, each following the same layout. Most cells appeared to be empty, unsurprising given that until recently, the Sidhe had employed permanent exile as a punishment for traitors. That decision had come back to hit them when the outcasts had rallied together and attacked Earth, dragging the Courts into war, but with death now permanent, it was easier for the Sidhe to execute traitors rather than jail them.

"Why wasn't he sentenced to death rather than being locked up?" The former Seelie Queen possessed a super-charged healing power which healed any injury in an instant, even the destructive magic of the Erlking's talisman, but Lord Daival had no such advantage.

"It was the Erlking's choice," he said. "He neglected to give specific instructions for Lord Daival's fate before his passing, only that he and the former queen should be given the tightest security."

Well, it clearly wasn't enough. I'd even managed to sneak off to talk to the Seelie Queen myself on the pretext of visiting my mother. I should have guessed Lord Daival would have been scheming, too, but I'd been fixated on protecting my family at the time.

When the guard used his talisman to unlock the door to the high-security area, a sudden pressure pushed against me from all angles, and the mark on my forehead throbbed, making my circlet feel uncomfortably tight. The glamour slid off my clothes, reverting them to the plain shirt and trousers I'd been wearing underneath my dress, but I doubted I'd be returning to the party after this. Beside me, Coral had gone quiet, her face pale.

The guard halted outside an open cell. The branches had retracted, revealing a dingy room the size of a cupboard. It was a dismal place to spend an immortal life, but Lord Daival had deserved it and so did his queen.

"What did he do, sneak out, steal a talisman, then sneak back in here and create an illusion?" I asked. "Seems kinda long-winded for an escape attempt."

"But an effective one," Coral said. "He must have stolen a security talisman, too, right?"

"He stole one from a guard on his way out," said the Sidhe. "It wasn't the only one of our talismans to end up misplaced during the attack on the Court, however."

Oops. I'd borrowed a guard's talisman myself to unlock the way to the Seelie Queen's cell so I could question her about the Erlking's death. At the time, the Sidhe had been on the brink of executing my mother for a crime she'd never committed, and besides, it hadn't been my actions that had led to the Sidhe lord's escape. "Did he use it to break into your weapons hold, then? Why do you keep other talismans within reach of the cells, anyway?"

"The talismans were among the possessions we confiscated from other prisoners," said the guard. "Including Lord Daival himself. Three are known to be missing, including his own."

"You kept them on the premises?" No wonder the guards seemed unusually subdued. They knew they'd really screwed up this one.

"His own magic was weak," the guard said.

"Which proves nothing, if he's claimed more than one talisman." The bloody fools had handed him the keys to the Court. "I would like to speak with the Seelie Queen. If she's using an illusion, too—"

"She isn't," said the guard. "There are no loopholes in the protections around her cell."

"Forgive me if I don't trust your word." My talisman glowed as my voice rose, and the guard's eyes rounded at the sight of the swirling light on my forehead. "The Seelie Queen and I have an understanding. For some reason, her plans involve keeping me alive, and I can use it to get her to talk to me."

Not strictly true, but the guard nodded. "Fine, but you will have ten minutes, and that's all."

Coral shot me a concerned look. "Are you sure?"

"I'll be fine," I said, though I felt my hands twisting together, gripping one another in the way they did when I was nervous. "You should stay here until I'm done. I don't want her playing mind games with you, too."

Mind games were all the Seelie Queen had left, locked in her cell for an indefinite sentence. I didn't *want* to talk to her, but to say I no longer trusted the Sidhe to do their jobs was an understatement. I needed to be certain she remained securely behind bars.

I already knew the way to the Seelie Queen's cell,

which lay at the dead end of a corridor, occupying a single section of wall. While neither of us could see the other, I felt her eyes watching me from behind the interwoven roots and branches, bringing goose bumps to my skin. I firmly gripped my left wrist in my right hand to stop the nervous motion.

"Hazel Lynn," she said. "Or should I call you Gatekeeper?"

What did she want me to do, profess my gratitude to her for kidnapping my mother and forcing her to relinquish her Gatekeeper powers to me?

"I was having a great time at my welcome party before I found out your assistant escaped jail," I told her. "I have to admit, I'm a little surprised he didn't come back to free you, too. Guess he wasn't so loyal after all, huh."

A chill breeze swept through the corridor, making me shiver. Here in the darkness, none of Summer's magic lingered, giving it a stifling, lifeless atmosphere that put me in mind of winding paths and trees frozen in time.

"I confess I've heard some interesting stories of how you thwarted Lord Veren," said the Seelie Queen. "I'm told there wasn't a trace of him or any of his companions found in the Vale. Nothing but ashes."

Fear clamped over my chest. She might not know I'd claimed the talisman, but if she realised I'd gone within range of the talisman's magic and survived, she'd know I was hiding information. Telling her about the stone Etaina had loaned me to protect me against the talisman's magic would give her another angle to use against me, so I simply said, "That's because you made them carry the talisman around until they disintegrated. Did anyone bother to warn them first?"

"They knew the risks."

I doubted it. "Well, Lord Fuckface is dead, and the Erlking's killer faces execution. You lost an awful lot of allies, Seelie Queen. I hope it was worth it to you."

"What does the heir to the Sea Court think about her brother's impending death?" she said.

I found myself doubly grateful that I hadn't brought Coral to speak to her. My friend was tough, but she didn't need to deal with the Seelie Queen's barbed comments on top of her brother's upcoming execution.

"It's not my business," I said. "Nor is it yours. I'd have thought you'd want to know all about the hopefuls who want to take the Erlking's place. Is that Lord Daival's goal? You rule the Vale, he gets Summer?"

She gave a delicate laugh. "Good guess, but I'm afraid you're going to be disappointed if you expect me to reveal my goals."

"Damn." I put on a mock-disappointed tone. "I really thought you'd tell me. Or at least hand me the blueprints to your evil plans."

"I can give you a clue, if you like."

"Depends what the catch is." I leaned closer to the cell wall, ignoring the cold tremor in my limbs. "I'm not promising you anything, and I'm certainly not involving anyone else in your schemes. What do you want?"

"Information," she said. "My servants are useful, but they cannot paint the full picture of life in the outside world the way you can. I will answer one question of yours if you do the same for me."

Hmm. "Ask yours first and I'll decide whether to accept your bargain."

A chuckle escaped. "You're as distrusting as ever, Hazel

Lynn. My question is this… what is your goal as Gatekeeper?"

She hadn't said I couldn't lie. An obvious oversight, especially as she couldn't see my face and read my body language. I cast around for whichever plausible answer would give her the least ammunition to use against me. If I tried a flippant answer like *to throw better parties than Lord Niall,* she'd know I was lying and clam up. I'd need to come up with something better.

To make sure the Sidhe don't kill each other.

To put a new monarch on the throne.

To undo the curse.

"To not lose the Summer Gate," I said. "Mostly because my mother would kill me."

"That is a satisfying answer," she said. "Now, you may ask your own question."

I opened my mouth then closed it again. Where to start? If I asked where Lord Daival was, I might not get an accurate answer even if she told the truth, because she couldn't have access to a constant update on his whereabouts.

"Choose wisely," she said. "It's up to you to decide what matters the most… your own personal curiosity, or the Sidhe's safety? Lord Daival, or me? Your own past, or the Court's future?"

I scowled at the cell wall. "I could ask you what in hell you meant by all that, but you'll only talk in riddles again."

My personal curiosity needed to stay firmly out of this one. As for the Sidhe, they faced threats on multiple levels and a single question wouldn't solve all of them. Lord Daival might be a pain in the arse, but he was harmless compared to his queen. She held all the cards here. Or she thought she did. Confident she might be, but there was a still a wall between us.

Your own past, or the Court's future?

What *that* meant, I could only guess. The past was past. As for the future...

She didn't know who the heir was, did she?

Lady Aiten's words replayed in my mind. Not only had the Sidhe yet to find the heir, the Erlking seemed to have left no record behind. Every day that passed without a new monarch on the throne made the Court vulnerable, not just to outside threats but to threats within their own borders. Look at those two brawling Sidhe at the party.

I drew in a breath. "My question is this: who has the information on the identity of the heir to the Summer Court?"

A low chuckle vibrated from behind the bars. "Clever mortal. You didn't ask if *I* knew, because your question wouldn't have come with a satisfying answer."

"Yes, yes, I'm very intelligent." Hardly. My sister was the smart one. I was just more accustomed to playing faerie games. "Answer my question."

"My answer is this," she said. "The Erlking gave the information on his heir to his personal sprite messenger, and nobody else."

My nails dug into the skin of my wrist. "What?"

"That is my answer."

Well, shit. The last time I'd seen the Erlking's sprite, he'd been living in the tunnels beneath his deceased master's territory. The only other time I'd set eyes on him had been when he'd delivered me the message telling me to investigate the Erlking's murder, and on neither of those occasions had he said a word to me.

"Does that satisfy you?" she asked.

"We're done with questions," I said. "Unless you'd like to tell me why he gave the information to someone who can't even talk."

"Oh, he can talk. My assistant is counting on it."

Please tell me she wasn't implying what I thought she was. "Lord Daival took the Erlking's sprite captive?"

She gave a soft laugh. "I imagine it wouldn't take long for that little creature to break and start spilling the Erlking's secrets. But I cannot see every event that occurs outside these walls, and I have not heard a word from my assistant since his escape. Perhaps the sprite managed to evade him."

Bile coated the back of my throat. She planned to have Lord Daival torture the information on the heir out of the Erlking's sprite. And then? He'd either capture or kill the next leader of the Summer Court.

3

I hurried back to the guard waiting outside Lord Daival's abandoned cell.

"Your friend went to see her brother," he said. "What is it, human?"

"I need to talk to Lady Aiten," I said. "Urgently."

His brow furrowed, but he led the way back through the doors and into the main section of the jail. The oppressive sensation of the magic-proofed spell lifted, but I hardly noticed. Panic whirled in the back of my mind. The Seelie Queen hadn't been bluffing, and Lord Daival had had ample opportunity to pay a visit to the Erlking's territory since his escape. I'd bet few people in the Court knew he even *had* a sprite.

Outside the jail, the guard gestured to the path leading back to the ambassadors' palace. "You'll find Lady Aiten at the palace. Your friend is with her brother."

"Tell Coral I'll explain later." I didn't want to worry anyone unnecessarily—mostly because when the Sidhe panicked, they blew shit up—but the situation locked grimmer than a troll's wardrobe. The Erlking's territory, abandoned and overgrown, didn't even register to the Sidhe as a place worth guarding. Lord Daival would have encountered no resistance.

Please say I'm not too late.

I tracked down Lady Aiten outside the ambassadors' palace, where she stood conversing with Lord Raivan. The blond Sidhe's flowery hat was lopsided, while his eyes held the glassy appearance of intoxication. "Lady Aiten, I need to talk to you."

"What is it, Gatekeeper?" She stepped smoothly away from her companion, her gaze flickering over my newly unglamoured, plain clothing. "Did you find what you were looking for in the jail?"

"Not exactly." I gave a brief scan of the area and checked nobody was eavesdropping in the bushes outside the palace doors. "Has anyone seen the Erlking's sprite lately?"

"His sprite?" she echoed. "Few know he exists at all. Why?"

"I need to visit the Erkling's territory. Now."

My frantic tone must have tipped her off, because she nodded without asking questions. "Come with me."

We passed through the palace grounds and out the gate, where the path changed at Lady Aiten's direction to reveal a winding forest track leading up to a pair of gates. Vines snaked up and down its spear-sharp points, and beyond lay wild forest as far as the eye could see. Lady Aiten extended a hand, revealing a knife gleaming with green light, and pressed it to point where the two gates met, causing them to swing open.

"You still have a security talisman," I observed. "Did you always have one?"

"Yes," she said. "Since the Erlking chose me to work for him. His original security team forfeited their talismans after the Seelie Queen's betrayal, and he distributed them among our new team."

"I hope Lord Farin has been relieved of his."

She cut me a sideways glance. "Lord Farin misplaced his talisman at Lord Niall's house, shortly before you informed us of the open doorway into the Grey Vale in the Erlking's territory."

Oops. In fairness, Lord Farin *had* fallen asleep on duty, and I'd borrowed his talisman for a good cause. Unfortunately, the killer had been one step ahead of me.

"I thought you were working against my family at the time," I told her. "Since you kept threatening to have me arrested. Besides, I was working on a hunch. I figured investigating alone would be less risky, given what happened to Lord Kerien."

"Be careful," she said. "I have warned you your Gatekeeper's title does not carry the protection it once did, which will only grow worse as long as there remains no monarch on Summer's throne."

"Believe me, I know." To say I had trust issues was an understatement, but the Sidhe were the ones who'd instilled a lifetime of wariness in me. Mum had taught me never to take them at their word despite their inability to lie, but the Seelie Queen's earlier statements had carried the chilling ring of truth. Lord Daival had come here after his escape, I was certain.

As for whether he'd found what he'd come for? That remained to be seen.

The Erlking's territory had grown wild in the short time since his passing. Thick foliage covered the exterior of the Seelie Queen's former house, where trees grew from floor to ceiling and the crater-sized hole in the floor was already choked with weeds.

"Sprite," I called, scanning the entrance hall. "Hey… sprite."

I climbed through a collapsed doorway and peered into the room beyond, but I might as well have tried to dig up a long-buried ruin. The Seelie Queen had left few traces of her old life here in her former home, and nature had reclaimed the rest. Tangled plants blocked the way into the tunnel through the trapdoor, and I couldn't picture even a sprite being able to squeeze down there into the darkness.

It took me even longer to find the clearing, trekking through dense forest choked with undergrowth. Most of Summer territory came equipped with a steady breeze to counter the heat, but my arms dripped with sweat by the time I tracked down the hunched shape of the Erlking's throne. Formed of the husks of rotting tree roots, it had since collapsed under a torrent of green moss and weeds.

I think he'd prefer it this way. Centuries of his life he'd spent sitting on that throne, unable to get close to anyone for fear of turning them to dust. He'd taken no pleasure in holding the talisman, and damn if I didn't want to raise him from death to ask how he'd resisted its call for so long. Even without its shadowy magic humming in my palms, the vivid memory of wrapping my hand around the hilt and feeling the whisper of its awakening conscious-ness was never far from the forefront of my mind.

I turned my back on the throne, shoving fistfuls of undergrowth aside until I uncovered the tunnel entrance leading into the Erlking's underground quarters. I ducked under a tree root into the tunnel, branches scraping my arms. In the wide cave ahead, roots sprouted through the walls, while large sections of the tunnels had collapsed beneath nature's onslaught.

"Sprite!" I called into the tunnel, but no answer returned. I pushed a wad of tree roots aside and shoved my way forward, calling out, over and over again.

Every route seemed to lead back into the main cave, and no sprite appeared. I took the longest route into the forest, emerging in the spot where the murderer had slain the Erlking's security troll. Shoving branches aside, I burst above the ground and yelled, "*Sprite.*"

The forest caught my shouts and echoed them back at me, but no response came. Breathless and covered in scratches, I made my way back to the entrance. Lady Aiten stood beside the gate, without so much as a bead of sweat on her perfect face.

I halted, clutching a stitch in my chest. "The Erlking's sprite is missing. The Seelie Queen told me he's the only person in the Court who knows the identity of the Erlking's heir. I think Lord Daival came here after his escape…"

"And took the Erlking's sprite captive?" Her tone dripped with disbelief, but it sounded more like she didn't *want* to believe me than anything else.

"I believe so." I straightened upright. "The Seelie Queen told me it was his intention, and I've found no signs of the sprite here on the Erlking's territory. Don't forget the sprite was the one the Erlking trusted to deliver the message telling me to investigate his death."

Lady Aiten's face turned ashen. "I must inform the others."

"Don't make a big scene," I warned. "If you tell all the Sidhe, everyone will start panicking. Others might take advantage of the situation to put themselves forward as the potential heirs, like those two shapeshifters at the party. Best to keep it quiet for now."

Her lips compressed. "You will need to hold your tongue, too, mortal. If the other Sidhe find out you were the one to inform me of Lord Daival's intentions, they might well decide you are to blame."

That figured. It'd be easier to blame the human than admit to their own screw-ups. "I'm used to keeping secrets. But I do need to warn my family about Lord Daival's escape."

"Do that." Her words were as sharp as thorns. "You are not to come back to Faerie until I have decided what to do with you."

And to think I'd thought we'd begun to understand one another. I recognised the raw fear underlying her tone, so I let it slide for now.

Once we'd retraced our steps to the ambassadors' palace, I made for the gate leading back home. I'd been looking for an excuse to get out of the party, but an escaped criminal hadn't been what I'd had in mind. *Why didn't I ask the sprite if he knew who the heir was?* It wouldn't have been my first thought, but knowing the Erlking's commitment to secrecy, of course he wouldn't have told any of the other Sidhe. As to why the sprite hadn't just *told* the heir... well, the Erlking's murderer had still been loose in the Court at the time. The heir had likely survived this long because nobody had known their identity.

On the path, the Summer gate waited for me, formed of pointed hawthorn stakes coated with moss. Opening the gate still carried the same storybook air it had when I'd entered Faerie for the first time, as though my very bones knew I was treading in the footsteps of my ancestor, Thomas Lynn.

All the stories told that the young knight had been walking in the woods when a faerie queen had lured him through a gate. After a time, he'd escaped back to Earth, but the Sidhe were not to be defied. They'd come for his daughters when they were grown, the same way they'd come for me. At twelve, I'd woken to find magic coursing through my veins, the Gatekeeper's mark glowing on my forehead. It'd taken me a while to learn my new talents came with one hell of a sting in the tail, yet despite our mutual dislike, I'd come to suspect that the Sidhe needed the Gatekeepers as much as we needed them.

"Hazel?" Ilsa called from behind me. "You're leaving?"

I turned around, one hand resting on the gate. River caught up with Ilsa, but nobody else was within hearing distance. "Lord Daival escaped jail and kidnapped the Erlking's sprite. Who, the Seelie Queen just told me, is the only person in the Courts who knows the identity of the heir to the Erlking's throne."

Her jaw dropped. "Shit."

"Yeah, pretty much," I said. "I don't care if the Sidhe notice I'm missing, but Mum needs to know. I'm not leaving her alone at home with Lord Daival on the loose, besides."

"They won't notice you leave," said River, whose

stunned expression matched Ilsa's. "I'll stay here and keep an eye out for trouble."

"If you're sure." Ilsa gave him a quick hug, then walked after me through the gate.

In the garden of the Summer Lynn house, bright green lawns ran to the large manor house, while on the right-hand side of the gate lay the Inner Garden. A narrow entrance between thick hedges led to the pool of healing waters, and within, a dark shape floated below the surface.

"I don't suppose you know who the heir is?" I asked the Erlking's staff.

No reply came. Shadowy magic coiled around the staff's hilt, mingling with the vibrant light of the healing waters. Not Summer or Winter magic, but the magic of the Sidhe's predecessors, the godlike Ancients whose power put even the Sidhe to shame. After the Sidhe had kicked their gods out of their realm, all that remained were remnants of their power.

Remnant or not, there was *something* conscious present in the staff, calling to me and urging me to wrap my hand around the hilt. The staff had the power to turn Lord Daival to dust in a heartbeat, but I was fairly sure it wasn't healthy to keep re-claiming the magic and then giving it up. Besides, conscious or not, it was still an inanimate object with no knowledge of the Erlking's heir.

"Hazel?" Ilsa said from behind me. "Morgan's not around, but Mum's still up, and she's not in the shed. Want to come and tell her?"

I dragged my gaze away from the staff and turned my back on the still waters of the grove. "Sure."

I didn't miss the faint traces of concern in her expression which always appeared whenever I lingered too long in the grove. Being close to the talisman's magic was like walking into a faerie revel. One second you were perfectly in control, the next you were leading a naked conga line through Lord Niall's living room. However much the staff might tempt me, I had no intention of turning into the next Seelie Queen, thanks. Lord Daival's magic was weak, as far as I knew. I shouldn't need the talisman's magic to apprehend him.

Mum sat up in the living room, surrounded by stacks of paper on every available surface. Teetering piles occupied the armchairs, the coffee table, even the bookshelves. All were covered in scrawling handwriting, mostly hers and Ilsa's.

"You're back early," she said, stifling a yawn with the back of her hand.

I closed the living room door and cleared a stack of papers from the sofa to sit down. "Do you want the bad news or the worse news first?"

"Lord Daival escaped jail and kidnapped the Erlking's sprite." Ilsa sank into the sofa beside me. "Turns out the sprite is also the one person who knows who the Erlking picked to be his successor."

Mum dropped the page she held, which fluttered to the carpet. "If he comes here—"

"He doesn't need to," I said. "Our copy of the family tree is incomplete, and besides, we don't know who the Erlking chose as his successor. It might have been anyone."

"What did the Sidhe tell you to do?"

I fished the paper from the floor and handed it back to her. "Nothing. Lady Aiten is the only person who knows, aside from me, and she thinks the other Sidhe might pin the blame on me if they find out." The Sidhe were more than welcome to deal with him themselves, even if years of cleaning up their messes had instilled me with a permanent mentality of *if you want something done right, you have to do it yourself.*

"Sprites are considered inferior beings in the Courts," said Mum. "I would guess that's why nobody guessed the Erlking chose him as a confidant."

"Yeah, I know." I looked at my feet, guilt swirling within me. I should have taken the sprite with me, not left him to roam around the Erlking's territory alone.

"Did you say the *Seelie Queen* told you?" said Ilsa. "Are you sure she wasn't leading you astray?"

"She didn't lie." My hands fisted on my lap. "She told me unambiguously that the sprite is the only person who knows who the heir is, and Lord Daival intended to capture him. Given the sprite's absence, it's safe to say he at least tried."

Mum swore under her breath. "The sprite was the Erlking's most trusted advisor. They'll have known one another for centuries. I should have known he would have told the sprite and not his Sidhe advisors."

"Especially considering one of them used to be Lord Daival himself," I added. "Though I'm guessing the Erlking didn't expect his sprite to become a target."

Which left the Sidhe with a conundrum and a half. If the sprite told Lord Daival the heir's identity, the Seelie Queen's next step would be to get rid of the competition. On the other hand, if he perished without revealing the identity of the heir, the Sidhe wouldn't be able to crown their next monarch with the confidence that the Erlking would have backed up their choice. From what I'd seen at the revel tonight, it was safe to say some of them would object no matter who the Erlking nominated, but the odds of the Summer Court electing a new leader without bloodshed had plummeted below zero.

"I was afraid of this," Mum said. "Given how long it's been since the Court had a change of leadership, nobody would ever have been as widely supported as the Erlking. Most of the current Sidhe were born after he was crowned and have never known a world without him on the throne, much less had cause to wonder about who might succeed him."

"Then why bother with the family tree?" Lady Aiten had been the one to convince Mum to start it, since our house held the most books on the history of the Courts in the mortal realm, but it seemed a pointless exercise if the Erlking had his own plans. "Considering most names on the list don't match up with actual people, it's probably centuries out of date."

"I imagine they're code names," said Mum, indicating the sprawling lines on the page in front of her. "Even the Erlking's own name is unknown to the Sidhe. Most knew him as Oberon, his father's name."

Ilsa gave a nod. "She's right. The Sidhe are superstitious about names."

Didn't I know it. The brief shred of optimism I'd felt at the sight of the family tree's lines gradually filling in had disappeared when Mum explained that most of the names didn't correspond with any known inhabitants of Faerie. It seemed the Sidhe were paranoid about being recorded in the history books, so they'd used false names like the Lord of Sweeping Tides and the Lady of Tall Trees. On top of that, many of them changed their actual names and titles every other century out of boredom.

"They are." Mum laid down the page on the arm of the sofa. "However, Lady Aiten asked me to do this, and it's all I can do, without my magic."

The vulnerability in her tone struck me at the core. Mum had always seemed indomitable, unyielding, but losing her Gatekeeper's powers must have hit her harder than I'd realised.

"Then I'll help." I sat down beside her and picked up one of the books. "If we find out who the heir is ourselves, we can at least warn them so they can be on their guard."

Ilsa picked up a stack of papers and shuffled them like a pack of cards. "The Sidhe must know Lord Daival is hiding in the Vale. If they can get over their fears and go after him, they should be able to find him."

"Unless he doesn't want to be found." I flipped open the book. "Did I mention he also stole back his talismans from the jail's weapon stores? The guards keep everything they confiscate from their prisoners in storage."

Ilsa rolled her eyes. "I think immortality is the only reason the Sidhe survived this long at all. If they'd let natural selection do its thing, they'd have died out."

"No kidding."

Speaking of dying out, the odds of the next monarch living as long as the Erlking were pretty much zero. Securing leadership was an awful lot easier with immortality backed up by a talisman with the ability to reduce any threats to ashes.

One thing was clear: whoever succeeded the Erlking, the era of peace in the Courts had come to an end.

Mum, Ilsa and I stayed up into the early hours,

working on the family tree. Ilsa was the bookish one in the family, but I'd been spending longer than she had in the library this past week, scouring my family's collection of ancient tomes for any clues about the Erlking's staff. So far, I'd found little to go by. No Gatekeeper in history had ever claimed a talisman, much less one as destructive as the Erlking's staff, so Ilsa had suggested I might end up in the history books myself, assuming I lived that long. Personally, I'd rather go down in history as the Gate-keeper who freed her family from the curse, but after combing through so many books on Sidhe history, I knew more about the Sidhe's various interrelated bloodlines than I did my own family's.

I didn't remember falling asleep, but I woke under the hand-knitted throw on the sofa to Mum's voice saying, "Lady Aiten is here to see you, Hazel."

"Ugh." Had the Sidhe forgiven me already? *A likely story.* I pushed into an upright position, knocking a stack of cushions to the floor. Scraps of crumpled paper, empty plates of stale cookies and teetering piles of books occu-pied most of the remaining space, while on an armchair, a lump of blankets was all I could see of Ilsa.

I pulled a glamour on to hide my rumpled clothes, wild hair, and the dark circles under my eyes and walked to the door. Yanking the door open, I looked blearily at my visitor. While Lady Aiten looked like she'd rolled out of bed pristine and shiny, the mirror on my left showed me I'd left a gap in my glamour which showed my bright pink bra strap. Great.

"Lady Aiten." I surreptitiously pulled my glamour into place. "You haven't told the rest of the Sidhe Lord Daival kidnapped the Erlking's sprite, have you?"

"No," she said. "I did tell Lord Raivan, as he is trustworthy and loyal to Summer, and unlikely to place the blame on either of us for the oversight."

"I hope so," I said. "You never know who might turn on you now the Seelie Queen's got the upper hand. She and Lord Daival might be planning to murder the heir or manipulate them into acting as their puppet while they rule the Vale."

"Yes, I'm aware of that," said Lady Aiten. "In fact, many of us believe that the Erlking's wishes should be only one factor in choosing the next monarch of Summer. The Court as a whole needs to support the heir, or else there would be no peace."

I arched a brow. "Does everyone agree with you?"

"No," she said. "Many believe the Erlking nominated an heir and that nomination should stand, but others would prefer to put their own names forward. And still others would argue that the strongest Sidhe should be heir, and there should be a contest to determine who should wear the crown."

"That sounds like the Unseelie way," I remarked. "Don't they pass their ceremonial talisman around and let its magic destroy everyone except the person it deems worthy of holding it? I mean, it's efficient, I'll give them that."

"There is... merit, to that approach," she said. "However, the Erlking's talisman is far too destructive to be allowed to determine the heir, even if it wasn't missing."

Uh, yeah. Also, that would make me *the heir.*

"Does Summer have an equivalent talisman that might be an effective test?" I said. "I'm not saying Winter's approach is the best one, but being chosen by a talisman is more decisive than being picked by a person, and everyone would have to agree with the choice."

She shook her head. "There is no equivalent talisman here in the Summer Court. There *is* the Erlking's crown, but that contains no magic, and I've stored it in a secure location until the heir is tracked down."

The Summer Court wasn't a typical monarchy—the immortality factor meant most monarchs did not give up their thrones willingly—but everyone seemed to think the crown would go to the next of kin. Ancestry was seen as important, and for half-faeries, their sole connection to Faerie was via their family, assuming their relatives hadn't spurned their half-fae offspring. For instance, as the son of a major Sidhe lord, River had been gifted with one of Lord Torin's talismans upon his entry to the Court despite his lack of any experience with the faerie realms.

But for a monarch, just having the right heritage would never be enough. They'd need to know how to lead, and if the Erlking hadn't given his heir any instruction, they'd be at a disadvantage from the start.

"So," I said, wondering what she was getting at, "are you prioritising going after Lord Daival?"

"We are," she said. "We believe he must be hiding in the Grey Vale."

"I know." If any of the Seelie Queen's other allies had survived the Erlking's talisman, that's where they'd be hiding, too. "Are you sending a team in?"

"No," she said. "You will go into the Grey Vale and search for Lord Daival yourself, Gatekeeper."

4

"She wants you to go into the Vale?" said Ilsa. "Alone?"

"I've been there before." I'd stand a better chance of finding Lord Daival with the Erlking's talisman, but I wasn't that desperate yet. "I'm allowed to take iron with me, too."

Mum wasn't up yet, but Ilsa sat awake in the armchair, dishevelled and bleary-eyed. The house's magic had also conjured up breakfast, so I shoved a slice of toast into my mouth and made for the stairs to get dressed and stock up on weapons. Since my Gatekeeper status held no influence in the land of the outcasts, I needed all the iron I could get my hands on.

When I returned downstairs, laden with iron knives, I found Ilsa and River waiting in the hall, fully dressed and looking a little more awake.

"We're heading back to Edinburgh," she said. "Let me know when you get back, okay?"

"You should have told me you had a shift at the necromancer guild," I objected. "I wouldn't have let you stay up half the night working on the family tree if I'd known. This heir crap is my problem, not yours."

She yawned. "Maybe, but it affects the future of humanity, so..."

I shook my head at the portraits of Lynns in the hall. "Nobody in our family has even tried to be *normal,* have they?"

"I tried it for five years," said Ilsa. "Didn't quite stick. I don't think it's possible for a Lynn to have a regular life. No wonder people say we're all cursed, Gatekeepers or otherwise."

"Some of us don't mind." River took her arm and pulled her close to him.

I made gagging noises. "You two are too much to deal with on little sleep, you know."

I was only half joking. Ilsa and River had the kind of relationship that would probably never be in the cards for me. Since the Gatekeeper's rules forbade me from dating faeries, my only option would be to start a relationship with a human who didn't mind me staying in Faerie for weeks at a time and would tolerate being targeted by every hostile fae in the vicinity. No wonder Mum had never tried dating again after Dad left.

Sheathing my last knife, I went through Summer's gate into the Court. Brightness dappled the leaf-strewn path and shone through the windows of the ambassadors' palace, warming my skin beneath my thick, armoured coat. I'd need it where I was going, so I bore the discomfort and went in search of Lady Aiten. She stood outside the palace, her slim form clothed in green that blended with the surrounding foliage.

"You do have your own quarters here at the palace, Gatekeeper, and you're welcome to use them."

That was a not-so-subtle dig at me for spending my nights in the Lynn house in the mortal realm. "I assumed the party would carry on all night, and I'm a light sleeper. How am I getting into the Vale?" Only Sidhe could cross between realms at will, which left me at their mercy the instant I stepped onto the other side.

"This way." She beckoned me into the palace itself. No signs of the party remained, not so much as a wine stain on the floor or a discarded item of clothing in the bushes. Through a door on our left was a sparsely furnished room, hung with tapestries and marked with swirling symbols drawn onto the floor.

"You're opening a doorway into the Vale in here?" I guessed.

"Yes," she said. "This room is well-protected. If Lord Daival tries to invade the Court via this route, he will find himself surrounded in an instant."

You'd better be right. I'd prefer not to have to claim a talisman to get out this time around. They didn't exactly fall out of the sky on a regular basis even in the Vale.

"Good," I said. "How long should I stay?"

"You will stay there until you find Lord Daival, or else find proof that he isn't there." Lady Aiten faced me, her green eyes glimmering, every inch of her glowing with magic. A breeze stirred my hair, and then the room vanished as a doorway appeared at my back, propelling me out onto a path bathed in silver.

Trees flanked me on either side, bleached of colour, as though a filter lay over the whole world. Creepy even by Faerie's standards, the Vale was the polar opposite of the magic-filled Summer Court. No sun shone here, just that same constant greyish light, while the trees never regrew the leaves they'd shed before the Sidhe's magic had ripped this part of the world away, leaving it frozen in time.

Few came into the Grey Vale on purpose. Beasts too depraved for the Seelie and Unseelie alike wandered in search of prey, death-stealers sucked the life from any living creature they happened upon, while sluagh wandered the divide between death and life. Disembodied howling noises, rustling in the bushes and the sounds of some poor creature being torn to pieces greeted me like a rambunctious welcome party from the depths of hell.

In my first visit to the Vale—when the Seelie Queen had kicked me out of Summer in the hope that the Vale's monsters would keep me from interfering in her attempted coup—I'd nearly been murdered by a group of merrows and then been buried alive. Last time, I'd fought an armoured troll and a gang of murderous outcasts and only the Erlking's talisman had prevented me from becoming another corpse lost in the Vale. I'd escaped by the skin of my teeth both times, yet I had a leg up on most exiles because the Sidhe's last act before exiling someone from the Courts was to rip out their magic and leave them powerless. Ilsa had used the same spell to rid me of the Erlking's talisman, so I knew first-hand how painful it was, and without magic or weapons, I wouldn't last ten minutes here.

I drew my iron knife with a *snick* that echoed among the silvery trees. Grey paths extended left and right, but it didn't matter which I chose. If Lord Daival wanted to be found, I knew how to reach him.

"Take me to Lord Daival," I told the Vale, and started

walking, my footfalls cushioned by a carpet of silver leaves.

The path wound around corners and wove among the trees, the scenery bare and unchanging. In the Vale, nothing died, but nothing really lived, either. Hence why the Seelie Queen and her kind found it a perfect place to hide out and plot against the Courts. I kept my iron weapon at hand, tensing at every small noise, and with every step, my frustration grew. Where the bloody hell was Lord Daival? I'd have thought he'd *want* me to find him, so he could boast about defying the Courts the same way his precious queen had.

On the other hand, he and I both had equal control over the Vale's magic, and if he didn't want to be found, we'd end up locked in an eternal battle of wills until I got the upper hand. *Why did I let Lady Aiten talk me into staying here until I got my hands on the bastard?*

A bolt of magic whistled over my head, crashing into the nearest tree. Silently thanking the invisible shield of my family's name, I spun to face my attacker.

The path appeared the same as before, no disturbances at all—on the surface, at least. Squinting, I peered to the left, and another blast of magic raised the hairs on my head and skimmed my arm like a mild electric shock. Thorny vines sprouted where it struck the path, giving away its owner as a Summer faerie. Based on past experience, I'd guess a wraith—a dead Sidhe who'd perished here in the Vale, reduced to nothing more than magic and the relentless will to annoy the shit out of me.

"Look, mate, you've picked the wrong target," I said to the patch of empty air. "You can't kill me, and I can't kill you, and I have better things to do than play games with you. So if you don't mind..."

A rushing noise cut through my words, and a torrent of green light surrounded me in a whirlwind. Thorns protruded from the light, threatening to break through my shield.

My circlet glowed on my forehead. Green energy lit up my hands, forming a barrier between me and the whirling torrent of magic. It flickered around the edges, as did the thorns. *Aha. They're not real. The wraith is using illusion magic.*

I reached out, searching for the threads of magic encompassing the spell, and gave a firm tug. The illusion shattered in my hands, in a move I'd like to think Darrow would be proud of, and the whirling thorns disappeared. In their place, a shadow shaped vaguely like a person hovered before me. Magic pulsed around its edges, tinged with the green of Summer. A wraith, as I'd suspected.

"Hey, there," I said. "You're not much of a talker, are you?"

I'd never particularly envied Ilsa's gift for necromancy, but I wished I could just say *I banish you beyond the gates of death* and have the ghost vanish rather than following me for the next hour. Suppressing a sigh, I sidestepped the wraith, and the path vanished from beneath my feet.

The ground became transparent, and an odd cloud-like substance formed a bridge where the path had once been. Worse, the bloody wraith was still there, blocking the way onto solid ground. If I wasn't careful, I'd end up falling straight into whatever oblivion lay below the clouds.

"Seriously?" I stared at the point where I thought the

wraith's eyes should be. "This isn't gonna go the way you think it is."

A green-blue torrent of magic smashed into the wraith, sending it reeling backwards, and a tall, lean figure ran up the path to join me, his silver hair streaming behind him. There was only one person I knew who could use both Summer and Winter magic: Darrow.

The clouds dipped below my feet, but he was at my side in an instant, reaching out a hand. His skin was warm to touch, a welcome change from the chill in the air.

"Darrow." I stepped onto solid ground, unlocking my fingers from his. "Thanks."

Faeries didn't make a habit of using the word *thanks* unless they didn't mind owing the person a debt. Unfortunately, by faerie standards, I *did* owe him for saving my life. Like the wraith's trickery wasn't humiliation enough in itself.

Darrow straightened upright, his silver hair falling to his shoulders. His aquamarine eyes betrayed his status as one of the few hybrid half-bloods who'd inherited magic from both Summer and Winter. The Aes Sidhe were an independent Court who'd split off from Summer several centuries ago, but while their own magic might be unique, it resembled Summer's on the surface. On the other hand, his skills with glamour made the wraith's look amateur by comparison. The one time he'd hit me with it, I'd been on the brink of spending the rest of my life worshipping him —which was just one reason I shouldn't be glad to see him again.

"What are you doing in the Vale?" he asked.

"Looking for Lord Daival." I decided to opt for a

truthful approach this time around. "Did you hear he broke out of jail? You weren't at the party last night."

"I wasn't in the Court at the time," he said. "I didn't know about Lord Daival, but it doesn't surprise me."

"Then what are you doing here?" This seemed an odd time to pay a visit to the land of the outcasts. "Etaina wanted you to pick her some man-eating flowers, did she?"

"I'm here to look for the Erlking's missing talisman."

My throat went dry. I should have known the leader of the Aes Sidhe wouldn't lie down and accept my cover story that I'd left the talisman in the Vale after its magic had killed Lord Veren and his fellow conspirators. While Darrow had no more idea than anyone else of the talisman's real location, he'd suspected I'd omitted information when I'd told him of its fate.

"Really?" I arched a brow. "Isn't it safer in here, where its magic can't harm anyone?"

He gave me a look which implied my breezy tone hadn't fooled him in the slightest. "No. If another outcast claims the talisman, they might use it against the Courts. I've been searching for some time, but I haven't seen another person until now."

Crap. Had the Vale's magic brought him to me because I knew where the talisman was? "The Vale isn't playing nice today. Lord Daival must want to stay hidden."

"Are you sure you asked nicely enough?"

"Ha." I wasn't sure he'd meant it as a joke, but I was reasonably sure I knew more about the Vale than he did. "Maybe you should have covered the Vale in my Gatekeeper training if I was going to end up spending so much time here. Not that I'm volunteering to resume our lessons."

I wouldn't lie, I'd missed our sparring matches. I did *not* miss the bond he'd put on me when I'd agreed to take the Trials, nor did I miss having to duck around his attempts to corner me while I tried to investigate the Erlking's death. But if he found out I had the talisman in my own back garden, our alliance would come to a crashing halt and I would find myself at the mercy of his Court and its leader. However fun our banter might be, I wouldn't allow myself to become complacent.

A bright flash drew my eyes. The wraith was back, firing a bolt of vivid green energy at Darrow. I opened my mouth to warn him—he didn't have a shield like mine—but he sidestepped with dizzying speed and returned the wraith's attack with one of his own. I'd forgotten how bloody fast he moved. The wraith's half-hearted blasts of green light seemed dim compared to the vivid green-blue light gleaming in his hands. I joined him on the attack, but being dead, the wraith remained stubbornly present, a patch of shadows etched against the misty backdrop.

"Gatekeeper," it growled. "Your days are numbered."

Well, well. The wraith had a voice, after all.

"Hey," I said. "Where is Lord Daival? If you're gonna follow me around, you might at least make yourself useful."

Darrow's next attack blasted into the wraith, sending it flailing over the edge of the cloudy mass.

"Hey, we were chatting," I protested. "We had a real rapport going."

He scowled at the spot where the wraith had merged

with the clouds, and it didn't return. "The wraith wouldn't have been able to tell you his location."

The wraith might have backed off, but it'd given me an idea. If I couldn't find Lord Daival, I'd go with the next best thing: finding his allies. "Then I'll find someone who will."

"Go ahead." Darrow let me take the lead. He'd once admitted to being intrigued as to what I'd do next, but his unquestioning acceptance left me a tad flustered, especially as I had no idea if my plan would work or not.

I concentrated hard, my thoughts hammering in time with my steps. *Take me to someone who can tell me where Lord Daival is. Take me to someone who can tell me...*

The path warped and changed before our eyes. Ahead, a serpentine figure coiled around the base of a thick oak. Sharp teeth jutted from its jaws, dripping with venom, but its facial features otherwise resembled a man's. Curtains of raven hair hung to its shoulders, and a forked tongue flickered between its teeth.

"Human," said the creature.

"Hi," I said. "Can you tell me where I might find Lord Daival?"

"Lord Daival?" said the creature. "I do not know that name."

So much for that idea.

"He was the Seelie Queen's assistant once. He carries a bunch of talismans. Silver hair. Uh, not him," I added, when his gaze went to Darrow. "The Vale told me you saw him. He enjoys throwing thorns at people."

"Thorns," said the faerie. "The Lord of Thorns?"

"Is that what he's calling himself now?" I shot Darrow

a triumphant look. "Is this Lord of Thorns hiding somewhere in the Vale?"

"No," said the serpent. "The Lord of Thorns was apprehended in the Summer Court. The fool blew his cover."

Shit. Lord Daival *had* been arrested in the Summer Court… months ago. Right after I'd become Gatekeeper. If this guy wasn't lying, Lady Aiten had it wrong. Lord Daival wasn't in the Vale at all.

"Great." I took a step backwards. "Guess I'd better be going, then."

The serpent fae uncoiled, baring his fangs at me. "I'm not finished with you yet, Gatekeeper. I haven't tasted a human in a long time."

"My circlet would choke you." I raised my iron blade. "And so would this."

The serpent lunged at me. I swung the blade, clashing with its sharp teeth. Bracing my feet on the path, I pushed hard, driving its teeth away from my exposed skin. Spitting out venom and blood, the snake reared back for another strike.

I dodged to the side, dealing a vicious blow to its neck. The serpent hissed in agony, shaking its head and scattering droplets of blood onto the path. My blade cut into its scaled skin—once, twice, three times, each cut driving deeper until the blade came free, buried in its mouth.

While the beast writhed on the spot, I drew a second blade and severed its head. Darrow watched the creature's serpentine body hit the ground with a jarring thud.

"You let me do all the work." I stepped over to its prone head and yanked out my bloodstained blade.

"You had it handled."

If I didn't know better, I'd say he'd enjoyed the show, which was kind of flattering. He wasn't my mentor anymore, so there was no reason for him to take an interest in my fighting prowess… unless he'd been told to watch for signs of the talisman's magic.

I found myself fervently glad that the talisman had left no traces behind after my sister had removed its influence. It'd hurt like hell to have the talisman's magic ripped out of me, but Darrow, with his sharp eyes and his knack for asking the wrong questions, would have known right away. Had he been here every day for the last week, looking for the talisman? *I should have known Etaina would be bloody persistent.* I needed to get us *both* out of here before he realised the Vale hadn't been screwing around when it'd led him to my side.

I shook blood droplets off my blade. "Not going to chastise me for using iron?"

"No," he said. "It's a sensible choice for the Vale."

His praise always threw me off-balance because he delivered it in the same manner in which he did his criticisms—matter-of-fact, without any hidden meanings—which made his compliments land with more weight than they normally would. That made it harder to distrust him, that was for damned sure.

I stepped away from the serpentine monster's corpse. "The Lord of Thorns? I should have guessed Lord Daival would adopt his own fancy title."

A thoughtful expression passed over Darrow's face. "If he isn't here, he may be in Summer, hidden among the other Sidhe."

"Depends how good he is at using glamour."

Glamour was the Aes Sidhe's speciality, but Lord

Veren had walked among the Summer Court for days before anyone had realised he'd been using a powerful illusion to conceal the decaying effects of the Erlking's talisman's magic. Even Lady Aiten, who'd walked at his side, hadn't noticed until Ilsa had spotted his damaged soul using her spirit sight.

"Or he might be in Winter," he added.

"No chance. It's the Erlking's throne his queen wants." Which meant the odds of him hiding in Summer were stronger than the chances of him picking the mortal realm instead. "He's either in Summer or on Earth, but he'd need to stay close to the Ley Line to get into Faerie."

"Yes, he would." Darrow scanned the path. "How did you plan to get back into Faerie yourself?"

"Lady Aiten left me a door open." I turned on the spot. "I'll have to find it."

"I have a quicker way." Darrow took my arm. Startled, I tilted my head up at him, warmth spreading from his fingers through my sleeve.

Then the Vale disappeared, to be replaced by a wide chamber. Tunnels extended in all directions like the roots of a giant tree, under curved ceilings that made the space feel more enclosed, as though we stood miles below the earth.

He'd brought me into the lands of the Aes Sidhe.

5

The dome-like chamber was empty aside from the two of us, and I didn't have the faintest clue which tunnel led to the way out. The walls were formed of smooth, packed earth, dotted with glowing patches of fungi that provided the only real light source, the floor flattened by countless generations of footsteps.

I turned on Darrow. "You bastard. If I die here, my mother will personally hunt you down and feed your balls to one of the Vale's serpents."

"Then it's a good job I have no intention of harming you." His crisp, even tone betrayed his annoyance at me for insinuating Etaina planned to have me killed. I didn't believe she did—I intrigued her too much—but if she realised I'd taken the talisman for myself, there was no telling what she might do.

"You know Etaina didn't have any intention of letting me go last time," I said. "I gave you the stone back. Why is she so interested in talking to me?"

"I think you know the answer to that question, Hazel."

The way he said my name sent a thrill down my spine, laced with a suggestiveness that implied *he* was interested in me for very different reasons. But we'd gone down that route already, and now he'd tricked me into coming here, I'd rather flirt with a goblin than try to seduce him again.

Before I could say another word, the sound of voices drifted in from an alcove off the main cave. Darrow lifted his head. "She's addressing her Court. I would advise you not to interrupt her, Hazel."

He walked to the alcove, which turned out to contain a wooden door. Darrow pushed it open without a sound, revealing a large chamber the size of a wide hall. Towering tree trunks connected the earthen floor and ceiling like pillars, their branches forming arches overhead, while rows of Aes Sidhe stood facing an elevated platform, conversing in low murmurs. Surprise rooted me to the spot. I'd never seen more than one Aes Sidhe in the same room, unless you counted the moment Darrow and I had first arrived, but he'd been bleeding out at the time and I'd been too overcome with shock to take in the details.

Here, there were dozens of them, lined up like soldiers and dressed in brown and green attire. While their silky hair and striking features mirrored the Summer Sidhe's, their uniform appeared drab in comparison to Summer's bright finery and Winter's stark beauty. More like human clothing, an odd choice for a Court with a proclivity for glamour. I scanned the crowd, wondering if any of them might be Darrow's friends or family. His gaze, however, was fixed on the raised platform at the front of the hall. Clouds of fireflies drifted over the ceiling, coalescing above the platform and leaving the rest of the hall in relative darkness.

Etaina, leader of the Aes Sidhe, climbed onto the platform, sending silence cascading across the chamber like a waterfall. Stunning as ever, she had ivory-white hair which had made me wonder if she might be related to Darrow when I'd first seen her. Her green eyes were the same as any Summer Sidhe's, and her fine-boned features spoke of noble heritage. Silver trimmings edged her green cloak, the sole marks of elegance among the plainly-dressed soldiers.

"You have served me well." Her melodic voice echoed with each word she spoke. "You've upheld your vows and dealt with those who sought to do us harm."

Dealt with. I wondered if they had a prison here like in the Summer Court, or if they just put dissenters to death. The Sidhe here must have lost their immortality at the same time as the Courts, but given their separation, they must be even more behind on Court news than the half-faeries living in the mortal realm. Or perhaps not, if they had other spies like Darrow hiding in Summer or Winter.

The remaining fireflies gathered above the platform until the only sources of light in the room were Etaina's mesmerising green eyes. Her words meant nothing to me, but a peculiar sense of unreality gripped me, as though I'd slipped out of my body and onto another plane, casting all mundane senses aside. Was this how Ilsa felt when she used her necromancy skills to leave her body and wander around in the spirit realm? Even when I avoided looking directly at her, my body angled in her direction like the point of an arrow.

Darrow's hand squeezed mine, bringing me back to

reality with a jolt. The crowd stood mesmerised, still held under Etaina's spell, as her words rang out like heavenly bells.

She was pulling a glamour on her whole Court. Even Darrow's gaze was transfixed on the stage as though he'd quite forgotten I was standing there. I was tempted to tread on his foot to snap him out of it, but the spell broke when a rumble of voices rose from the crowd.

"We serve you, Lady of Light. We are sworn to you."

The instant Etaina stepped down off the stage, Darrow's fingers closed around my arm, urging me back towards the door.

Shaking my head to clear the fuzziness caused by Etaina's glamour, I ducked into the chamber we'd arrived in. A raven-haired Sidhe female with dark skin and green Summer eyes exited the hall behind us.

"Darrow," she said, in sour tones. "What is the Gate-keeper doing here?"

"She's come to see Etaina," Darrow said.

"No, she hasn't," I said. "Darrow whisked me away here, but I need to get back to Summer before they come looking for me."

Not that anyone in Summer knew this place existed. If it wasn't in the Courts, I could only assume we were in a liminal space somewhere, but with no doors or windows, it was beyond me to figure out where. Perhaps even below the Summer Court itself, buried deep in the hillside in a place where the other Sidhe would never find us.

The woman's gaze lingered on Darrow with more than a hint of dislike. "Nobody leaves here without permission from our leader."

"Fine." I put on a smile. "I'm interested in learning

more about your Court, so that works for me. Nice show, by the way. Does she normally use her power to turn you all into obedient servants or is this just a special occasion?"

Darrow gave me a warning look, which I ignored. If he didn't want me to comment, he shouldn't have hauled me into his Court against my will in the first place.

The other Sidhe stepped aside as Etaina strode into view, her elegant brows lifting at the sight of me.

"Gatekeeper," she said. "I told Darrow to bring me the Erlking's talisman, and instead he brought me the reason for its absence."

"You wished to speak with the Gatekeeper," said Darrow. "I searched the Vale extensively, but I found no signs of the talisman. However, Hazel was there on a mission of her own, so I thought it wise to bring her in to fulfil her end of your bargain."

Because there was no way I'd agree to come here if asked. Not only had Etaina made no secret of her desire to own the Erlking's talisman, but she also had no love for the Gatekeepers and seemed convinced that my ancestor had *stolen* the Sidhe's magic. I was in no position to argue, since Thomas Lynn had vanished not long after his daughters had become the first Gatekeepers, and whichever Sidhe had initiated the original Gatekeeper's pact remained a mystery even to our family. Etaina, however, had been alive in the days when the Erlking had taken his throne, which meant she far outclassed me in terms of knowledge.

"Very well," she said. "The Gatekeeper and I will speak alone."

She swept down the corridor, leaving me with little

choice but to follow her to her office. The high-ceilinged room was furnished in oak wood, with towering bookshelves covering the three walls and a desk and chair in the centre. The absence of any windows meant the only light in the room came from groups of fireflies flitting around the ceiling and the magic shimmering in Etaina's vibrant green eyes. Lady of Light, her people had called her, probably because she was the only source of light and colour in this underground realm.

"How deep underground are we?" I asked.

"I believe we came here for me to question you, Hazel Lynn," she said. "If you stay here long enough, you may find out."

No thanks. "At which point does this turn from a friendly chat into a hostage situation? Because I didn't bring any spare clothes, and I have several angry Summer Sidhe and a mother with a collection of iron knives waiting for me back home."

"It depends if we can come to an agreement, Hazel," she said. "I'll start by asking what you did with the Erlking's talisman."

Can't say I didn't see that one coming.

"The talisman was lost in the Vale," I told her. "Its magic destroyed Lord Veren and the other traitors, and only the stone you loaned me stopped it from killing me, too. Darrow was injured and my mother had no way out of the Vale, so my sister and I left the talisman behind in order to help them escape."

"Am I to understand that your sister carries a talisman of her own?" said Etaina. "She's human, is she not?"

I'd known Darrow would tell her, and Ilsa didn't mind being used as a cover story. Her talisman did give her the ability to cross realms, though it exacted a heavy toll on her when she used it, but it wasn't implausible that she'd have used her talisman to get us out of the Vale once our adversaries were dead.

"She is," I said. "She's also a necromancer. If you want to ask about her talisman, you're welcome to speak to her instead of me."

"Perhaps I will," she said.

Had she meant that to sound like a threat? At a guess… yes, she had. I gave her a smile. "Sure. Ilsa's more than happy to give a demonstration. Her talisman can raise and banish the dead."

Her brows crept up at my words, but she betrayed no other reaction, to my disappointment. The Sidhe feared death beyond all else, and most of them pretended Ilsa's talisman didn't exist for that reason alone. If Etaina thought Ilsa might summon a plague of zombies, I'd hoped that would put a lid on any ideas she entertained of dragging my family members here to interrogate them about the Erlking's talisman.

"You brought Darrow back to the Court with you, too," added Etaina. "If I'm to believe his story, you priori-tised saving his life over making sure the talisman stayed out of enemy hands."

"The enemy was dead, I told you." What was she getting at now? "It wasn't like I could take the talisman back into the Court. I had to leave it behind."

She gave me an assessing look. "I find it hard to believe you had no plan for disposing of the talisman once the enemy was dead."

"If you ask Darrow, you'd know I'm not a planner, not

by any stretch of the imagination," I said. "I like living on the edge."

Or rather, the Sidhe always screwed up my plans, forcing me to think outside the box.

"Yes, he did mention you had an unpredictable streak," she mused. "I also find it difficult to believe that Darrow was unable to track down the talisman when it has no wielder. What were you doing in the Vale?"

"I was on a mission for my Court," I said. "If it'd involved the talisman, I'd have asked for a loan of another one of those stones of yours. I take it you gave one to Darrow? You wouldn't have sent him out into the Vale alone without protection from the talisman's magic."

Perhaps I should have kept the stone rather than handing it back to her, but I hadn't wanted to owe her another debt, and I'd hoped keeping my word would be enough to get her to leave me alone. I didn't even want to tell her about Lord Daival, much less how he'd kidnapped the Erlking's sprite. Given that she was old enough to remember the Erlking being crowned, though, *she* might know who his heir was. *And she'll just tell you for free, will she?*

Cold magic slid over my skin like silk, probing beneath the surface. A gasp caught in my throat when it tingled up my arms, tracing the symbol on my forehead. Images of yawning chasms and starless skies appeared in my mind, and I shuffled my feet to remind myself they were firmly planted in reality. My hands knotted together, the nails digging into the skin of my palms.

Then, to my relief, the sensation lifted. Had she been testing to see if I carried the talisman's magic? She had nothing on me, but the intrusion left me reeling. Not least because I'd had a mere taste of the true extent of her power, and it left a sour, metallic taste in my mouth.

"You are in no position to judge what I wouldn't do, Hazel Lynn," she said softly. "I want the Erlking's talisman, and if you give it to me, I will tell you anything you desire to know."

"I'm not making a bargain with you." I kept my words measured, my voice steady. "There's nothing you can tell me that is worth betraying my Court."

"I think you know the talisman has the potential to affect far more than just the Summer Court, Hazel."

"Yes, but it belonged to the Erlking." Not only would I be betraying Summer if I gave it to her, but I'd also be betraying my family, and everyone else who might be affected if she turned the talisman on her fellow Sidhe. Humanity had paid a heavy enough price for the Sidhe's inability to think of anyone outside of their narrow boundaries. I didn't trust her to have humanity's best interests in mind any more than I did the Sidhe in the Summer and Winter Courts.

"The gods are waking," Etaina said. "The talisman yearns to be wielded, and if nobody makes that choice, it will do so itself."

"You're talking like talismans have feelings." Chills brushed the nape of my neck, mimicking the sensation of shadows wrapping around my fingertips, pushing me to unleash their wrath.

"Feelings?" she said. "Not in the same sense as we do, but they have desires, impulses, and no weaknesses and attachments. They want to be wielded, but they won't hesitate to manipulate their owner or turn on them if they find someone they deem more worthy."

"Guess the staff did find the Erlking worthy, then."

Etaina didn't like that, not a bit. Her eyes went even colder than before. "Talismans might be sentient, but that does not mean they cannot be manipulated."

What was she implying? That he'd taken it without permission—or stolen it?

"The Erlking spent decades or centuries cut off from his own Court to keep that talisman from harming anyone," I said. "You, on the other hand, kidnapped and manipulated *me*, so I'm less inclined to believe you wouldn't turn the talisman against my Court, given the chance."

"Are you quite certain?" she asked. "You remain loyal to the Erlking, even though you know nothing of who he really was, or what he did to your family?"

Damn her. She dangled answers like a carrot on a stick, and a traitorous part of me wanted to speak the truth just to see her confidence break, her eyes widen in disbelief that a mere human had tamed the talisman she'd been unable to claim.

Okay, that's definitely the talisman talking. I don't even want the bloody thing. She'd already laid out the price for information, and it wasn't one I was willing to pay.

"I remain loyal to my family," I said in clear tones. "To keep them safe, I choose to stand beside my belief in the Erlking."

The wristband engraved with our family name, Lynn, tingled on my wrist beneath my chilled skin. A reminder that no matter how she tried to probe me for answers, my resolve would remain as unbreakable as iron.

Her eyes flared, the green glow brightening, but she didn't strike me. "How disappointing. Leave, then."

I turned and left, a knot in my chest unravelling. I'd escaped unscathed this time. Darrow stood outside the doors, and I wondered how much he'd heard of our conversation.

"She dismissed me," I told him. "Where's the way out?"

"My sprite will take you back to Summer," he said. "He dislikes crowds, so I believe he's in my room."

Guilt churned in the pit of my stomach, a reminder that the Erlking's sprite remained at Lord Daival's mercy. I'd really thought I'd find him in the Vale. Now I'd ended up delaying, and thanks to Etaina, I'd come close to compromising the Court's security to boot.

"How generous of you," I said. "Almost makes up for you telling Etaina every single word I spoke to you. I suppose you also shared every detail of the time we spent together when you were my mentor."

All our training sessions, arguments, the time he'd accidentally blasted me with his glamour… even our hot make-out session at Lord Niall's party. If he was bound to her, he'd have had to spill every detail, yet I couldn't imagine him telling Etaina he'd pressed his body to mine and kissed me until my nerves ignited.

"Not everything," he said, his voice quieter than usual. "I didn't intend to deceive you, but I knew you'd put up a fight if I invited you here."

"Damn right I would." I folded my arms across my chest, shoving all memories of the party aside. "You screwed me over when you kidnapped me in the middle of an important mission. It better not have been longer than a day at home, otherwise shit is going down."

From Mum, not the Sidhe. The Sidhe didn't value my

life *that* highly. They'd be more likely to assume I'd deserted and hunt me down as a traitor.

"I'll keep that in mind." He led the way down a corridor towards his own quarters, where he opened the door to a sitting room furnished in similar pale shades to Etaina's office. Clusters of fireflies hovered beneath the ceiling, while the room contained little aside from a few wooden chairs and a cabinet. It had a musty, unused air, suggesting he hadn't spent much time here recently. If he'd been trekking all over the Vale in search of the talisman, it was no wonder.

"Nice place you have here," I commented. "Must be quiet, unless your neighbours are the type to have midnight revels."

Darrow glanced at me. "The Aes Sidhe are not like the Sidhe who live in the Courts."

"You mean to say they don't throw parties?" I grinned. "Lord Niall would hate it here. So would most Summer Sidhe, considering there's no windows or doors or any way to get close to nature."

"We have everything we need." His firm tone told me he'd seen through my half-hearted attempt to get him to let a clue slip about our location.

I smiled innocently back. "I bet you do. How many people does she have spying on the Courts on her behalf? Must be a fair few. And in the human realm, too. You're half-human on both sides, right? How'd that happen?"

"Unless it is more different for humans than I've been led to believe, the usual way."

My mouth parted in surprise at his comment, then I let a grin slide onto my lips. "So what was it, a wild night of passion or a drawn-out star-crossed-lovers kinda thing?"

His brow quirked. "Did you ask your parents how they conceived you?"

"No, but my dad left before I was old enough to ask," I said. "It's not much fun being tied to Faerie if you're human."

"I suppose it isn't." He crossed to a wooden door at the back of the room and rapped on it with his knuckles. "Hummingbird?"

I blinked in confusion, then remembered his sprite's name. "Maybe you'll have to show me the exit after all. I know we're near the Ley Line."

He tilted his head. "What makes you say that?"

"No Lynn is allowed to wander too far from the Ley Line without suffering backlash, even non-Gatekeepers," I said. "Given that I'm still standing, we must be close to the rest of Faerie."

His brow furrowed. "Still standing?"

"If I walk too far away from the Ley Line, I get so dizzy I pass out cold, and if I were to, say, fly to another county, the vow would rip me in half," I went on. "The Sidhe don't like to lose track of what they believe to be theirs. Still think my ancestor did this to his descendants on purpose?"

"Nobody knows the nature of the bargain Thomas Lynn struck," he said. "You're tied to the Ley Line because it's the part of the mortal realm that's the closest to Faerie, correct?"

"You've got it," I said. "Me, more than the others. Mum can leave, technically, but it's not like there's an abundance of jobs open to former Gatekeepers."

Even my siblings had had trouble hanging onto ordinary jobs, since our Sight attracted any Faerie within a mile. The Ley Line started at the tip of Scotland and travelled through the middle of the country, which didn't make it much easier to guess our current location, especially if we were in a liminal space between Faerie and Earth.

He turned the handle of the door and walked through. In a moment of curiosity, I strode after him and stuck my foot in the doorway before he could close it.

Behind the door lay a bedroom as plain as the living room, containing pale wooden furniture and few personal trappings. Weapons—knives mostly—were lined up on a wooden table, while a bookcase stood in one corner, filled with volumes in both faerie languages and Earth ones. Various outfits ranging from armour to finery hung on a rack against one wall, the only source of colour in the room.

"I guess Etaina's trusted advisor doesn't have time for hobbies," I observed. "You might have used magic to brighten up the place a bit, though. Don't you have glamour for that?"

Darrow snapped his fingers at the bookcase and his sprite rose into the air in a haze of dust, making me cough. In the spot where he'd been lying, I glimpsed an open volume of the complete works of Shakespeare marked with a postcard-shaped bookmark which depicted a bright field. Darrow slammed the book closed before I could snoop further.

"He fell asleep reading?" I stifled a laugh. "I should introduce him to my sister."

The sprite flew around Darrow's head, whispering in his ear. "He'll take you home now."

"Aww. Can't I nose around and see if I can unearth your secret diary?" I jokingly reached for the shelf, and his hand snapped out, catching my wrist. "Whoa."

My heart gave a stutter. His face was inches from mine, his eyes narrowed and startlingly bright with magic. Coldness and heat tingled in his fingertips, rippling up my arm.

"Ah. Sorry. Didn't mean to touch your stuff." I dropped my gaze self-consciously, catching sight of the edge of the postcard with the field, poking out of the book. "I should head back to Summer. They're expecting me."

Darrow released my arm, something like an apology in his eyes, but he didn't speak. Hummingbird flitted over to me with swift wingbeats like his namesake, and cold light engulfed us, sweeping us away to the Summer Court.

6

Darrow and I landed side by side on the path outside the ambassadors' palace. Hummingbird fluttered around our heads, his pointed ears pricked and his beady eyes alert.

"Are you going to tell me how you transported the two of us out of the Vale without his help?" I asked Darrow.

"Etaina gave me a transportation spell, single-use only," he answered. "Hummingbird, you can go now."

The sprite gave a bow, then he disappeared in a puff of light.

"You're coming with me, then?" I asked Darrow. "The Sidhe won't like that. They might put on their own interrogator hats and ask you who you're working for."

"That won't be an issue," he said, with absolute confidence. *Right... his glamour.* While I'd never seen him use his ability to its full extent except for that one time he'd blasted me during training, the reason he'd got the job of training me was because he'd used glamour to talk his way into Summer without anyone asking questions about his real Court. Really, it was no wonder I'd suspected him of murdering the Erlking.

"Have it your way, then." I headed through the oak doors into the palace, spotting Lady Aiten waiting beside the door to the tapestried room. "Hey, Lady Aiten. You can close the doorway now. Darrow brought me back."

I hoped she'd ask how—as a half-Sidhe, he shouldn't have the ability to cross between the Vale and the rest of Faerie—but she simply frowned at me. "Am I to take it that you successfully found Lord Daival? I don't see him with you."

"I searched, but I was told he hadn't been seen in the Vale since before his arrest," I explained. "Perhaps he did the same as Lord Veren and hid among the Sidhe here in the Summer Court."

Her eyes flared with green light. "If there's the slightest possibility he is here in the Court, then you are to track him down yourself, Hazel. Darrow, since you're here, I will give you permission to question any Sidhe you might want to, and if either of you sees anything suspect, you will report it to me."

"Of course," said Darrow.

What the bloody hell was he playing at? He couldn't possibly think the Erlking's talisman was here in Summer, could he? "What's to stop the other Sidhe from turning me into a lawn ornament if they feel I'm accusing them of being traitors?"

"I'm sure if you apply your mind to the task, you'll think of something, Gatekeeper." She waved a hand in dismissal. "Find that friend of yours. She's in the garden. I will close the doorway to the Vale."

I hope a death-stealer got out of the Vale and chewed all

your tapestries. She knew perfectly well the Sidhe were as likely to confide their secrets in me as a troll was to develop a sense of personal hygiene. Then again, if having Darrow at my side meant he wasn't probing my family on Etaina's command, I'd take it.

"Which friend?" said Darrow.

"I'd guess Coral," I said. "I'm not subjecting *her* to the wrath of angry Sidhe either, come to that. You're welcome to deal with that part yourself."

I wouldn't get any peace until I delivered Lord Daival to Lady Aiten, dead or alive, so I might as well start somewhere. Besides, I did want to check in on Coral, after I'd been forced to leave her behind at the jail.

"How much glamour did you use on her, anyway?" I said to Darrow out of the corner of my mouth. "She gave you the job without even asking what you've been doing for the last few days."

Darrow didn't answer. Come to think of it, he could probably ask any Sidhe to spill their secrets and they'd trip over themselves to do so. If he had one fraction of Etaina's skills, the guy had been holding back most of the time I'd known him.

Fucking glamour.

I found Coral in the back garden, sitting on a bench to watch sparring matches between some of the other half-Sidhe. With my promotion to Gatekeeper, there'd no longer be any need for them to live in the underground training grounds, so I'd convinced Lord Raivan to let them move into the palace. There was no shortage of spare rooms, since nobody else lived in here, and it was the safest place for mortals here in the Summer Court. After all the half-Sidhe had done to keep me alive during my Trials, the least I could do was ensure they had a roof over their heads.

I waved at Coral. "Everything okay here?"

"There you are." She sprang to her feet. "Did Lady Aiten really send you into the *Vale?* Alone?"

"I ran into an old friend." I indicated Darrow, who dipped his head in acknowledgement.

"Our task is to find the escaped criminal Lord Daival," said Darrow. "Lady Aiten believes he may be hiding here in the Summer Court."

"We haven't seen any signs of him," Coral said. "Willow and some of the other half-Sidhe searched the whole house during the party last night. They found a group of piskies partying in the attic and a troll who got stuck in a painting, but no Lord Daival."

Hmm. "Everyone at the party was glamoured halfway to hell, which doesn't help. You should have come, Darrow."

"Yeah, why weren't you there?" asked Coral. "Uh… not that it's any of my business."

While she and Darrow might both be half-Sidhe from other Courts working in Summer, he'd never been particularly friendly with the others and held himself at a deliberate distance from them the same way he did everyone else. He'd claimed it was due to his glamour being harder to hide the closer he grew to people—and to be fair, he had a point. Look how I'd managed to crash into his orderly life and unwittingly became the first person in the Courts to learn the truth of the Aes Sidhe in centuries.

"I had business elsewhere," he responded. "I've offered to accompany Hazel to question the Sidhe."

"Meaning, I'm not going to question them directly,

because I don't have a death wish," I interjected. "If I wanted to hear the latest gossip about the Sidhe, who'd be likely to talk?"

"Piskies," she said. "They're not the best choice if you don't want word of your mission to spread across half the Court, though."

"No thanks," I said. "Tell you what... do the other half-faeries have orders?"

"We're waiting for them." Coral dropped her voice. "Between you and me, the others... well, they don't really have anywhere else to go. They're either estranged from their Sidhe families or not considered a high enough priority to be invited to permanently stay in the Court."

"Oh." Coral herself was the heir to the Sea Court, so I'd forgotten how rare it was for a half-faerie to have a stable station in Summer or Winter. "If they want to carry on working as my bodyguards, then they're welcome to stay here in the palace. Is it okay if I put you in charge of them? Don't let anyone risk their safety, but if they can find anyone willing to spy for us, it would be welcome. Maybe ask some hobs or sprites who work in close proximity to the Sidhe who can see if any of them might working with the outcasts?"

"Of course." Coral smiled. "They'll be grateful you let them stay."

I didn't even know I had the authority to make that decision. The Sidhe had eased up on their attitude towards their half-human offspring in the last year, allowing those who had relations in Faerie to come to the Courts. However, the half-bloods' safety depended on the generosity of their fae relations, and they weren't allowed to own property as the Sidhe were. If I had to guess, these particular half-Sidhe had applied to work for the Gate-keeper because they *had* no relations in Faerie, or at least none who would give the time of day to a mortal. Good old-fashioned Sidhe prejudice.

"No problem," I said. "Can you get daily updates from everyone, like you did when they were my bodyguards?"

"Sure," she said. "What about you?"

I turned to Darrow. "Am I supposed to give you orders, too? Or do you want to resume your old role as mentor, minus the bond?"

"We can create another one if you like." From his tone, I couldn't tell whether he was being serious or not.

"No, thanks." A binding spell that told him where I was at any given time was the last thing I needed. "You volunteered for this job, so I assume you have no shortage of ideas as to how to track down our escapee. What do you want to do, lift rocks to see if Lord Daival is hiding underneath them?"

I was starting to regret telling him I'd been searching for Lord Daival in the Vale to begin with, though Darrow's ability to see through glamour would be an asset if he'd concealed himself here in the Court. Short of knocking on everyone's door and ordering Darrow to ask some pointed questions, though, I couldn't think of a more efficient method to find the Sidhe's wayward criminal.

"I think your plan has merit," said Darrow. "Do you believe his goal is to free the Seelie Queen?"

"Yes, I do." Before or after he'd killed the heir, I didn't know. Not that I'd be mentioning *that* detail to Darrow, with Etaina implicitly listening to every word I said to him. "I already questioned the guards at the jail and searched the Erlking's territory, and he wasn't there."

I didn't need to bring up the sprite. Lord Daival's interest in the Erlking's ex-wife was enough of an explanation for him to show an interest in that area of Faerie, after all.

"The Erlking's territory," he repeated. "Do you think he means to reclaim the Seelie Queen's home?"

I shrugged. "If he doesn't decide to set up a new Court for her in the Vale, it's as good a guess as any. If I were him, I'd run as far away from Faerie as possible, but he does whatever the Seelie Queen tells him to do even when she's behind bars. Kinda sad, really."

His jaw locked. "In the Courts, most have little choice but to obey the person who has the most power, especially if one has little of their own."

His words carried a ring of truth, as though he spoke from experience. "Lord Daival doesn't serve her because she's more powerful than he is. He's just a greedy sycophant. And I reiterate: she's behind bars. There's nothing she can do to stop him fleeing for the Vale. Granted, she's the reason he was exiled in the first place, because he betrayed the Courts for her."

"There's more than one kind of power one might wield over another," he said.

Like you and Etaina?

The phantom touch of her magic shivered across my Gatekeeper's mark. She'd scared the living shit out of me earlier, and the way she'd mesmerised her entire Court frankly disturbed me. Could Darrow do the same? He'd used his power exactly once, when I'd goaded him into giving it his all, and it'd damn near turned me into his willing servant for life. If she had a hold over even him, then her power must be off the charts. And he still thought she was the right person to wield the talisman?

He turned away. "We have a criminal to find. Let's get started."

———

It turned out wrangling lesser fae to spy on the Sidhe was a trickier job than I'd anticipated. After a frustrating afternoon giving repeated instructions to hobs and sprites about who to spy on and what information to listen out for, I returned home with the suspicion that I might have had better luck finding Lord Daival if I'd wandered around turning over every rock in the Summer Court instead.

The sight of Mum's half-assembled family tree in the living room did not improve my mood, but my sister did. Ilsa glanced up from the sofa and gave me a wave.

"Aren't you supposed to be patrolling with the necromancer guild?" I asked.

"Got the rest of the day off." She yawned. "Didn't have much to do, so..."

"So you decided to come here and research the Erlking's concubines instead of, like, going bowling with River or something."

"River is training a new group of novices at the guild," Ilsa said. "Besides, this is good research for my PhD proposal."

I lifted the topmost page. "Was the Erlking's firstborn son's codename seriously Lord of Thunderstorms?"

"According to more than one source." Ilsa took the

page back and set it down on the pile. "He was born over nine hundred years ago, died during the battle with Winter, reinvented himself as Lord Striking Thunder, died in a battle with a bunch of sluagh, and I think he became Lord of the Meandering Path afterwards. No idea what name he goes by now."

I groaned. "It's like looking for a penny in a troll's nest. I can see why some people at the Court want to just nominate their own heir and be done with it."

She rubbed her bloodshot eyes. "They do?"

"Some of them do." I sighed. "I wish I'd known the Erlking better. Then I might have an idea of who he'd choose as his successor."

"How was your day, anyway?" Ilsa asked. "The Vale wasn't too heinous this time?"

"I ran into Darrow." I sat down and conjured up a plate of cookies and a glass of water. "He hauled me off to speak to the Aes Sidhe, the dickhead. Don't worry, I didn't give anything away."

Ilsa picked up a cookie. "What the hell was he doing in the Vale?"

I downed half the glass of water. "Looking for a certain talisman, because the universe can't just give me one dilemma at a time to deal with."

I summarised my adventures in the Vale, my unexpected trip to the lands of the Aes Sidhe, and finished with Lady Aiten's ultimatum.

"That's such bullshit," said Ilsa. "It's not your job to spy on the Sidhe, and it's not supposed to be your responsibility to deal with Summer's criminals either."

"I used to do it often enough even before I became Gatekeeper," I reminded her. "Besides, Lady Aiten doesn't want to spark a panic by letting the other Sidhe know that the Erlking's sprite might have told the enemy the heir's identity."

"Understandable, but that doesn't mean she has to throw the whole burden on you." Ilsa turned a cookie over in her hands. "If we assume the sprite will give in, though, the heir will have no idea Lord Daival is coming."

"Bit hard to warn the heir when we don't know who it is," I said. "I didn't tell Darrow that part, so I don't know why he's latched onto the idea of inviting himself to help me out. Unless he thinks the talisman is in the Court. I'm lucky he didn't follow me home."

"Is that why he wants to find Lord Daival, do you think?" she asked. "He thinks he has the Erlking's talisman?"

"Never thought of that," I admitted. "But Darrow knows the talisman can't be hidden in Summer without someone noticing, and if he thinks Lord Daival has it, it makes no sense for him to waste his time searching the Court."

"He must believe sticking with you will get him what he wants, then," said Ilsa. "Or rather, what Etaina wants. Sounds like he's her lackey, for the most part."

"Yeah." I brushed crumbs off my knees, a hollow sensation forming in my chest. "I guess he is."

It shouldn't matter to me in the slightest, but the bitter sting of disappointment I'd felt when he'd hauled me into the realm of the Aes Sidhe mingled with annoyance with myself for ever believing he might be different to a typical lackey who would slit my throat if a higher authority ordered him to. Perhaps I'd thought he might be different because he had an unusual level of authority for a half-

Sidhe, but most of that was his use of glamour to get his way, and he hadn't used it when he was at home in his own Court.

He must have a trusted position if Etaina sent him on missions, though, yet in the times I'd seen him among the Aes Sidhe, he'd never been surrounded by a throng of admirers. Then again, Etaina herself didn't seem well-liked. Worshipped, yes, but not liked.

"You know how lifelong vows go," said Ilsa. The hint of sympathy in her voice made me feel even more wrong-footed. "Etaina seems like a total bitch."

"She is." I took another cookie. "She dropped another bunch of cryptic hints which were supposed to tempt me into handing the talisman to her in exchange for information. She said she was surprised I'd side with the Erlking after what he did to my family."

"Seriously?" said Ilsa. "Sounds like a bluff to me."

"I'm not planning on setting foot in that place again if I can help it," I said. "I may have mentioned your talisman again, by the way. I didn't *exactly* say you'd flood the place with zombies if she tried interrogating you, but it was implied."

Ilsa snorted. "Did you get any more clues about where the Aes Sidhe's realm is located?"

"It must be near the Ley Line," I said. "I'd have felt more strong side effects from the curse if it wasn't."

"Good point." Ilsa lifted a stack of notes. "That gives you a reference point if you get stuck there without Darrow's sprite to help you escape."

There came a knock at the door. "Speak of the devil…"

I peered out the window and glimpsed hooded faces and long cloaks. Not the Aes Sidhe, but a cult of weirdo rebels who believed the Erlking was the next messiah. Just what my day needed.

Ilsa put the notes down and pulled her talisman from her pocket. "Want me to raise a zombie to chase them off?"

"For all we know, they'd mistake it for the Erlking and put a crown on it." I walked out of the living room and down the hallway to the front door, yanking it open. "Can I help you fine gentlemen?"

The sarcasm flew right over their heads. "We have come to see the Summer Gatekeeper."

"That's me," I said. "If you're going to ask me if I'm prepared for the rapture, I'd be happy to introduce you to my own version."

When a group of them had crashed Lord Niall's party and one of them had pretended to be the Erlking himself, the Sidhe had retaliated by using thorns to shred them from the inside out. You'd think that would have been enough of a deterrent to stop them causing trouble, but apparently not.

"We are here on behalf of our king," said the hooded Sidhe at the front of the huddle of rebels.

"He's got you delivering messages from beyond the grave now?" I said.

"He will rise," said the Sidhe. "The Lord of Thorns will bring him back to us."

The what? "Lord of Thorns?"

The faerie in the Vale had called Lord Daival by the exact same title. It might be a coincidence, but the Erlking's worshippers were driven by some weird internal drive to ignore all logic and were easy targets for manipulation. I could just see them falling hook, line and sinker for the words of a new leader who promised the return of their king.

"And where is the Lord of Thorns?" I asked.

"We will be meeting at sunset tomorrow, at the hill west of the human village," he said. "There will be wine and festivities to celebrate the return of our lord. He is deeply invested in the placement of the rightful monarch on the throne."

I bet he is, if he's secretly supporting the Seelie Queen. On the other hand, what better shot would I have to find Lord Daival without having to send sprites to hide in the Sidhe's underwear drawers?

"Okay," I told them. "I'll come."

Alone. After Darrow's underhanded manoeuvre, I was far from in the mood to play nice with him, and a group of rebels should be no trouble to handle.

Closing the door, I returned to my sister. "Guess I'd better get my best arse-kicking party gear ready."

"I was going to suggest putting up a sign in the window saying *no door-to-door salesmen or weird faerie cultists,*" she said. "What did they want?"

"They're working for someone calling himself the Lord of Thorns, the same title someone in the Vale gave Lord Daival, and they're holding this party tomorrow in his regard. Might be a dead end, but what the hell."

If it *was* him, it seemed Lord Daival had wasted no time in recruiting a group of new supporters, ones who were willing to believe anything that aligned with their unfailing faith that the Erlking would return from death.

Sure wish he would *come back. That would solve almost all our problems.*

I woke to the sound of high-pitched screaming from the garden. Blinking in confusion, I turned to my bedroom window and squinted at the dark lawn. No signs of movement stirred the grass, but the screaming drifted from somewhere near the house.

I trod downstairs, my soft footsteps drowned by the clamour from outside. I crept past the living room, spotting Ilsa sprawled out on the sofa, and opened the front door.

As I stepped outside, the screaming stopped, but the creepy silence lingering over the lawn was somehow worse. The hairs rose on the back of my neck as I crossed the garden, and magic tingled in my fingertips.

The talisman.

Dread took the wheel, steering me to the Inner Garden. Inside, the water's glimmering light has dimmed, and several bodies floated face-down. Small, pointy-eared bodies. Bile rose in my throat. They were fire imps, floating dead in the water. Drowned? Or killed by my talisman's magic?

Shadows wrapped around the staff, creating rippling circles in the pool water and creeping along the bank like malevolent tentacles. Had the talisman ensnared the imps from a distance? They wouldn't have wandered over there of their own accord. *That is seriously fucking creepy.*

I reached for the water, and faint threads of shadowy magic brushed my hands. My heart climbed into my throat.

"Did you lure them here?" I whispered to the staff.

The shadowy magic crept closer, and my heart jolted

in my chest. Half of me feared it'd try to claim me again, the other half feared I'd be rejected. Without the stone, I had no defence against its destructive power. Vulnerability scraped me to the bone, and I muttered a curse under my breath. Some people had talismans which healed their injuries or alerted them to danger. What did I have? A talisman that lured innocent creatures to their deaths.

"Hazel?" Ilsa peered through the gap in the hedge. "What are you doing, sleepwalking?"

"More like talisman walking."

Her eyes widened at the sight of the imps' bloating bodies. "Shit. They weren't there the last time I looked."

"I guess the staff got hungry. Or bored." My skin shivered with revulsion, at least half of it levelled at the part of me drawn, against all rationality, to feel its magic in my hand once again.

It yearns to be wielded, and if nobody makes that choice, it will do so itself. Etaina knew it well. She was prepared to handle the fury of a talisman which had endured countless years of isolation in the hands of a man who refused to use its magic.

Okay, stop that. Don't try to work your magic on me. I'm not your pawn, and I will not bend to your will.

I gave the magic a firm shove, and to my surprise, the shadowy threads withdrew beneath the water. Did the talisman still recognise me as its wielder even after I'd rejected it?

Coldness frosted the surface of the water, turning it to ice. Not the talisman's magic.

Ilsa cursed. "There's something else in the garden."

My Gatekeeper's mark reacted with a twinge of warning. I backed out of the grove, and a shadow swept across the lawn, shaped like the vague outline of a person.

"Wraith," said Ilsa.

"Gatekeeper," growled a voice.

"Great. This one talks." I readied myself to attack, but before my Gatekeeper's magic could spread to my hands, the talisman's shadowy magic lashed at the wraith, smothering it in a dark embrace.

The wraith let out a piteous howl, flailing, but the shadows held tight. As well as draining the life from anything it touched, the talisman also fed on magic—and now I had my answer as to whether it worked on the dead. I stared, transfixed, as the wraith became more transparent and its magic unravelled, drawn to the talisman's shadowy outline in the water.

Ilsa pulled out her own talisman, a book with the image of a raven on the cover.

"I banish you," she said. "Go in peace."

As her magic extended soft blue threads, what was left of the wraith evaporated into fragments, and the talisman's remaining shadowy tendrils retracted back into the pool. I released a slow breath, my heart hammering.

"Where the hell did that thing come from?" I said. "I thought they'd left you alone for months now."

"They have," said Ilsa. "I think it came after you, not me."

Bloody hell. Had the wraith been drawn to the talisman, too? Was it putting out some kind of signal that only faeries could hear? I *hoped* it was only faeries.

"The wraith's magic froze the pool," I whispered. "Do you think the Erlking's talisman is weakening its healing power?"

Concern flickered across her face. "Maybe."

"We'll have to avoid any fatal injuries, then." My flippant tone didn't land, because if it was true, we were in a shit-ton of trouble. Despite the number of people on my team, I'd never felt as alone as I did when I looked back at the talisman's shadowy form beneath the water.

If it had only been here a few days and had already started luring in prey to feed on, how long before it started to do the same to other living things... even humans?

7

After a sleepless night, I headed back into Faerie for another thrilling day of wrangling hobgoblins and elves in the hope of finding the so-called Lord of Thorns's current hiding place. I'd have preferred to nap until the party tonight, but Darrow or Lady Aiten might come sniffing around the house if I didn't show my face in the Court.

I must have looked rough even with the bags under my eyes glamoured, because Darrow's first words to me upon my arrival in the ambassadors' palace were, "Late night? You didn't go to Lord Niall's revel, did you?"

"Didn't know he had one," I responded. "A wraith showed up on my lawn in the middle of the night. Guess it followed me from the Vale. Anyway, you couldn't pay me to go another of Lord Niall's revels, unless he's hiding Lord Daival in his basement."

"Not according to the three hobs who were spying on the event," he said. "Your employees are waiting with an update."

"They aren't my employees." Spotting Coral inside the entrance hall, I made my way over to her. "What's the latest?"

"Nothing so far," she said. "I sent a few people to watch Lord Niall's revel, but they didn't see any suspicious signs."

"Not even those rebels?" Lord Niall had skewered a few of them with thorns last time, so even they should have enough sense not to crash another of his parties. Instead, it seemed they were organising their own revel with Lord Daival himself at the helm. I wouldn't have minded telling Coral about tonight's event, but not in front of Darrow.

"Nope," said Coral. "Didn't stop Lord Niall from marching around in circles jabbing his talisman at anything that looked him funny. I think he's paranoid."

"Not enough to stop hosting parties, evidently." I turned to Darrow. "Any other ideas? If Lord Daival didn't show up to cause trouble at the party, the odds of him being here in the Court are pretty low."

"If that's the case, why did Lady Aiten argue against telling the other Sidhe?" he said. "Doesn't that imply she thinks there's a strong chance the traitor is here?"

Nope. Just the heir, whose identity might be compromised right now. I wasn't comfortable with leaving the Erlking's sprite to endure torture while I waited to ambush Lord Daival at the revel tonight, but he'd doubtless be lying low until then.

"Perhaps she thinks he's recruiting." Which he might well be, considering how many of the Seelie Queen's allies had died in the Vale when I'd claimed the talisman.

"Gatekeeper." Lord Raivan beckoned me over to one of

the tapestried rooms. His eyes were red-rimmed, while the smell of elf wine hung around him. "Come and speak with me."

"Lady Aiten sent you, didn't she?" I obligingly followed him through the door. "She told you everything?"

"She did," he said. "I'm surprised you aren't making a more active effort to search for Lord Daival in the Court, given your evident compassion for non-humans."

"I *am* making an active effort." Come to think of it, he was the Sidhe least likely to get under my feet if I told him my plan. "I have a lead, but I'll only let you know what it is if you agree not to tell Lady Aiten until it's confirmed. I don't want the whole Court involved."

"Why me and not Lady Aiten?" he asked.

"She screwed me over when she decided to hide the crown on my family's property without my permission," I said—truthfully. "You never worked for the Erlking, so you have nothing to hold over my head." *Also, you're not the one who gave me this absurd quest and refused to listen to reason.*

"Very well," he said. "State your case."

I took in a breath. "Another group of Sidhe who believe the Erlking is still alive showed up at my house trying to recruit me. I have reason to believe they're working with Lord Daival and he's brainwashed them into thinking he can bring back their king." I summed up last night's unexpected visitation. "I don't know for sure if it's him, but those guys would have stopped talking if I'd told them to get lost. If I play along and show up at the party, I can bring Lord Daival straight here to the Court."

"And what do you intend to do until then?" he asked.

"I thought I might try to figure out who the heir is

first, but I wouldn't know where to start," I admitted. "You know Lord Daival has the Erlking's sprite, right? Can you tell me his name?"

"Nobody was close to him aside from the Erlking," he said. "He rarely left his master's side. He trusted you, and you remain the only person who's seen him since the Erlking's death."

He just had to play the guilt card. "I find it hard to believe there isn't a living soul in the Courts who's set eyes on him."

Lord Raivan glanced at the tapestry, a pondering expression on his face. "There was an incident some years ago, in which a thief in the employ of one of the monarchs of the borderlands managed to break into the Erlking's territory. It's possible he might have spoken to the sprite."

"The borderlands?" I said. "Let me guess… it was one of Lady Hornbeam's people."

While the borderlands technically belonged to the Courts, they were ruled by some particularly nasty Sidhe who had no issues with shooting humans full of arrows if they dared trespass near their property. They also had zero respect for the Gatekeepers. Lady Hornbeam was the worst of the lot.

"It was," said Lord Raivan. "However, the borderlands have recently gained new leadership, following Lady Hornbeam's death."

"She's dead?" She wouldn't be missed, that was for sure, but after centuries of immortality, it must be jarring for the Sidhe who'd seemed like permanent fixtures in the Courts to suddenly cease to exist.

"She is," he said. "Lord Kerien was acquainted with their current leader, and he told me the very same thief who once broke into the Erlking's home is the new Lord Hornbeam of Half-Blood Territory."

Huh? "Did you say Half-Blood Territory?"

His mouth twitched with evident distaste. "That's what they're calling themselves. Their lands are of no concern to the Courts, so they're welcome to keep them."

Reading between the lines, I surmised that he'd opposed the idea of the half-bloods claiming their own territory but had been outvoted. Now the same guy who'd once tried to steal from the Erlking was their new leader? Dude had balls, that was for sure. "Would this monarch be interested in claiming the Erlking's throne?"

"No," said Lord Raivan. "That is… he has expressed no interest in leaving the borderlands. Therefore, you must visit him in person if you want to find out what he knows."

Hmm. The borderlands were volatile by reputation, though the half-faeries should be less difficult to deal with than Lady Hornbeam and her crossbow-wielding guards. Paying a visit seemed a decent enough diversion until the gathering tonight, and one that might turn up some useful information, too. Besides, I had to admit I was kind of curious to meet the guy who'd once tried to steal from the King of Faerie.

"I'm going to the borderlands," I told Darrow as I left the room. "Also known as Half-Blood Territory. I'm told their new leader might have some ideas about where Lord Daival is hiding." *Not to mention the heir.*

"The borderlands are no place to wander alone," he said. "If I'm to assist you in your questioning, I will need to come with you."

He sounded peeved at being left out of my meeting

with Lord Raivan, but that's what he got for shoving his way into an investigation that wasn't his to begin with. What did he expect me to do, let him in on private Court matters, and allow Etaina to have a say in selecting the next monarch? It was bad enough that she was holding information about the Erlking over my head. I didn't need to give her any more leverage.

"You needn't be so distrusting," he said, as we walked out of the gates and turned down the path away from the palace. "We're in your Court now, and I will play by Summer's rules while I'm here."

"That implies you don't play by our rules when you're elsewhere," I pointed out. "I might add that you're working for another Court whose leader tried to blackmail me into handing over something that used to belong to Summer, so anyone would distrust you."

"I desire nothing from Summer," he said. "Only the pleasure of your company."

I frowned, trying to puzzle out whether he was being sarcastic or not, but his tone was neutral. "Why, I'm flattered. Would you trust me if our positions were reversed?"

"No, but you and I see things differently, Hazel."

My heart skipped a beat. I might not be able to control my reaction to the way he said my name, but trusting him was a different matter altogether. "Like Etaina? Do the Aes Sidhe choose their leader based on bloodline? Who's the heir?"

I expected an evasion or a lie, but he said, "Etaina has ruled fairly for centuries, and she will rule for a long time to come."

"She seemed pretty disdainful of the Erlking for doing

the exact same," I commented. "What's her past with that talisman? Does she want to be the wielder?"

"No," he said. "Nobody should wield that staff."

"At least we agree on one thing." The memory of creeping tentacle-like shadows infiltrated my mind, along with how they'd lured those imps to their deaths. "How do you know she'll keep her word?"

"She will," he said. "She understands the talisman in a way few others do. Would you trust anyone else to use it in an honourable manner?"

Well, no. "No, but from what I've seen of her, I wouldn't trust her with a dangerous magical artefact with the power to disintegrate her enemies and bring the Courts crashing to their knees."

She had quite enough power already, with her glamour skills and ability to turn anyone into a devoted worshipper. Including Darrow, unless he had some personal reason for his faith in her. Based on what I'd seen, though, she didn't deserve mine. A true leader wouldn't need to put her entire congregation under a glamour to ensure obedience. Bringing that up wouldn't do me any favours, though, so that was a conversation for another day.

We turned off the main path, where thick, tangled forest blotted out the sunlight and filled the air with wild scents and wilder sounds. I did my best to tread lightly, but Darrow's utter silence was impossible for my imperfect human feet to achieve.

The borderlands, as their name suggested, lay between Summer and Winter and didn't belong to one particular Court. They'd once been divided between a number of Seelie and Unseelie families who declared frequent wars on one another over territory, and on my last trip here, one of Lady Hornbeam's soldiers had almost skewered us all on the spot because Ilsa's boyfriend had insisted on picking a fight with him. Hopefully, Lady Hornbeam's replacements hadn't inherited her fondness for torturing humans.

"I hope this half-blood king is kinder to outsiders than Lady Hornbeam was," I said. "She used to keep humans in cages and force people to duel to the death for sport."

"What did Lord Raivan tell you of this king?" Darrow asked.

"That he's a thief," I said. "By reputation, he's a sneaky bastard. He once tried to rob the Erlking and now it looks like he's stolen a throne, too."

"Reputation isn't everything," said Darrow.

Huh. Was that an attempt at an apology for the comment he'd made when we'd first met, implying I was a ditzy human who had no idea how dangerous the faeries were? Admittedly, I'd cultivated that reputation for a reason during my days as heir because it ensured the Sidhe would underestimate me and give me information they would never normally tell a human. Now I was Gatekeeper, though, I couldn't hide who I was, even out here in the borderlands.

"Sometimes it is. Look at Lord Niall." I dug my hands in my pockets, wondering how much further we had to walk. "Did you see Lord Raivan earlier? He was blatantly hungover halfway to hell. He must have drunk an ocean of elf wine last night."

Movement slithered in the undergrowth, raising the hairs on my arms. A sluagh, half spirit, half corporeal, rose from the bushes and settled into the form of a ghostly humanoid figure.

I drew an iron knife. "You're not supposed to be here."

"It's from the Vale." Darrow's shoulders tensed. "The borderlands are close to the land of the outcasts."

I gave him a sideways glance. "You never mentioned you'd been here before."

"You never asked."

I lunged at the sluagh, but the iron blade passed through its semi-transparent form. *Dammit.* I tugged at the knife's handle, and a torrent of ice-cold air slammed into me from behind. A second sluagh had joined the first, its rippling form resolving into a giant insect-like creature with way too many legs. Jets of a foul black substance shot from its mouth, splattering the ground at my feet. That would be a pain to clean out of my shoes.

Darrow's icy magic smacked into the second sluagh, freezing the venom before it touched me. With a nod of acknowledgement, I sank my knife deeper into the first sluagh, seeking its beating heart. A shower of dark blood told me I'd found my mark.

Darrow circled the second sluagh, aiming a blast of magic that sent it reeling backwards into the path of my blade.

"Nice teamwork." I yanked my knife out of the sluagh, and its formless body collapsed.

Pain speared my arms as the blade-like branches of a tree wrapped around me from behind. *Not* a sluagh. Sharp, finger-like branches climbed up my shoulders, grabbing for the circlet.

"Hey! Hands off." I swung my foot back, slamming it

into the tree trunk, but the angle of made it impossible to drive the blade into the wood and make it let me go.

Darrow lunged at the dryad himself, and its sharp branches went for him instead. I shouted a warning, but the instant the branches made contact with him, he vanished.

A moment later, a second Darrow pounced on the tree from behind, his blade sinking into one of the branches that held me. That was enough for me to free my right arm, and my iron blade sliced the branches clean off, sending a spray of sap the colour of blood onto my shoes. Yanking my other arm free, I pivoted to find myself faced with a grey-trunked tree inset with a feminine face. Dryads were typically bright and vibrant, but not a single leaf grew on the tree's branches and the dryad's face was grey and wrinkled.

She'd also tried to strangle me, but now I saw the lifeless colour of her trunk, I suspected she'd tried to grab my circlet because she needed magic. Her tree was dying, the life bleeding out of it as though touched by the destructive power of the Erlking's talisman.

Before I could quite consider what I was doing, I called my Summer magic and pressed my hands to the bleeding trunk. After a few moments, the grey colouring turned a healthy brown, and leaves began to sprout from its branches again. The dryad's gasps evened out, and her eyes brimmed with gratitude.

"Thank you, human," she murmured. "A favour I will grant you."

"Can you point us in the direction of Half-Blood Territory?" I asked.

A branch extended, pointing northwest into the trees.

"Go in peace, human. You will face no more enmity from me."

I nodded in acknowledgement and began trekking northwest.

Darrow gave me an odd look. "Why did you heal her? Did you know she'd point us in the right direction?"

"No, but she was dying."

Confusion wrinkled his brow. He didn't get it, and I wasn't sure I did either. Once, Darrow had told me he thought attachments to others were nothing more than a liability, but his own actions in helping me proved he didn't always follow that rule. On the other hand, while I didn't normally save the lives of people who tried to kill me, there was something weird about the dryad's desperate state. Was it a consequence of the Vale being close to the borderlands, or some insidious aftereffect of the Erlking's death?

"You might want to glamour your clothes if we're visiting a monarch," Darrow said.

"Fair point." I pulled a glamour on, adding a few embellishments to cover the damage and make me look a little less like I'd just taken a bath in oil-like slime. Darrow could glamour circles around me, though, and between one blink and the next, he was as pristine as ever. His silver hair was glossy, and his clothes gleamed, looking more like he was on his way to a fancy event than a walk through one of Faerie's most dangerous regions.

His eyes flared with magic. "We're being watched."

Without a sound, a number of figures emerged from the trees, dressed in dark clothing and wielding bows, spears and swords. A smile curled my lip. "I guess things haven't changed much here, then."

8

I faced the group of armed strangers. "We're here to speak to the leader of Half-Blood Territory, on behalf of the Summer Court. It's about the Erlking."

"We know of the Erlking's passing," said a bow-wielding female half-Sidhe with ebony skin and braided hair. She was clad in some kind of brown-grey armour that didn't give away her Court designation. Nor did the others', though I'd automatically classified them as Summer due to Lady Hornbeam once owning this territory. Now I looked closer, some of them had blue eyes which signalled Winter heritage.

A female half-faerie with pale skin and long dark hair stepped forward. "I'll take you to him," she said. "I can't promise Lady Whitefall will be accommodating, however. We've had a lot of trespassing incidents lately."

"Trespassers?" *Like Lord Daival?* With a glance to make sure the archers weren't going to fire at my back, I walked after the half-faerie with Darrow at my side.

A short distance away lay a palace, surrounded by

wooden fences of interwoven thorns. While the thorns mimicked Summer's style, the palace's bone-white walls put me more in mind of the Winter Court. As we walked through a gate to the oak wood doors, a male Summer half-Sidhe walked out to greet us. A thin scar bisected his cheekbone, while his unembellished clothing resembled that of the guards. Only the silver crown atop his shoulder-length dark hair gave away his identity as the new Lord Hornbeam.

I'd also seen him once before, minus the crown. "Princeling? *You're* the new leader?"

He cocked a brow. "You again? The Gatekeeper pretender?"

"I'm the official Gatekeeper now," I told him, "and I'm here on behalf of the Summer Court and the Erlking."

At least he wasn't pointing an arrow at my skull, but let's just say we'd got off on the wrong foot during my last visit to the borderlands. He was the same guy who'd threatened to hand me over to Lady Hornbeam for bringing my siblings into the Court. Now I thought back, River had recognised him as Lady Hornbeam's thief, but I'd never got his name.

"Who is it, Cedar?" A female half-Sidhe strode out of the doors to join him. Her hair was the same colour as the snow-white walls behind her, while power thrummed in her bright blue eyes. Her armoured outfit mimicked Cedar's, but an identical silver crown sat atop her head.

A Summer and Winter half-Sidhe ruled side by side? In the mortal realm, it'd go unremarked upon, but Faerie had been divided between Summer and Winter from the start, even in the borderlands.

"These two are here from Summer." Cedar's lip curled. "On behalf of the deceased Erlking, allegedly."

"I'm Hazel Lynn, Gatekeeper of the Summer Court," I said to the newcomer. "I came to speak to... to whoever rules the borderlands, I guess."

"That would be us," said the woman. "I'm Lady Whitefall, joint ruler of Half-Blood Territory."

"Since when?" I tried to keep my tone non-confrontational, but I could hardly believe the Sidhe had let them take over the whole of the borderlands without a fuss.

"Since all the ruling borderland Sidhe died or turned traitor," said Cedar. "Including Lady Hornbeam."

"Damn," I said. "You two seemed pretty tight. I'm surprised."

Lady Whitefall gave him an uncertain look. "Do you know her, Cedar?"

"We met," he said. "I found her trespassing on Lady Hornbeam's territory some months ago with a troop of humans."

"With my family," I corrected. "To warn the Summer Court of an impending coup. He and my sister's boyfriend nearly got into a punch-up over a talisman and he threatened to shoot me."

Lady Whitefall looked like she was trying not to laugh. "Your past comes back to haunt you again, Cedar. We don't run things the same way Lady Hornbeam did, don't worry. Humans are welcome here. You'd better come in. Oh, and you can call me Raine."

Well, damn. I'd come here expecting a trap and found something far weirder. While I hadn't ruled out the possibility of the half-bloods turning on us, this Cedar was a world away from the prickly thief who'd threatened to shoot me on behalf of his unforgiving queen.

A high-ceilinged room off the main hall greeted us, dominated by two towering thrones. On either side, tapestries cloaked the walls, depicting lush forests and fields, snowy wastelands and frozen lakes.

"We want half-faeries from both Courts to feel welcome here," explained Raine. "Like they do in the mortal realm."

I studied her, noting her accent was plainly English despite the lilting cadence common to half-bloods. "You grew up there."

"Right." She nodded. "What did you call yourself, the Gatekeeper? I've heard about you, but Cedar didn't mention you'd met."

"We didn't exactly have time to stop and chat," I said. "Also, I wasn't Gatekeeper at the time. I was the heir."

Cedar's eyes raked me up and down. "You're human, right? The Sidhe didn't mention that part. I was told you were peacekeepers."

"We are." If Raine was new to Faerie, most half-bloods in the mortal realm knew little of the Gatekeepers, but it seemed Lady Hornbeam had neglected to share information on the Courts with her soldiers, too. It surprised me the Sidhe had told them anything at all, actually, but perhaps they'd struck some kind of bargain when the half-bloods had taken over this territory. "That is, we're peacekeepers between humans and faeries."

Cedar's gaze went to Darrow. I tensed, expecting him to blast the two of them with glamour, but half his attention was on the tapestried walls. "I am Darrow, an ambassador assigned to help the Gatekeeper with her mission.

Did the Courts give you permission to rule over the borderlands?"

"Of course," said Raine. "We take care of the borderlands, and they leave us alone, for the most part. Nobody else wants to live here, so it worked out pretty well."

The half-faeries living in the ambassadors' palace might be interested to know this place existed. Those who were lucky enough to be invited to live in Faerie were forced to depend on the generosity of their Sidhe families, which was often lacking. On the other hand, there must be another reason Raine and Cedar had convinced the Sidhe to hand over the borderlands to them. What powers did they possess? Cedar carried no weapons save for the crossbow strapped to his back, but the bright glow in Raine's eyes signalled strong magic, while a similar glow came from a long sceptre strapped to her side. Threads of power brushed against me, cold and sharp and disconcertingly intelligent. "You have a talisman."

"I do." She lifted the talisman—a sceptre the colour of ice, with the blue glow of its magic shimmering around the tip—and its chilling touch slid beneath my skin as though probing the depths of my soul. I forgot to breathe for an instant. While not a single drop of the Erlking's magic ran in my veins any longer, some deep intelligence in the talisman recognised me as a kindred spirit. "That circlet on your head..."

"Oh, it's not a talisman." I buried my cold hands in my pockets, trying to quell the lingering sense of disquiet. "It's a ceremonial circlet, that's all."

"You didn't come here to discuss talismans," said Cedar. "Why did you come?"

"There is a criminal loose in Faerie," said Darrow.

"Lord Daival. We wondered if you'd seen any signs of him in the borderlands."

"Lord Daival?" Cedar frowned. "I know of him, but no, we haven't seen any Sidhe here for a long while. Is that all?"

Darrow gave me an expectant look, and for once, my mind went blank. "Uh, not all. I also heard you once tried to steal from the Erlking, and frankly I'm intrigued enough to want to hear the story for myself."

Amusement flickered in Cedar's eyes. "That's still going around?"

"It's true, isn't it?"

"Yes, it's true," he said. "There's little to tell. I stole a security talisman, slipped through the gates and was caught in the act by the Erlking himself. He knew me for Lady Hornbeam's child thief, so he sent me on my way without punishing me."

"While you were there, did you see anything odd?" *Really specific, Hazel.* "I mean, which part of his territory did you see?" *Like his talisman?*

"Not much." He gave a smile that softened his features considerably. "I found my way into the forest, and as luck would have it, I ran into the Erlking himself coming the other way. I never found his quarters."

Hmm. The Erlking presumably hadn't been carrying the talisman on him at the time, but perhaps he left it behind whenever he wanted to walk in the woods without turning everything he touched into dust. It must be tiresome having to keep an eye on it for every waking moment.

From Darrow's expression, he knew I was probing for information, but not my reasons. I hastened to say, "That's all we wanted to know. I should mention we were attacked by sluagh on the way here. Is that common in the borderlands?"

"Very common," said Raine. "Vale beasts often trespass here. That's why we have fences around the palace, to keep them out."

"What about the Sidhe?" I asked. "Do they often come this way? Would an outcast be able to hide in the forest?"

"Not as well as they would in the Vale," said Cedar. "We send frequent patrols around our territory. Nobody would be able to evade our attention for long."

I guess not. With Darrow hovering over my shoulder, I didn't dare ask any questions that alluded to the heir or the sprite, but hours remained until tonight's special event, and the question of the heir's identity loomed larger than ever. It was unlikely a group of half-Sidhe in the borderlands knew who the Erlking had nominated to be his successor, but if Lord Daival was a no-show tonight, I'd regret not trying harder to find him.

"Is there anyone else who might help?" I asked. "The Sidhe don't want word to spread of Lord Daival's escape, but given his closeness to the Seelie Queen, we're concerned he might come back to break her out of jail."

"You could always try the memory-eater," said Raine. "She can extract information from the memories of those around her. If Lord Daival passed her way, she'll know where he was heading."

"Extract memories?" I raised an eyebrow. "That sounds unpleasant."

"It is," said Raine. "She also tends to require a price for her services. Fair warning."

That figured. On the other hand, if this memory-eater

could extract *anyone's* memories, might she know the identity of the heir? The Seelie Queen had been adamant only the sprite knew, but she'd told the truth according to what she believed. If this memory-eater had ever met the Erlking and read his thoughts… *damn. That's one hell of a power.*

"Whereabouts does she live?" I asked.

"On the east side of the borderlands," said Raine. "Follow the path into the forest and head for the clouds. I'll just go and fetch something you'll need to take with you."

She slipped through a wooden door at the back of the hall which I was positive hadn't been there beforehand. Cedar, meanwhile, paced away from the throne to speak to the dark-haired female soldier from earlier. I watched him for an instant, wondering how he'd talked the Sidhe into letting him become the new king. While he carried no talisman like Raine's, being trusted to steal from the Erlking required uncommon skill, and it was no mean feat to go from Lady Hornbeam's lackey to a leader in his own right, either. If I didn't know Darrow would pass on every word we spoke to Etaina, I'd have asked him more questions.

Darrow, however, seemed more interested in the bright tapestries clothing the walls. In the picture to our right, frost-crowned trees overlooked a meadow of autumn-yellow flowers, like an amalgamation of Summer and Winter. The one closest to us depicted a flock of horses galloping across a plain. Not just horses—the one in the lead boasted an impressive horn. I reached out to the painting and stroked the unicorn's forehead.

"What *are* you doing?" Darrow wanted to know.

I lowered my hand. "What? I like unicorns. Always wanted to see one."

He eyed the beast's magnificent form. "Why?"

"No idea. Probably because one hasn't tried to kill me yet." My impression of horses had somewhat soured after a rogue kelpie had nearly drowned me in a loch when I was six years old, while I'd found imps adorable until a group of them had tried to set me on fire in junior school.

"Hmm." Darrow's expression was unreadable when he studied the tapestries, though when he saw me looking, he averted his gaze. Did he feel guilty for admiring another Court? A Court that wasn't buried underground, and which didn't involve swearing any vows of service or facing brainwashing glamour—and was ruled by two half-bloods at that. In Faerie, stumbling across a unicorn was far more likely than any of those things.

I turned to Cedar. "Do you require your citizens to swear a vow, like the Courts do?"

His eyes narrowed. "Certainly not."

I blinked at the vehemence in his tone. "Just wondered. It seems…"

Too good to be true. I wouldn't have minded living in a place like this, even as a human. I'd never be completely at home living among the half-faeries, but my position set me too far apart from other humans aside from my family, and the Sidhe didn't do friendship, only alliances.

"We allow people to opt in, rather than forcing them." Raine slipped through the door back into the hall, the tapestries fluttering in the breeze stirred up by her arrival. In her hand dangled a small bag, which she handed to me. "The Sidhe don't like it, but they gave up the borderlands and now they have to live with whatever we decide to do with them. I think Lord Kerien hopes the Vale's monsters will drive us out."

"Lord Kerien?" I pocketed the bag. "You know he's dead, right?"

Her eyes widened. "When?"

"I thought everyone knew." That explained why they weren't up-to-date on recent events in the Courts. Lord Kerien had been the main ambassador between mortals and the Sidhe before his death. "He was killed while investigating the Erlking's murder, murdered by one of the faeries who conspired against Summer on the Seelie Queen's orders."

Raine turned to Cedar with a troubled expression. "I didn't hear. Did you?"

"Lady Whitefall!" One of the archers from earlier ran into the room, his clothes bloody and torn. "There's been an attack."

Raine's expression hardened, and she pulled out her sceptre. Cedar reached for his crossbow, moving fluidly to the door.

Outside, the sound of screaming came from somewhere near the fence on our left. A roar followed, and we ran towards the fence to find two giant trolls bearing down on a group of half-faeries. Two arrows flew from Cedar's bow, burying themselves in the troll's shoulders, while Raine swung her sceptre, sending a jet of icy energy into the monster's eyes.

The second troll swung hands encased in iron chains which suggested it'd run away from the Vale. I jumped in with my blade, sinking it deep into the troll's thigh, but the troll shook off the iron wound and swung its chains at me. I ducked under its arm, and Darrow stabbed it from the side, fighting with a sharp ferocity that surprised me. His usual cool manner had cracked, his blows swift and ruthless, his mouth set in a hard line.

Darrow's blade cleaved through the meat of the troll's ankle. The troll bellowed in pain, its stump of a leg gushing blood. It stumbled into the path of my blade, which sank deep into its neck. More blood gushed, the troll's death rattle ringing in my ears.

Raine and Cedar moved toward the bodies of their fallen soldiers. Cedar's hands glowed with the familiar glow of healing magic, but from his grim expression, it was too late for at least one of the victims.

My throat closed up. "Is there nothing we can do?"

"No," said Cedar, his voice soft. "I'm afraid there isn't."

It hurt to leave them like this, but neither of us had healing magic. If Lord Daival was behind the attack, I had yet another incentive to skewer the bastard. "I'm sorry."

Silence lingered over Darrow and me as we left. His expression remained preoccupied, remote, but my mind kept spinning in circles. Had Lord Daival sent those trolls to attack Half-Blood Territory? If they'd come from the Vale, surely not, but I couldn't help wondering if our own presence here might have triggered their arrival.

Even if not, the sluagh's appearance earlier and Raine and Cedar's comments reminded me of the borderlands' proximity to the Vale. They must have known what they were getting into when they'd built their home here, and I could only hope they continued to thrive in defiance of anything the world threw at them. A land where anyone in Faerie might walk freely was a rare thing indeed.

After this, the idea of making yet more bargains with a fae by the name of the 'memory-eater' was not an appealing one, but when I spotted another patch of dying trees on our right-hand side, it brought a reminder that the Vale wasn't the only source of trouble in this part of Faerie. Something was wrong, and at this point, any answers would be more than welcome.

I just hoped this memory-eater's price didn't turn out to be as impossible to pay as Etaina's.

9

Darrow and I followed Raine's directions to the east of the borderlands, where I pulled out the small bag she'd given me. Inside were a handful of small berries and a note that read, *you'll need to eat these to breathe in the memory-eater's territory.*

"We have to eat these?" I sniffed at them, recalling Coral's lessons on detecting poisons, but didn't pick up on anything untoward. The berries smelled of wildflowers, and when I tossed one into my mouth, it tasted more like floral-scented soap. I pulled a face as I chewed. "To breathe... I guess the memory-eater must live somewhere the air isn't breathable."

Darrow held out his palm. "I heard she lives high up in the clouds."

"You didn't mention you'd heard of the memory-eater before." I handed him the remaining berries and he popped one into his mouth.

"I've heard of most of the fae who lives outside the boundaries of the Courts," Darrow answered.

"Not them." I jerked my head over my shoulder in the general direction of the palace. "Half-Blood Territory is a new addition."

Not an unwelcome one, either. I debated asking if seeing the half-bloods' palace had caused him to rethink his decision to stand by Etaina's draconian orders, but he spoke first. "I believe we're being watched."

I glanced up, following his line of sight. The clouds appeared to hang lower than they had before, brushing the tops of the trees and cloaking them in whiteness. Wood imps peered from holes in the tree trunks, but that wasn't what made the back of my neck prickle as though unseen eyes stared down at us from the clouds.

As we went deeper into the woods, the clouds lowered even further until they swirled around our ankles and obscured the ground, in a manner disconcertingly similar to the creepy clouded path in the Grey Vale. A sudden rush of vertigo hit me when I saw the tops of the borderland's trees *below* us. The path had turned vertical, and we'd been walking upright without noticing.

"I'm guessing this is the reason for the berries." I turned to Darrow to find him staring white-faced at the clouded path. For someone who'd grown up underground, walking into the sky must be even more overwhelming than it was for me. "Want to turn back? I can go and see the memory-eater alone."

If anything, I'd prefer it that way. If she could read the minds of every single person who passed her way, did that mean she knew I'd claimed the talisman? Would she be able to show anyone else that memory if they asked?

I think coming here might have been a mistake.

Without warning, Darrow disappeared, sinking through a carpet of cloud into the treetops below.

"Darrow!" Alarm lanced through me, and the ground dipped beneath my feet. I scanned for a way down, and a long-limbed faerie rose from the clouds and blocked my path. Her white hair was long and braided with thorny branches, while her wings had odd rainbow patterns which gave her an oddly child-like air in contrast to her wrinkled face. A pair of eyes brimming with intelligence and cunning looked me up and down.

"Hazel Lynn," said the faerie. "You have passed your Trials, but your tests as Gatekeeper have yet to truly begin. You have an interesting road ahead of you."

"Where is Darrow?" I glanced below, but puffy clouds covered the view beneath my feet.

The winged faerie studied me, a hint of wickedness in her wire-thin smile. "You wanted him gone, did you not?"

"I didn't want him to fall to his death." If the trees had been as close as they looked, he would have had little trouble catching his balance and climbing to the ground, but that didn't mean I appreciated her trickery. "Also, are you reading my thoughts right now?"

"They call me the memory-eater for a reason," she said. "Whenever a person passes within range of my domain, their memories flood into my mind, every last one of them. I know the truth of you, Hazel Lynn. I know what it is you crave."

"I didn't come here to talk about me," I told her. "Have you seen Lord Daival recently?"

"I do not see with my eyes as you do," said the memory-eater. "I cannot see his location, only his memories and others' memories of him. The Lord of Thorns has lived a long life, mortal, and I will show you one memory, just one. Choose wisely."

Hmm. "Have you seen any recent memories of him kidnapping a sprite?"

She leaned forward, excitement suffusing the craggy lines of her face. "He has committed a heinous crime, oh yes, in capturing an innocent creature to torture for information."

My remaining hopes that the sprite might have escaped elsewhere evaporated like mist. "Will you show me? What is your price?"

"I will show you one memory in exchange for another, mortal."

"Exchange?" I looked into those ageless eyes. "You consume memories, don't you?"

"I do, mortal," she said. "You're not the first to come here looking for answers, but I am no powerless being for the powerful to torture and lock in a cage. Are you sure you want the truth, Hazel Lynn?"

Okay... "Can you just show me the memory?" My heartbeat kicked into gear, my body tensing in anticipation of an attack.

Then the clouds rose up, drawing me into their embrace.

———

I lay in a light doze, summer air drifting through the open window and bringing the scents of night-blooming flowers. Through lidded eyes, I took in the familiar outlines of the furniture in my bedroom back at the Lynn house.

Footsteps sounded, then a whisper, soft as a caress. "This is the one, is she not?"

I shivered. No human voice spoke in such a melodic cadence, like music formed into words. My eyes itched to open further, but my eyelids felt heavy, weighted. Two dark shapes passed within my line of sight, one tall and feminine, the other shorter and stockier.

"Yes, my Lady," murmured a deeper voice. "She is the one."

Panic gripped me, and a sudden blaze of silver light dragged my eyes open. Pain seared the skin of my forehead as the Gatekeeper's mark imprinted itself on me, imbuing me with the magic of Summer.

I jerked out of the memory the instant I recognised it as such, finding myself standing in the clouds once more. They'd thinned out, revealing the spear-sharp treetops below. I should be alarmed that there was nothing solid beneath my feet, but it was the dream that made me reel in shock.

Was there really someone else there the night I was chosen as Gatekeeper? The voices had been too quiet to make out any signs of familiarity, but I'd always thought the Gatekeeper selection was totally random. After Morgan hadn't been chosen, the choice had been a fifty-fifty split between Ilsa and me, and I'd assumed we'd both had an equal shot.

Had the Sidhe spied on us since infancy? They visited our house whenever they wanted, everyone knew that, but if it was true, the memory-eater had done far more than read my memories: she'd teased out details I hadn't known were there. I tried to recall the two figures I'd seen in the memory, but the image was already fading, and doubt filtered in. *It's a trick. A glamour. It must be.*

The memory-eater appeared before me, her rainbow wings beating. "Intriguing, no?"

"What was that in aid of?" My hands curled into fists. "I told you to show me a memory of Lord Daival, not one of my own memories. Assuming it wasn't a trick."

Her wicked smile returned. "I saw the memory in your mind, and I know how deeply you yearn for the truth. Many questions gnaw at you, and you will never be at peace until you gain satisfying answers."

My hands clenched and unclenched at my sides. "I came to answer a specific question, and that's it. I want to know where Lord Daival is hiding so I can tear into him with a sword."

"Is revenge your primary motive?" she said. "I think you're lying to yourself because you fear the price you must pay to gain the answers you crave."

The image of the talisman flashed through my mind. I might have to test the limits of what I was willing to do to keep my own secrets one day, but I'd come here on a mission and I was damned if I let her distract me from it.

"How often do you get visitors from the Courts?" I asked. "Because I'd have thought they'd want to use your power to spy on their enemies."

Fury snapped through her expression. "I am no servant of the Sidhe, and I never show any memories without a price."

"Then what was your price for that memory you showed me?" I folded my arms. "You never told me which memory you wanted from me. It seems to me that you change the rules whenever it suits you."

"This is my domain, human," she said. "The rules are mine. I gave you one memory for free, but for your impertinence, the next will require a higher cost."

I'd walked right into that one. "What cost?"

"Tell me which memory you desire to see and I will answer you, mortal."

I drew in a breath. "What is your price for letting me see Lord Daival's most recent memory?"

'Most recent' ought to tell me his current location, surely. Why had I ever thought a rogue fae would show me anything but trickery and deceit?

"I will show you the memory of the one you seek in exchange for a promise," she said. "One further favour you will owe me. Do you accept those terms?"

A favour? She couldn't ask me to do anything that contradicted my binding to the Summer Court without it rebounding on her, so that was probably the best I'd get. And better than giving up any of my own memories.

"I accept."

The clouds enveloped me once more, and my vision darkened. In the gloom, a tall, silver-haired Sidhe paced before my eyes, muttering to himself in the faerie tongue. Earthen walls formed a wide space beneath a domed roof. *Is he in Faerie or the mortal realm?* No obvious landmarks caught my eyes, as Lord Daival continued to mutter and pace.

I startled at the word *sprite,* spoken in the faerie language. I wasn't exactly fluent—when the Sidhe spoke to me, their magic made me capable of understanding every word as though it was English, so I hadn't had all that many opportunities to practise—but I recognised the gist of his words. He was angry with the sprite. *Is it because he's refusing to give in and share who the heir is?*

If so... there might be hope for his survival, after all. *Hang in there. I'm coming after you.*

The memory faded away, and the clouds reappeared beneath my feet. The memory-eater had vanished from sight. Nothing remained but clouds, treetops, and a bright sky without sunlight. All I'd gleaned from the memory was that Lord Daival was angry with the sprite, most likely for refusing to spill the Erlking's secrets... but not his location.

"You might have given me a clue as to *where* that cave is," I said, but the memory-eater didn't reappear. I should have figured she'd find a way to weasel out of giving me answers.

Irritation scratched at me like an itch. *Many questions gnaw at you, and you will never be at peace until you gain satisfying answers.* She thought she knew me, and hell, maybe she did. She'd read my every thought, and if I could bargain with her to gain access to another person's memories, anyone might come here and do the same with mine. Like Darrow, wherever he was. I peered down through the clouds, but the ground was too far away. I'd need to climb down to find him.

I took another step, and the clouds vanished beneath my feet. Cold air rushed past, branches scraped my face, and my circlet flared up, green light spreading to the trees and urging them to break my fall.

My hands snagged a thick bough, jerking my body to a stop. I hung suspended for a moment, judging the distance to jump, then dropped to the earth. Soil cushioned my feet, and the earthy smells of the forest surrounded me on all sides.

Well, that's one way to climb down.

"Was it worth the sacrifice?" said the memory-eater's voice from within the fog-drenched woods. I snapped my head upright, but the faerie wasn't speaking to me.

Darrow stood not ten metres away from me, watching the memory-eater's winged form hovering between the trees.

"Was your position worth the price you paid?" the memory-eater went on. "Was it worth her life?"

"That is not your place to judge." There was something oddly raw in his tone. "You know nothing of me or the choices I have made."

"Oh, I don't need to know your thoughts to understand your choices," she said. "I've seen many like you... many who bind themselves with chains, who walk a path they know will lead to ruin.'

Worth her life? Whose life? Had someone close to him died?

"You can only see the past, not the future," Darrow told her. "You can't know where my path will take me."

"I am no oracle, but the past allows me to predict the future with startling accuracy," she said. "I have seen many like you end up the same way. I know what it is you crave."

"Then you can tell me where the talisman is," he said.

My breath stoppered in my lungs. *No. please, no.*

"You want it not for yourself, and that will ruin you," she said. "You are the master of your own fate, even with the tethers that bind you. The Ancients' magic has a will of its own, and there is nothing it likes more than a willing pawn."

An image entered my mind, unbidden: Darrow lifting the talisman, its shadows wrapping around his wrist. Raw jealously pierced me to the core.

Stop that. It's not yours. I'd fought too damn hard to fall to the very magic that had led the Sidhe to exile the gods from their realm. The memory-eater might be full of shit, but her words about the talisman fit with what I'd seen and heard so far. Still, I was no pawn, and I was under no illusions about the origin of its power.

I didn't think I'd moved or made a sound, but something must have tipped Darrow off as to my presence. His head tilted my way, and the memory-eater vanished into the surrounding mist.

Darrow spoke without looking at me. "This was a mistake," he said. "The memory-eater has no true Court. She can strip out our secrets and hand them directly to the enemy."

"I'm not sure she will," I said. "Don't get me wrong, she's unpleasant, but from her reaction when I suggested she could make a fortune from spying on the Sidhe, she thinks they're beneath her."

He turned around to face me. "You said what?"

"It slipped out. Not my smartest moment." To say the least. "She showed me Lord Daival is hiding in a cave, so she couldn't have been too offended."

Darrow made a noise that almost qualified as a sigh, and an inexplicable smile quirked my lips. "I assume she's gone, but I confess, I've lost track of the way back."

"You and me both." What with all the mist, it was a little

difficult to tell. Nobody had ever mapped Faerie, because while some parts—like the path back into the mortal realm—remained in more or less the same place, while others moved around on a whim. Trees came to life and walked off. Whole sections vanished with no explanation. The Sidhe, with their ability to use their magic to hop around effortlessly, seemed oblivious to how frustrating this was to the rest of us mere mortals. The memory-eater's realm didn't seem to be anchored to the rest of Faerie, but there must be a way out.

"What did you promise her in exchange for what she showed you?" Darrow asked.

"A favour," I said. "She can't make me do anything to betray the Court, so if she wants to use me for revenge on the Sidhe, it won't work out for her. What about you? Did she show you anything?"

"No. She tried."

He'd resisted her temptation, unlike me, but it didn't matter to him whether we found Lord Daival or not. "I swear we should be out of this fog by now."

Darrow cursed under his breath. "We're still in the memory-eater's domain."

Damn her. What was she devising now?

"You haven't called your favour yet," I said to the forest. "Either tell me what you want or let us go and stop these games."

"You're free to go." Her voice drifted from the mist, with a barely concealed laugh. "If you make it to the other side of the mist, that is. But you won't sniff *me* out so easily, Gatekeeper."

An odd choice of wording. Was she referencing the time Darrow had challenged me to go through a hedge maze without him catching me? I *had* sniffed out his magic, which might sound a little weird, I'd intended to use all the resources at my disposal. If she wanted to strike fear into my heart, she'd have to do better than that.

"I'd rather not sniff you out at all, thanks." I took a step into the misty forest, away from her laughing voice.

At once, a vivid image showed before my eyes—a field, bright with yellow flowers. I instantly recognised it as Summer's meadow, the one near the boundaries of the Court, where Lord Raivan spent his free time.

"Stop staring," said a voice from beside my shoulder.

"I've never seen grass before," I said—or rather, the person whose eyes I saw through did. A young male, I'd guess. "Real grass, I mean."

"If you want to impress the Lady, I wouldn't get distracted by scenery, Darrow."

Holy shit. I was in Darrow's memory?

The scene lingered for an instant before vanishing from sight, depositing me back in the mist. There was no sign of either Darrow or the memory-eater, but his memory had pulled me in, as vivid as the bright yellow flowers blanketing the grass.

Why had she shown me Darrow's past? To goad me with glimpses of the history he wouldn't tell me, or to taunt both of us at the same time? Had she shown him the same, or…?

Fear slithered through me. If I'd seen Darrow's past, then he might have seen mine at the exact same instant. If so, one wrong step would reveal the truth we wanted to conceal.

The mist would show Darrow exactly where the Erlking's talisman was hidden.

10

I remained rooted to the spot for an instant, the mist swirling around me and masking the trees from sight. That crafty bitch had played us for fools. This was her idea of a game. Win, and she'd let us leave. Lose, and we'd know the truth of one another. I'd bet she'd seen into my memories and my decision to hide the talisman and drawn her own conclusions about what I had and hadn't shared with Darrow. Likewise, she'd viewed something in his history that he wanted to hide from me. The memory she'd hinted at when they'd spoken to one another.

Would I be willing to kill Darrow to keep the talisman secret? Would he rather see me dead than share the truth he wanted so desperately to hide? I couldn't answer either of those questions with certainty, but I knew I'd regret taking Darrow's life. If he backed me into a corner and tried to steal the talisman for himself, though? The talisman's whispers in my mind suggested it hadn't relinquished the idea of me wielding it despite Ilsa ripping the magic from me.

Perhaps I ought to be flattered that it'd chosen me above all the Sidhe, but I knew better. The talisman's sole agenda was to lure its wielder into using its magic to cause as much destruction as possible. The Erlking had resisted for centuries, a feat few others might have achieved. I wouldn't live for as long as a Sidhe, though, and the future of the staff remained as misty and unclear as the forest.

Even the memory-eater doesn't know its fate. She can't see the future, like she said. I'll break out of her trap and find a way to beat them all at their own games.

Taking in a steadying breath, I walked on through the mist. Within a few seconds, the image of a tunnel appeared before me, lit with clusters of fungi beneath a curved earthen ceiling. Another of Darrow's memories.

I—or rather, Darrow—walked through the tunnel into the darkness, following the sound of breathless laughter. "Hurry up," called a little girl's voice. "You're as slow as a troll."

"Am not." Darrow caught up to the girl, who halted at the tunnel's end to wait for him. Her pointed ears and bright green eyes designated her fae status. Half-Sidhe, like him. "See, told you we were going the wrong way. We're lost."

"No, we aren't."

"Are too."

Their laughing voices faded into the mist, and I caught my balance against a tree trunk. Darrow's youthful laughter sounded in my ears, bringing an odd ache to my chest. Who was the girl in his memory?

I shouldn't be seeing this. The memory-eater was toying with us, and for all I knew, Darrow was watching me hide the talisman in this very moment.

I didn't care if he spied on my childhood. He was welcome to see me sleeping through classes at school and getting into fistfights with the local half-faeries. I wouldn't even mind if he saw the time I'd played strip poker with a group of half-goblins—long story—or the night I'd got myself trapped inside a dryad's tree after spilling whiskey on her roots. *Anything but the bloody talisman.*

Gritting my teeth, I walked on. Image after image hit me, none longer than a few seconds—Darrow exploring the tunnels, sword-fighting with other faeries, watching Etaina address rows of uniformed soldiers. The girl from the first vision appeared frequently, though I never heard her name. I did my best to keep my attention on the forest, but given the thickness of the mist, I might have been walking in circles for all I knew.

Pushing a low-hanging bough aside, I walked into a bustling cave filled with music and laughter. The sound of a harp playing formed a backdrop as I danced with a girl —the same girl as before—her arms wrapped around my shoulders.

"Told you you'd enjoy it," she said, her eyes sparkling with mischief.

Her mouth moved closer to mine—or rather, his.

Whoa there. Not sure I want to see this.

As I pulled back, I hit my head so hard on the low-hanging branch so hard I saw stars. *Ow.*

The pain brought a rush of clarity. I'd been moving through the mist while I'd been in the memory, but I'd still been present in the real world at the time. The mist had been enchanted to show memories as I walked, and like all glamours, it could be broken.

I held out my hands to grab the strands of magic that made up the illusion, but they passed through empty air. If Darrow hadn't managed to undo the spell yet, then it must be more advanced than any I'd dealt with before. Unsurprising, given that the mist covered the whole forest, but there'd be cracks in the memory-eater's armour, ones that would allow us to break out.

I clenched my fist over the mist, and triumph surged as it began to turn solid beneath my hands. Then the threads gripped back, wrapping around my arms like vines. Sharp and tight, cutting off my circulation. Mist swept along my arms, up my spine, around my legs, tightening as it did so. *Dammit.* Now the forest knew I'd seen through the trick, it planned to devour me alive.

Fighting panic, I twitched one hand, then the other, trying to free myself. The mist held fast, tendrils covering my arms, yet there was one section they hadn't touched.

The iron band on my wrist. *It can't be touched by faerie magic.*

I focused all my attention on the iron, twitching my arm to move the wristband down to my hand. Inch by inch, it moved, until the threads twisted away from my right hand, avoiding the iron.

Yanking my hand free, I pulled my iron knife from its sheath. The blade severed the mist, and a familiar scent of oak and ash washed over me. Fighting harder, I cut the mist away. I couldn't see Darrow, but he must be close.

"Darrow, I'm over here!" I yelled. "Help me get this mist off me, won't you?"

Footsteps sounded, and Darrow pushed through the mist, his eyes fixed on the blade in my hands. "Hazel, what are you doing?"

"Cutting off the..." I glanced down, only to find the mist had vanished from sight. "It's all a glamour. All of it. What did you see? I saw—"

"Your memories," we both said at the same time.

"Nothing incriminating," I added. "You?"

"No. Your childhood, mostly."

From his expression and tone, he showed no indication that he'd seen me claim or hide the talisman. "You didn't see the strip poker incident, did you?"

"Do I really want to know?" he said.

"No." A grin tugged at my mouth, mostly relief. *She didn't beat us.*

The memory-eater loomed before us, her rainbow-striped wings beating. Her craggy face was lined with unrestrained rage, and magic spun from her fingertips in the form of misty vines.

I raised my blade, but Darrow got there first. His sword pierced the faerie's heart, and her shrieking died along with the remains of the mist.

"Damn." I took in a breath. "I didn't know she could be killed."

"Everyone can," he said. "Even immortals."

The hard rasp within his voice surprised me. *He's pissed at her. Or me.* It was no more my fault than his, but he knew I'd pried into memories I didn't have the right to see.

Questions buzzed in my mind like a swarm of persistent wasps, and my jaw ached with the effort of not blurting them out. Relief that my history hadn't been exposed mingled with guilt over what I'd seen of Darrow's past. In particular, the girl. It was a wild leap to assume she was the person the memory-eater had referenced, but the two had seemed very close in their memories, yet I hadn't seen her in the time I'd spent in the Aes Sidhe's realm. Hadn't him exchange a friendly word with anyone at all, in fact.

When we left the forest behind and reached the ambassador's palace, Darrow departed with obvious relief at no longer having to prolong the awkward silence. I, meanwhile, headed into the main hall.

"There you are, Hazel." Coral's expression brightened at the sight of me, at least until she saw my bloody clothes. I'd forgotten the memory-eater had knocked off my glamour. "What have you been doing, wrestling a troll?"

"Among other things," I said. "We went to Half-Blood Territory and had a run-in with some Vale beasts."

"Half-Blood Territory?" she echoed. "I thought you were going to the borderlands."

"The half-faeries rule the borderlands now," I explained. "They're also open to accepting anyone from any Court, so you and the others have somewhere to stay if shit hits the fan. Or if anyone here doesn't want to answer to the Gatekeeper."

"I'll let them know," she said. "They'll appreciate it. Did you think the half-bloods might have seen Lord Daival in the borderlands?"

"It was worth looking around," I said. "They hadn't, though. Any leads?"

"Nope," she said. "We even tried the mortal realm. I wondered if you'd run into him, considering how long you were gone."

"Nah, we didn't leave Faerie." Perhaps the memory-eater's realm had caused us to miss a few hours. If more time had passed than I'd thought, I needed to get ready for the evening's event with the Lord of Thorns. After all the trouble I'd been through to gather information, it'd be a fine thing to lose the one solid lead I'd had. "Can you tell Lady Aiten I went home? I need to talk to my family."

"Oh, sure," said Coral. "I didn't see anyone near your gate, don't worry. Are you okay, Hazel? You look kinda… frazzled."

"Yeah. Lucky escape, that's all. I should go home and clean up."

And ready for a night of music and revelry. Or creepy chanting and human sacrifice. With the Erlking's deluded followers, one never knew what to expect.

Seeing the Lynn house again brought a rush of unexpected emotion. While I'd seen one lone memory from my own history, my visit to Half-Blood Territory reminded me I'd been lucky in so many ways. I'd had an unconventional childhood, but the Gatekeeper's mark scared off most mundane threats, while I also had a guaranteed home and a job for life, which was more than many humans could say. If those half-faeries could beat the odds and establish a Court in the heart of Faerie, I could find a way to thwart the Erlking's talisman and rescue his captured sprite.

I allowed myself one glance to confirm the talisman was still in the Inner Garden, then I headed for the house.

I found Mum sitting in the living room with a mug of cocoa and the Erlking's family tree laid out on the floor in front of her.

"Hey, Mum," I said.

She eyed my bloody clothes. "What did you get up to, Hazel?"

"Well." I put on a cheery smile. "I met the new leaders of the half-faeries, made a bargain with the memory-eater in exchange for a useless memory, and otherwise wasted my time wandering around the forests of the borderlands."

"The *memory-eater?*" she said. "You didn't see her alone, did you?"

I wish I had. "No. Darrow went with me, and then he decided to stab her to death for tricking us."

Mum shook her head. "Better hope she *is* dead if you struck a bargain with her. What memory from your own history did she show you?"

My hands knotted in my lap. "The night I was chosen as Gatekeeper."

I described the memory, recalling the soft voices and the sound of footsteps. Had the Sidhe truly visited me in my sleep and picked me out as Gatekeeper, and if they had, why hadn't the people from the vision ever spoken to me face to face? I wasn't sorry Darrow had skewered her, but I couldn't help wishing I'd dragged more information from the memory-eater. If I hadn't let her distract me with her cryptic hints, she might have shown me the Seelie Queen's own history. Or the Erlking's. I'd bet few other faeries with her particular skill set existed, too.

Mum's expression clouded. "I don't remember any visitors the night you were chosen, but the Sidhe do as they wish."

"No shit." I leaned back against the cushions. "I'm staying here tonight, but I might be back late. There's a faerie party happening in the hills near the Ley Line."

Mum lifted her head. "Is it linked to your mission for the Court?"

"Actually, it is, for a wonder," I said. "If Lord Daival shows his face, anyway. Even if not, it'll be my pleasure to deal with a group of annoying cultists who think the Erlking is their undead messiah."

I was hardly in the mood for a party, but with any luck, Lord Daival would be waiting for me. Then Lady Aiten's ridiculous demand would be done and dusted, and I'd ensure neither he nor his queen would ever see the light of day again.

11

I surveyed my reflection, a scowl on my face. The rogues hadn't given me a dress code, and my usual attire of gold and green seemed too bright for a gathering of people who worshipped a dead man. When I tried glamouring one of my dresses from green to black, though, I looked like I was on my way to a Goth rave.

One way or another, nobody would ever mistake me for a Sidhe cultist. I wasn't tall and lithe like the Sidhe, but strong and curvy and muscled. Add in the circlet on my head and hiding in Faerie was pretty much a no-go. I'd have to dress up as the Gatekeeper no matter what, and hope that the rogues' inexplicable desire to have me on their team outweighed the convenience of bumping me off.

In the end, I went with a plain green dress and left my hair in loose curls. Ten minutes before the event kicked off, I walked out of the Ley Line into the mortal realm. I'd get some odd stares if any humans saw me wandering around the hills in fancy Sidhe clothing, but the muddy country lane was a safe enough distance from the village. I bloody well hoped Lord Daival would show his face after all the time I'd wasted getting ready.

As I walked, I scanned the hills for any signs of the so-called Lord of Thorns. Despite the silence, a prickling wariness rested between my shoulder blades. I'd felt secure in my decision to go in alone, but I'd been accustomed to having Darrow with me at these events, and his absence disconcerted me. *Honestly, Hazel.* Did I really miss having a stoic companion who sulked in the corner during parties?

"Hazel!" Coral called after me. "What do you mean by going to a gathering of rogues and not inviting me?"

I rotated on the spot. To my astonishment, Coral wore a modest dark dress beneath her cloak, like she was on her way to a funeral. "How'd you even hear about it?"

"From the other half-faeries, of course," she said. "I wasn't sure if you'd been invited, but now I can go in as your bodyguard."

"You'll have to pretend to be a fanatic," I reminded her. "Or tell them you want the Sea Kingdom to be annexed by Summer again. Either way, just talk about how the Erlking is the next messiah and you'll be fine."

I was the one who might have trouble holding my tongue, especially after a glass of elf wine. I needed a stiff drink, considering the day I'd had, but I might have to refrain if I didn't want to end up fighting an entire cult single-handedly.

"No problem," she said. "We're almost there."

Reaching a dip in the hills, I spotted two cloaked Sidhe standing on either side of an opening in the hillside.

"Hey, there," I said, when they looked up and saw us.

"I'm Hazel Lynn, and this is Coral. We're here to meet the Lord of Thorns."

"His Lordship may not grace us with his presence tonight, but we are honoured to have you join our cause, Gatekeeper," said the cloaked guy on the right.

Sure you are.

Coral and I descended into an open space beneath the hill, lit by a thousand fireflies glittering under the curving earthen ceiling. Banquet tables and barrels of wine covered the back wall of the cave, while fae music filled the air, eerie and mesmerising. *Oh good. It's a real party, without evil chanting and human sacrifice.* Some of them even looked like they were having a good time.

Not all of them, of course. As I'd expected, the cultists wore long cloaks and drifted around like necromancers with pointed ears, but other guests were dressed in Summer finery. Others wore human clothes together with dazed expressions as though they'd been whisked here from the mortal realm and weren't entirely sure how they'd ended up at a faerie revel beneath the earth. Clusters of half-faeries conversed in groups, some of whom I recognised as Coral's fellow spies. Despite the crowdedness, a jolt of recognition hit me as I looked around.

"This is where I saw Lord Daival," I whispered to Coral.

"Saw him? When?"

"In a vision a faerie showed me when I asked to see his most recent memory," I murmured. "I'll explain later. People are staring."

My circlet had begun to draw attention, and many of the cloaked figures grouped closer together. I held my head high, resigned to playing the part of the Summer

Gatekeeper for the night. While Lord Daival had been in the cave recently, he wasn't here now. Maybe he'd gone to put on his best glamour for the party.

Coral leaned in and whispered, "I'll go and check the food for any poison, and make sure nobody's prepared to ambush you."

"To be honest, I'd rather they get it over with." I waved her off, scanning the room for any signs of Lord Daival. Personally, I'd prefer to get into a brawl with some rogues than flirt with them in the hopes of finding out where their Lord was hiding, but it seemed he planned to make an entrance or not show his face at all.

My gaze panned across two half-satyrs dancing in clip-clopping circles and tripping on one another's hooves; an antlered female Sidhe with cerulean hair grinding against a dazed-looking human male; and a winged half-faerie grabbing handfuls of buzzing fireflies and swallowing them whole, her entire body glowing like the lights on a Christmas tree.

And then I saw the one person who I'd never expected to see at a gathering of fanatics from Summer: Holly Lynn, my cousin, and Gatekeeper of the Winter Court.

Holly had dyed her hair black and cut it to shoulder length and she wore dark clothing which blended into her surroundings, but her blue eyes shone as bright as any Winter Sidhe's, and on her head lay a circlet near-identical to mine. Studded with white gems, it gleamed with icy magic. Like the humans, the Winter Gatekeeper looked as though she wasn't quite sure how she'd ended up here.

Nor was I, for that matter. How had the Winter Gate-keeper come to be invited to a Summer gathering intended to celebrate the Erlking's return? It didn't seem as though she'd brought any companions, either, though surely even the cultists would draw the line at inviting Unseelie Sidhe to witness the Erlking's revival.

Holly caught my gaze, her shoulders tensing at the sight of me. "Hazel."

"Hey," I said to her. "You got an invite, too, huh?"

Her gaze flicked to my circlet. "I didn't know you'd be here."

"Likewise." I hadn't seen Holly in weeks, but she'd had an even tougher start to her tenure as Gatekeeper than I had, including the death of her mother—twice, after she'd tried to use necromancy to cheat death. "What on earth did the Sidhe say when they invited you? Because they made me some absurd promises about getting to be the Gatekeeper who stood beside the rightful leader of Summer. Somehow I doubt they'd say that to a Winter Gatekeeper."

"You'd be surprised," Holly said. "They told me it was an exclusive event for anyone who supports the Erlking's return to power."

"Why would the Winter Gatekeeper support the Erlking?" I frowned.

"Stability," she said. "The Unseelie Queen doesn't want a war with the Seelie Court. We don't know who might end up taking his place and claiming his crown, so the Erlking's return works in Winter's favour."

Oh. I'd forgotten Holly had seen the Erlking's talisman in action and witnessed its destructive power. Considering the Unseelie Queen had ruled for at least as long as the Erlking had, she might well have seen it for herself at one point or other. If she thought the Erlking's replacement might claim his staff, it was no wonder she'd support his return, even if it was impossible.

Bloody hell. How did I end up stuck between every powerhouse in Faerie while in possession of the only weapon that might start and end a war all at once?

"Believe me," I said, "I wish he hadn't died. I really do. But death is final. He's not coming back."

"How do you know?" Holly said. "We don't understand how immortality works, but the Sidhe do."

I opened and closed my mouth, knowing her mother wasn't far from her thoughts. The former Winter Gatekeeper's final act had been to attempt to turn herself into an immortal, and in the process, we'd learned that the Sidhe's original source of immortality had been the blood of the gods whose magic they'd stolen. When the last storage of the Ancients' blood had broken, the Sidhe's immortality had come to an end. That didn't mean the Sidhe had accepted that eventuality, but the cultists' denial was on a whole other level.

"There's a reason there's no such thing as necromancy in Faerie," I whispered. "These people are nothing but fanatics. If they die, there's no do-overs. Same with the Erlking."

"Your point?" Holly's mouth set in a stubborn line. "Better to keep an eye on them than be taken unawares."

"I'm not disagreeing." I turned outward to scan the cave in case Lord Daival had entered while we'd been talking. "But these guys are a few sandwiches short of a picnic basket, and they'll skewer us all if we wreck their fantasies."

"I was raised by a woman who wanted to become immortal," she said through gritted teeth. "I've known manipulation since I could walk, and even more since I gained the Gatekeeper's magic. Trust me, I know every trick they might use to brainwash me, and I won't yield."

Her words conjured the memory of voices in a night-time room bathed in summer air. I turned to face her. "When you gained the Gatekeeper's magic, do you remember that night at all?"

She blinked at me. "Why on earth do you want to know that?"

"Because the Sidhe paid a visit to my family that night and picked me as the Summer heir in person."

Holly sniffed. "Am I supposed to be impressed? There's only one of me."

Oh, crap. I'd hoped to find out who the mysterious Sidhe in the vision was, but it'd slipped my mind that Holly had been forced into her position because she had no siblings and no other potential Winter Gatekeepers waiting in line. Because of that, part of me had once hoped that I might be able to get her to help me with my plan to undo the vow binding our family to the Courts. I hadn't reckoned on us winding up in this mess, though.

"I know," I said. "I meant the Sidhe visited me as a child and chose me. They spied on my siblings."

"Did you expect me to be jealous or something?" she said. "If you're telling me to watch my back, I don't need a bodyguard to do that for me."

"Ouch." That was Holly for you—cold and sharp as a thorn bush encased in frost. Yet I'd seen her at her most vulnerable and I knew she must be worried about her own Court if she'd come here alone. "All right, I'm going to go and mingle."

Holly seemed content to hover in the shadows, but she

was far from the only wallflower present. Groups of cloaked Sidhe gathered along the walls, conversing in whispers. Perhaps they were exchanging tips on how to run an evil cult.

I made for the dance floor instead, and within two minutes, I found myself struggling to extricate myself from a Sidhe who seemed to think I was someone called Catriana and kept trying to pull the circlet out of my hair. He'd turned his cloak into a toga and was totally naked underneath, and when I shoved him away from me, he nearly pitched forward into the wine barrel.

"Careful." I grimaced at his clammy touch as he grabbed my arm for balance. "Let go of—"

"Gatekeeper." Another Sidhe stepped in front of me, one of the cloaked group who'd visited the Lynn house to invite me here. "You came."

"I did." *Though I'm having a lot of regrets right now.* "Where is the Lord of Thorns?"

"He will come in time."

"How much time? I need my beauty sleep." I was bloody exhausted after the day I'd had, and despite the abundance of food on offer, my appetite was non-exis- tent. Luckily, the toga-wearing Sidhe had wandered off, leaving me with the newcomer.

He leaned closer. "You may dance with us all night, human, and feel none of it tomorrow. The king will rise from the ashes and bless us all with his presence."

Uh-huh.

The music grew louder, and as the Sidhe paired off, I let the newcomer pull me into a dance. "When you say rise from the ashes, do you mean that in a literal sense?"

Unbidden, the image of the former Winter Gatekeeper

turning into a wraith filled my mind. No way. Even they wouldn't be *that* desperate.

He took my hand and twirled me with such speed that I found myself glad I hadn't imbibed any of the faerie wine. I staggered away, and Coral caught my arm, helping me catch my balance.

"Willow saw something," she whispered. "And I thought you needed rescuing."

"Cheers." I gladly left the dance floor with Coral to walk over to Willow, a pretty half-Sidhe with olive skin and dark hair. She wore a white dress patterned with wildflowers. "Did she get an invite, too?"

"I invited her," Coral admitted. "To help spy on the enemy. We need as many eyes as possible."

"Are you sure that was your only motive?" I grinned at her. I knew the two had hit it off, but not that they were still in contact now Coral had become their heir of the Sea Court. Anything that took her mind off her brother's fate was a good thing, as far as I was concerned.

A flush darkened her cheeks. "No, but she did see some of the cultists acting oddly. Odder than usual, I mean."

"Hey." I smiled at Willow. "What did you see?"

She gave a nervous glance at the buffet table. "Some of the Sidhe were moving barrels around the tunnel back there, and… it might have been a trick of the light, but I swear one of the barrels was full of blood."

Blood? My stomach lurched. "Uh, whose blood?"

"I don't know," she said. "Not Sidhe. Smelled fresh, though."

"What're they doing, summoning a redcap contingent?"

The word *summoning* blared through my mind like an alarm bell. My siblings dealt with enough summoning-related trouble at the necromancer guild to know that any magic involving blood in any capacity was bad news. When I'd thought of human sacrifice earlier, I hadn't *actually* expected it.

I made my way to the wine barrels, snatching up a glass on the pretext of filling it with elf wine. Stepping around the barrels at the front, I walked towards the back, which extended into a dark tunnel.

A pair of bright green eyes shone from the gloom, resolving into the shadowy form of a cloaked Sidhe lurking behind the barrels. "What are you doing, mortal?"

"Oh, sorry." I gave a giggle. "I'm afraid I'm lost."

The Sidhe eyed the wine glass in my hand. "The wine barrels are over there."

"I heard you were keeping the good stuff back here." I gave another giggle, my gaze darting to the barrel to the left of me. One glimpse of the crimson liquid inside the barrel confirmed Willow's suspicions.

"Who told you that?" The cloaked Sidhe took another step closer to me, his hood slipping over his pointed ears. "Get out of here."

I leaned over the barrel and feigned a gasp. "Is that *blood?* What are you *doing* with that?"

I raised my voice loudly enough to reach the Sidhe near the wine barrels. The music quietened, but two more cloaked Sidhe stepped in to join their companion.

"Keep her quiet," one of them hissed.

A pair of hands clamped over my shoulders. Quick as a flash, I spun, kicking the intruder in the shins. His grip broke, and I rammed an elbow into his throat. I saw Coral weaving through the crowd towards me, but a wall of cloaked Sidhe blocked her way, trapping me in the narrow tunnel with the barrels.

"Whatever you're hoping for, it won't work," I warned them. "Only necromancers or witches can use blood magic, and it doesn't work with whatever *that* is. Also, using blood magic this close to the Ley Line is more likely to send you into Death than bring anyone back."

"I told you we needed fresh blood," said the cloaked Sidhe on the right.

Ack. "Didn't you hear a word I said?"

The point of a sharp blade kissed my throat. "Your blood will fuel this sacrifice, and the king shall rise again."

You have got to be shitting me. They thought they were raising the Erlking, but blood sacrifices tapped into dimensions beyond death, ones which made Faerie look like paradise. It was bad enough when humans tried to raise the dead, but faeries had zero understanding of the boundaries of life and death here in the mortal realm. They must have heard some version of the truth—that the Ancients' blood bestowed immortality—and had sought to recreate it.

The slight problem was that they'd got the source wrong. The blood in the barrel didn't belong to a god, and neither did mine, but using me as a blood sacrifice on the Ley Line might well kill every single person in this cave.

12

Think, *Hazel.* Four or five cloaked Sidhe surrounded me, while the barrels of blood or wine blocked my escape route. A sharp pain stung my neck, and I leaned back from the blade's edge, calling on my Gatekeeper's magic. Aiming the green glow at the earthen floor, I searched for any signs of life beneath the ground.

As my Summer magic reached below the earth, a torrent of roots burst upwards into the cave. Feeding more magic into the roots, I willed them to grow faster, thrusting like spears from the cave walls and ceiling. Fragments of soil rained on our heads, splashing into the wine barrels.

The hooded Sidhe wielding the blade backed up a step. "Stop that, human."

Too late. The roots continued to grow, fuelled by my Gatekeeper's magic. The music jarred to a crashing halt, while the dancing broke up, shouts of alarm echoing off the ceiling.

"The cave's collapsing!" someone yelled.

Might have overdone it a little.

I threw up a shield above my head and shoved my way through the cloaked Sidhe. They let me run, trying in vain to drag the wine barrels out of range of the falling earth. Emerging into the main cave, I grabbed Coral's arm and pulled her after me into the crowd of fleeing faeries.

Roots popped out the earth, knocking over the guests like skittles, while the despairing shouts of the panicking Sidhe came from the very back of the cave.

"Serve them right if they get buried along with their precious wine barrels." I elbowed past the hooded cultist who'd danced with me earlier and let Coral and Willow overtake me, glancing behind to make sure the Sidhe hadn't resumed their attempt at blood magic.

From the back of the cave, a bubbling crash sounded, and a torrent of wine swept through the cave, swirling around our ankles. That was enough for the remaining Sidhe, who joined the crush of people fleeing the cave. Winged piskies, cloaked cultists and bewildered humans tripped over one another in an effort to get outside.

When we reached the mouth of the cave, I ducked after Coral and Willow, emerging onto the hillside. A wave of earthy wine followed, flowing down the grass and into darkness.

"There'll be some really drunk highland cows wandering around here for the next week," I remarked. "I didn't mean to bring the whole place crashing down."

"I'd take a collapsing tunnel over a blood sacrifice." Coral reached for Willow and brushed earth from her shoulder.

"You ruined everything," said a dishevelled half-Sidhe

whose wine-dampened hair clung to her face like seaweed. It took me a moment to recognise her as Aila.

"You're welcome." I scanned the guests for Holly but saw no signs of her. Given our proximity to the Ley Line, I wouldn't blame her if she'd sneaked back home early. Watching Aila leave, I turned to Coral. "You didn't invite her, too, did you?"

"Of course not," said Coral, shaking wine droplets off her cloak. "I suppose she thought it an honour to get an invitation."

"That, or she's joined the cult." It wouldn't surprise me. Aila was the sort of half-faerie who bore a bitter and irrational hatred towards humans, as though she blamed us for her own mortality. She'd despised me without reason ever since I'd first set foot in Summer. A cult dedicated to immortality would be right up her alley.

Lights flared on the hillside, heralding the arrival of several Sidhe on horseback. Lord Raivan led the way, stopping at a safe distance from the flowing wine river, and the cultists continuing to wade out of the cave.

What a waste of time. The bloody Lord of Thorns wasn't even here, and we hadn't found the Erlking's sprite, either. Where had Lord Daival sneaked off to in the time that had passed since I'd seen him in the memory-eater's vision? For all I knew, she'd been trolling me and had shown me a memory from a week ago. That's what I got for expecting anything remotely helpful from a faerie.

Coral nudged me. "Look who's here."

Darrow caught up to the Sidhe, and he looked pissed. Uh-oh. I'd bet he'd pressured Lord Raivan to tell him everything, and he was not pleased that I hadn't chosen to confide in him.

Sighing inwardly, I walked over to him. "Fancy meeting you here."

Darrow eyed the collapsed cave under the hill and the river of elf wine trickling out. "Your work, I presume?"

"The outcasts planned to enact a necromantic ritual, with no knowledge of necromancy," I said. "It went about as well for them as you'd expect."

"How long have you known?" he said. "Is this what the memory-eater showed you?"

"Does it matter? Lord Daival wasn't even here." Why did he have to butt into every part of my life? It wasn't as though I was the one trying to conduct necromantic rituals on the Ley Line or start a cult to raise a dead man. "He's probably sipping wine on a desert island laughing at us. I really thought we had him."

My forehead gave a sudden throb, and green light flared from my circlet like a torchlight in the darkness.

Darrow frowned. "What—?"

"It's a warning." My gaze fell on a dark shape hovering above the Ley Line. *A wraith.* "The bastard went after my family."

Darrow made to follow me, but I shook my head at him. "Go back and tell the Sidhe there might be an attack on Summer's gate."

"Why?" he asked. "They can help you—"

"Like hell they can," I said. "This is personal. If Lord Daival is on my family's property, I'll kill him myself."

I could only hope he decided I'd acted out of reckless bravado and nothing more, but I didn't have time to conjure a better excuse. I broke into a full-on sprint into the Ley Line's path, crossing over to the Lynn house. Following the tug of the circlet's warning magic, I leapt over the fence and sprinted around the manor to the back garden.

On the lawn, Lord Daival stood over Mum, thorny vines flowing from his hands and wrapping around her ankles and wrists. Her hands and arms were bleeding, and an iron knife lay at her feet. I snatched it up and pointed it at Lord Daival's throat. *Fucking talismans.*

"Get away from her," I growled. "I thought your Queen wanted me to rule at her side, not turn you into a pincushion for attacking my mother."

"You should be dead," he said, unconcerned by the iron's proximity. From the bright glow of his thorns, they were the product of a talisman's magic, subtle enough to get around our family's shield.

"You'd be dead, too, if their attempt to sacrifice me had worked." I thrust the knife at him, but the thorns rose into the air, yanking the knife from my grip and tossing it away. "Didn't you even bother to read a basic guidebook before forcing your people to use necromancy on your behalf? Or didn't you care if they brought about a second faerie invasion?"

I pushed my Gatekeeper's magic at his thorns, demanding they release Mum, but they held fast. Gritting her teeth, she kicked the knife back towards me, only for more thorns to materialise and tug it away once more. Sweat stood out on her forehead, while blood slicked her wrists and ankles.

"Let. Her. Go." With each word, I pushed more magic into the thorns, drawing on the power of my circlet, but Lord Daival simply conjured more thorns in each hand. When Mum broke free, a fresh pair of vines ensnared her, gripping tight.

Then a blanket of icy cold fell over the lawn, followed by a shadowy form. *Oh, there's the wraith.*

"Go to Edinburgh," Lord Daival commanded the hovering dark shape. "I'm sure your siblings will have sensed the disturbance on the Ley Line by now, Hazel. They'll be right in the wraith's path."

"What the hell did they ever do to you?" I spat, resuming my attack on his thorny vines.

"Your family is the reason for my imprisonment," he said. "You wronged my queen, and you'll pay for it."

Damn him. He hadn't just been trying to summon the dead—his intention had been to draw Ilsa and Morgan's attention to the Ley Line and punish my entire family in one instant. My circlet ignited in tandem with my rising anger, and the thorns binding Mum's wrists released her.

Lord Daival went for me instead, thorn-coated blades in each hand. I dodged one, but the edge of the other nicked my arm, drawing blood. Cold magic brushed my skin, signalling the wraith's presence. *I can't fight them both at once.*

The wraith gave a sudden, piercing scream. The sound ripped through my eardrums, and a whirlwind of icy air tore the grass from its roots and the leaves off the bushes. Lord Daival stopped mid-strike as a wave of shadows engulfed the struggling wraith.

"What is this?"

The wraith's icy magic vanished beneath the shadows, and its struggling screams died to nothing, revealing silence behind. Even Lord Daival stood frozen to the spot, his expression transfixed, his thorny blades dangling at his sides. The lawn was a wreck, the hedges stripped to the bones, and the Inner Garden lay open for all to see.

Even from a distance, the waters appeared cloudy and dull, the staff floating on the surface in a pool of shadows.

"It cannot be," murmured Lord Daival.

No.

Panic drove me forward, a knife in my hand. He tore his gaze from the talisman and deflected my blow with the side of his left-hand blade. The right blade swiped at my hip, sending thorns to ensnare my ankles. I tripped, stumbling on the spot, as he spun out of reach of my knife.

Mum lunged at him from behind, but he darted out of reach, too fast for her to catch. Thorny vines entangled my feet, climbing up my legs and piercing the skin underneath.

Lord Daival's second blade clashed with mine, and a second tendril of thorns wrapped around my upper arms. The vines crept higher, poking through the thin fabric of my dress, as his blade skimmed my throat. "Surrender."

"I claimed the talisman," I gritted out. "If you strike me dead, the talisman's magic will destroy you before you can deal the final blow."

I hope. The talisman's shadows hadn't stopped him tying me up with thorny ropes or devoured him like they had the wraith. What was it playing at? *Go on. Kill him.*

"You led the Sidhe to believe the staff was lost," he said. "Devious work, for a human. However, I would like to know how you tricked it into serving you."

His gaze slipped to the talisman, and I brought my knee up into his groin. The thorns' sharp pain deepened, but Lord Daival staggered, cursing, right into the path of Mum's knife. The blade sank into his shoulder from behind. At once, his face greyed with the effects of the iron, while the thorny vines relinquished their grip on me. An alarming amount of blood soaked through my dress, trickling down my bare arms and legs.

"Get him!" I yelled at Mum. "Hit his heart this time."

Lord Daival roared in fury, pulling the knife from his shoulder and throwing it at me. I dove to the ground to avoid it, right onto a bed of thorns. My vision turned fuzzy, my limbs heavy and throbbing with pain.

"You *will* yield the talisman to me," said Lord Daival. "For every day you fail to surrender, a new potential heir will die. This, I promise you."

"Go fuck yourself with a thorn bush." I lifted my head, willing my body to move. Blood darkened the grass around me. Too much blood. I tried to reach for my weapon, but my hand closed on empty air. My vision faded in and out, and when it cleared, Lord Daival had vanished.

"He hopped through the Ley Line." Mum stood over me. "Hazel. Stay with me."

Her hand grasped my wrist and released it at once. Shadows curled up my arms and around my hands, caressing me like a cool breath of air.

"Stop that!" I gasped. "Don't you dare attack my mother."

The shadowy tendrils of magic tightened, tugging my body across the lawn. Mum cursed, grabbing for my arm, but I shook my head, understanding what the talisman was doing.

A moment later, the waters of the healing pool closed over my head, and all went dark.

———

"The water healed all your injuries," said Mum. "That's the good news."

"The bad news is that Lord Daival saw the talisman." And it was more the talisman's fault than mine. The bloody thing had been trying to get the world's attention ever since I'd left it in the grove and would have probably hopped out of the waters and terrified some poor human next, but that didn't stop me from feeling like I should have done more to stop it. "And it tried to attack you."

I'm in way over my head with this one.

I lay under a blanket on the sofa and sipped at a mug of a blood-replenishing potion Mum had insisted on making me. It tasted of ogre piss, but after a few sips, I felt less shaky and more like chasing down Lord Daival. After a nap, that is.

"It didn't, Hazel," said Mum, draining the rest of her own mug. I'd insisted she got into the waters as soon as I'd regained consciousness, and the marks from Lord Daival's attack had faded from her wrists. "The talisman pushed me away from you, yes, but I didn't feel any adverse effects from its magic."

"I guess it was focused on me not dying." I took another sip of the foul liquid. "It still views me as the wielder, for some reason."

Not that I couldn't have reached the waters with Mum's help anyway, but it'd pushed her away. Like it wanted to protect its owner. Why?

There came the sound of a key turning in a lock, then hurried footsteps. A moment later, Ilsa burst into the living room. "Hazel? What did you do?"

"Lord Daival. Thorns. The usual." I should have figured she'd come here as soon as she saw the disturbance on the Ley Line. "And an attempted necromantic ritual that went wrong. Don't worry, I dealt with it."

"So that's why there are so many Sidhe on the hill near the village," she said. "Wait, tonight was that party with the cultists, right?"

"You've got it." I put the mug down. "The cultists tried to do a necromantic ritual the wrong way, then figured sacrificing me would do instead. I collapsed the tunnel on them and wasted several barrels of perfectly good elf wine. Oh yeah, and Holly was there."

"*Holly?*" said Ilsa.

I told her everything, from my conversation with Holly to Lord Daival's attack on our house. Including my utter failure to stop him from laying eyes on the talisman.

Ilsa remained silent for a long moment. When I was on the brink of drifting off to sleep, she said, "It's not your fault, Hazel. Like you said… the talisman wanted to make itself known. And now Lord Daival thinks you're the wielder, he's going to think twice before trying another direct assault on the house."

"He can still target you and Morgan," I mumbled into the blanket. "He blames our entire family for the Seelie Queen's imprisonment. And he promised to kill one potential heir every day until I give him the talisman."

"It's a bluff," said Mum. "From what you said, it doesn't sound like the sprite gave in and told him the heir's identity."

"He's still a prisoner." My gut tightened. "No matter what, innocent lives will be lost."

With the Sidhe, 'innocent' was a relative term, but I wouldn't stand for anyone trying to use my talisman as leverage against the Summer Court and its inhabitants.

He had no right to play executioner when he didn't get his way.

"You can't do anything about him while you're resting, Hazel," said Ilsa. "I'll tell Morgan, and we'll be ready for a potential attack in Edinburgh. You focus on what you have to do."

"Kill Lord Daival. That was supposed to be the easy bit." I rested my head against the cushions. "The Sidhe are going to have my head for this."

13

The Sidhe did indeed have my head—metaphorically speaking, anyway.

"What do you mean, he escaped?" said Lady Aiten, confronting me in the tapestried room the following day.

"Lord Daival turned me into a human pincushion and left me bleeding out in my own garden," I told her. "Trust me, nobody's more annoyed about this than me."

"Lord Raivan claimed you were certain he'd be at this gathering of rogues," she said.

"That's where I was, until I found out he went after my family instead." While I'd fully recovered from the thorns, my tolerance for Sidhe bullshit remained below zero. "When I had him cornered, he hopped through the Ley Line and vanished. The cave where the outcasts had their party used to be his hideout, so I don't know where he went this time."

"Did he say nothing of his intentions?" she said. "No mention of the Seelie Queen?"

"No, but…" I paused. "He told me he plans to kill all the potential heirs to the Summer Court's throne. One each day as long as he goes free."

Lady Aiten's features tightened. "Then you will find him again, and you will not allow him to escape this time."

Easier said than done. That thorn magic had cut straight through my magic-proofed shield, and now Lord Daival knew the location of the Erlking's talisman, he'd be unlikely to make a second attempt to get into the Lynn house. But there was no sense dwelling on past regrets. I'd nail the fucker next time and make him pay for threatening my family.

"Also," she added, "why did you not inform me of your intentions to infiltrate the outcasts' gathering?"

"Because I knew you'd blow my cover," I said. "Did you manage to arrest them all, at least?"

"Yes," she said. "They will be put to death along with the other traitors in one day's time."

That meant Coral's brother would die tomorrow, too. She'd known it was coming, but that didn't mean it wouldn't hurt like hell.

"As for you," she went on, "you will resume your search for Lord Daival and return the Erlking's sprite to us."

Back to square one. "I'll do my best to, but his cave is buried in elf wine and I don't have any other leads. Has he been seen in the Court? Because if he's going to keep his promise and go after the heirs, he'd need to break into Summer. Today, in fact."

"We're watching every passage in and out of the Court, but his own magic allows him to cross into any area of

Faerie at any time," said Lady Aiten. "You must intercept him first."

You're asking me to do the impossible. "Why not set up a trap for him here in Faerie? It seems more efficient than traipsing around the Highlands in the hope that we find him squatting in a cave somewhere."

"I have given you orders, Gatekeeper," she said. "Do not fail again."

"I'm not the one who let him break out of jail." The Gatekeeper's mark on my forehead lit up in response to my growing anger, and its green glow enveloped the room.

"Do *not* use your power against me, Gatekeeper," said Lady Aiten in a soft, deadly voice. "You don't want me as an enemy."

"I don't want Lord Daival as an enemy, either," I said. "It's your Court and your heirs he's after, and if he figures out you're using me as a shield, he'll find a way around it. You can't run away from this, Lady Aiten."

Magic crackled in her eyes, inches from touching me yet unable to do so without bouncing off my shield. "I think you should leave, Gatekeeper."

With pleasure. I slammed through the door and found myself nose to nose with Darrow. I hadn't seen him since last night, so I'd assumed he'd gone with the Sidhe to drag the conspirators back into the Court.

"Is he really threatening the heirs?" asked Darrow.

"You were eavesdropping." I took a step back. "Not cool, Darrow. Yes, Lord Daival threatened to kill the heirs, and yes, Lady Aiten still wants me to take him on alone. Considering I haven't the faintest idea who the heir *is*, any Sidhe in the Court night be the target."

We'd have to get every Sidhe in the entire Court in the same room to stand a chance of isolating the heir and keeping them from harm, which seemed a taller order than Lady Aiten having a change of heart and deciding to do her own dirty work.

"Has she told the other Sidhe?" he said. "If they found out, she'd have to allow them to have a say in how we approach the issue."

"There'd also be a mass panic. Or rioting, considering half of them fancy themselves as the Erlking's successor already." There must be a way to get them into the same place without rousing suspicion, right? I twisted my hands, thinking hard. Then I had it. "Throw a party."

"Excuse me?" he said.

"I'll ask Lord Niall," I went on. "He doesn't need an occasion for a celebration. Make it a major event and invite every Sidhe in the Court. We'd have to warn them of a potential attack, so they're not all totally addled when he shows up, but even his thorns aren't enough to protect him against a room full of angry Sidhe."

Instead of the heir, he'd find himself with a hundred blades at his throat. Once we had him, we'd save both the heir *and* the sprite all at once.

Darrow studied me. "You know, Hazel… that just might work."

"Glad you have faith in me." For the first time since I'd been handed the mission, a current of determination rushed through me. I'd ensure Lord Daival took his last breath without ever revealing the talisman's location, and I'd save the Erlking's sprite from any further torture at his hands.

To start off with, I went looking for my new friend

Lord Raivan. As per usual, he paced around the golden meadow near the palace, waiting for any humans who might come to the Court with requests. The meadow's glow brought a memory to mind—a memory that wasn't mine, of Darrow's fascination with the expanse of grass. Now I thought back, I'd seen the same image on the postcard he'd used as a bookmark in his room, too. *Okay, time to put your curiosity away, Hazel.*

Lord Raivan gave me an expectant look. "Yes?"

"I have a question for you," I said. "Do you know how often Lord Niall hosts revels?"

"As often as possible, generally," he said. "Why?"

I took in a breath. "I got a tip-off that Lord Daival intends to murder one of the Sidhe today. He hasn't specified who, but I believe he plans to take them unawares when they're alone. I told Lady Aiten, and she seemed unconvinced that I could get all the Sidhe into one place at the same moment. I think Lord Niall would beg to differ."

His gaze sharpened. "You wish to lay the bait for him?"

"Better," I said. "I'll have Lord Niall do it for me. Spread the word among the Sidhe that a vast celebration will be happening today. Say, midday. Just make sure nobody walks alone in the Court before then, because he's planning on sneaking in and out without being detected. He thinks it'll frighten you more."

"You assume he can best us?"

"One of you?" I said. "Yes. He has multiple talismans, and he retains his ability to move around Faerie at will. Wouldn't it be better to force him to confront the entire Court head-on? It's the opposite of what he wants, and that way, you can give him the beating he deserves."

From the glint in Lord Raivan's eyes, I'd hit the right notes. The Sidhe were proud, but they also enjoyed spectacle and hated traitors with every fibre of their being. The idea of taking out Lord Daival in as public a manner as possible would be a popular one.

"I agree," said Lord Raivan. "I will ask Lord Niall to begin preparations immediately, and I'll speak with you again in one hour."

"Sorted." I grinned. "Good luck."

I'd just have to hope that Lord Daival wouldn't strike before then, but he ought to at least give me a head start. I would be ready for him this time.

Next, I went through the gate to the Lynn house in search of Mum. I found her in the shed, hammering away at a punching bag.

"Hazel." Her fists bounced off the bag. "Did Lady Aiten send you home in disgrace?"

"No, but I have a plan." I outlined the details to her. "It's not perfect, by any means, and for all I know, the heir is more than a match for Lord Daival. But this way, he won't be able to sneak around and slit throats behind the scenes. The Sidhe will corner him."

"And you're forcing the Sidhe to do the work themselves," she said, a note of approval in her tone. "How did Lady Aiten react?"

"I haven't told her yet," I said. "She's so intent on making me be the one to face up to Lord Daival that she's leaving her own Court members vulnerable to attack. She'll thank me later, when she's over the shock."

"The celebration will be at Lord Niall's," said Mum. "That ought to mean nobody can get through the Summer gate, but I'll ask Ilsa and Morgan to come to the house."

"Why?" I asked. "Do you think he'll ambush you again?"

"No." She resumed punching the target. "I intend to be the one to deal the killing blow, and to do that, I need to be at the party. That means someone else will have to watch the house."

Oh... kay. There was no arguing with Mum when she was in this kind of mood, so I ducked out of the shed, mentally running through the list of things I needed to do. Wrangling people into line—especially Sidhe, with their tendency to overreact at the slightest provocation—was not in my skillset, but Lord Niall would take care of the location, the catering, the music, and the elf wine. Especially the latter. That left me without much to do except prepare for battle and strap on as many iron knives on as possible.

I was too tired from the last disaster of a party to face another one, but I at least knew to avoid wearing a skimpy dress this time. Instead, I picked a gold-and-green outfit with built-in armour and strapped knives to my thighs, ankles, and arms.

When I was checking my reflection in the mirror, Ilsa walked into my bedroom. "What's this I hear about you organising a party? You're dressed like you're on your way to fight a war instead."

"That's because I am." I fitted another sheathed knife into the cleavage of my dress. "Lord Niall is organising a party as bait to lure in Lord Daival and kill him before he murders the heir."

"The *heir* will be at the party?" asked Ilsa. "I thought nobody knew who it was."

"If every Sidhe in the Summer Court shows up, the heir will be among them, theoretically."

"Even if it is a trap, you can't go to a fancy ball wearing armour," said Ilsa.

"All right." I glamoured a dress on top of my clothing, but the glamour refused to stick. "Too much iron."

Morgan entered my room behind her, pursued by Pepper, his pet cu sidhe or faerie dog. "Why're you dressed like an assassin?"

I reached down to pet the faerie dog, who ran around me in excited circles. "Get out, both of you. You've made your point."

Five minutes later, I wore my least skimpy dress and as many iron knives as I could realistically fit underneath. Pepper whined and avoided me, which I hoped was a sign that I was wearing enough iron to give Lord Daival a really hard time. The hilt of a blade pointed out of my cleavage and I pushed it out of sight. "I should have just gone with the armour. This isn't going to work."

"Sure it will," said Ilsa. "You're just nervous."

"Because Lord Daival wiped the floor with you last time," Morgan said.

"Oi." I scowled at him. "Watch it, you."

"I'm more concerned the Sidhe will boot you out for carrying enough iron to poison half the Court," Ilsa interjected.

I sighed and removed one of the knives from under my dress. "It'd at least stop any of them from dragging me into an unwanted dance."

"I thought you liked dancing with the faeries," Morgan said.

"Not tonight. Today, I mean." This party was all business. I couldn't fail this time. "The Sidhe might not know Lord Daival's coming, but I do."

"You didn't tell them?" he said. "You sure they'll be sober enough to fight, or do you expect them to just throw him into a wine barrel and be done with it?"

"That would work," I said testily. "Morgan, stop poking holes in my plan."

"What?" He picked up Pepper, who'd started to growl at the knife I'd dropped on the floor. "You told me to come here. Mum said you need both of us."

"To keep an eye on the Erlking's staff," I said. "And watch out for wraiths, who are apparently Lord Daival's new BFFs."

"Are you sure he won't come here again?" Morgan adjusted his grip on Pepper. "Because I can deal with ghosts, but not freaky thorn magic."

"I doubt he'll risk attracting the talisman's wrath," I said, "but if I don't do this, the heir dies today. Probably the Erlking's sprite, too. On top of that, Lady Aiten will have no choice but to reveal the truth to the other Sidhe, and all hell will break loose."

In short, the perfect opportunity for Lord Daival to sneak into the jail and set the Seelie Queen free to claim the Erlking's throne.

Ilsa's expression clouded. "What do the Sidhe think of your plan? And Darrow?"

"Darrow was fine with it last I heard, but he doesn't know it's today," I said. "I told Lord Raivan to put the idea in Lord Niall's head. Lady Aiten is the one who forced me to go after Lord Daival alone, so it's not my problem if she doesn't like my methods."

"No kidding," said Ilsa. "Are you okay? After those

thorns, I mean?"

"I'm good. I'm more concerned with the fact that he saw the staff." If he mentioned it in front of anyone at the Court, I'd be royally screwed, but what else could I do? If I claimed the talisman again, the Sidhe would exile me, and besides, I wasn't convinced it'd let me go this time around.

Morgan glanced over at the window. "Have you moved it?"

"I can't," I said. "Nothing can contain that thing except the waters of the pool in the grove, and not forever. Their magic is already weakening."

Ilsa's eyes widened. "You never said."

I shrugged, wishing I hadn't brought up the subject. "That's because I've been bouncing from one crisis to another ever since I became Gatekeeper. Your job is to stop anyone sneaking through the gates while Mum and I are at the party. We'll deal with the rest later."

I was well aware that 'later' kept being pushed further and further into the future, but even claiming the talisman wouldn't stop Lord Daival from killing the heir, considering nobody knew the identity of his target. I'd let the Sidhe take him out and wash my hands of the matter before considering the talisman's fate.

My plan had to work. I'd make sure of it.

14

Half an hour later, what seemed like the entire Summer Court filled Lord Niall's estate. I'd left Ilsa and Morgan at home with a stack of instructions, while Mum had talked me into asking Lord Raivan to move the Summer gate closer to Lord Niall's house to layer the bait for Lord Daival.

You wouldn't think the whole event had been put together at the last minute. Faerie music filled the air, flipping from melancholy to joyful, while magic shone from every bright flower and glittering fountain. The Sidhe danced with abandon, the elf wine flowing freely, and none showed any signs of the revel being an elaborate trap to lure in an escaped convict.

Mum stood in the corner, wearing an expression that suggested anyone who tried to speak to her would find themselves with a knife at their throat. *Yeah, she and Darrow really would get along.* Not that I'd seen him so far. Coral and the other half-faeries surrounded the estate ready to intercept Lord Daival and his allies, but my former mentor hadn't showed his face yet.

Too restless to keep still, I walked around the main room, weaving between the fountains and tables and statuary. I paced until my feet ached and the knives strapped to my thighs, arms and chest chafed against my skin. Nobody asked me to dance—they could sense the iron even if they couldn't see it—which was fine by me.

The sky darkened overhead, though it should still be daytime here if you followed Earth logic. In Faerie, a day could last forever or a second depending on what the Sidhe wanted.

I rounded a corner and spotted Darrow making his way towards me, sidestepping two goat-footed satyrs and a giggling nymph.

"What is this?" He indicated the room at large, from the finely-dressed courtiers to the barrels of wine.

"A party," I told him. "Didn't we talk about it earlier?"

"I didn't know you planned to do this today," he said. "With so little time to prepare for an attack."

"For whom?" I asked. "It had to be today, because Lord Daival said he'd kill one heir per day." At his suspicious stare, my heart sank. Had he figured out Lord Daival's threat had been about more than taunting me, and that there was something he wanted from me in exchange for sparing the heir's life?"

"Has it occurred to you that this threat of his might have been intended to deflect attention from his larger goal to break the Seelie Queen out of jail?" said Darrow. "He might be planning to take advantage of everyone's attention being here."

Oh, no. He's just being a dick instead.

"Yes, I'm aware of that. That's why there's extra security there. Lord Raivan saw to it." What was his problem? "Did you just come here to criticise all my ideas? If you wanted to help carry in the wine barrels, you could have just asked Lord Niall. I'm not in charge, as far as any of the Sidhe know. I'm the woman behind the scenes, that's all."

"You certainly work fast." He gave the room another scan, his gaze picking out the guards stationed beside each door and window. "Or Lord Niall does. Lord Raivan, too. What made you decide to pick him as a confidant?"

"He doesn't ask questions." Why, did it bother him that I hadn't chosen him instead? He was acting bloody weird. I gave him a surreptitious look and spotted a wine glass in his hand, while his eyes seemed to shimmer brighter than usual. "Are you *drunk?*"

He couldn't have got smashed in such a short space of time, surely, unless he was more of a lightweight than I was.

"Does it matter?" His voice didn't slur, but it was hard to tell with half-faeries.

"Damn," I said. "You beat me to it. What brought this on?"

"Whoever said there had to be a reason?" His gaze flicked around the room as though unwilling to focus on my face. "You didn't tell them they might be attacked?"

"Can you imagine the ruckus if I had?" I stepped out of range as one of the Sidhe fell headfirst into the water fountain, splashing everyone in the vicinity with glittering foam. "Trust me, if Lord Daival shows his face, he'll be surrounded in seconds. I've got it covered."

"I suppose you have." His finger brushed my chest, and

I stiffened, confused, until I realised he was moving one of my knife sheaths out of view. Not feeling me up. *Behave, Hazel.* "You might want to hide the iron. Do you usually keep your weapons in such prominent places?"

"Prominent?" I shot him a grin.

His finger left a trail of heat across my collarbone, sending warmth pooling in the pit of my stomach. "I'm saying you're wearing so many iron knives that if you try seducing another Sidhe, you might knock them unconscious."

I stifled a laugh. No wonder he'd resisted my attempts to get him drunk if one glass had such a strong effect on him.

"I'll keep that in mind," I said. "I'll let any Sidhe I seduce know you're so concerned for his safety."

"Who?" The word came out so fast that my brows shot up. Was he *jealous?* Of a hypothetical Sidhe who didn't actually exist? I had no plans to seduce anyone—including Darrow, for that matter—but damn if this wasn't an entertaining conversation on multiple levels. Had I finally caused him to crack, or was there some other reason he'd dipped into the elf wine as soon as he'd walked in here?

He frowned. "What are you grinning at?"

"You." I took his wrist. "What're you doing, drowning your sorrows?"

Might his encounter with the memory-eater be preying on his mind? It was as good a guess as any.

He loosened his arm from mine. "Not in a literal sense, I take it."

"Figure of speech," I said. "And for me, it's more like drowning my minor annoyances. Lady Aiten is the most ungrateful Sidhe I've ever met, and that's saying a lot."

I picked up a wine glass of my own from a passing hobgoblin, sniffed it for poison, and took a sip. One glass would be fine, but any more than that and I risked compromising my fighting skills.

"I didn't know you came close to death at Lord Daival's hands," he said. "If I'd known he was capable of that, I would have come with you."

There was something odd in his tone. Worry? "You mean if you'd known he'd kick my arse? What makes you think you could have done any better?"

Even Darrow would have had his work cut out fighting against those thorns. I didn't know whether to feel insulted that he thought himself more capable of beating Lord Daival than I was or flattered that he'd been worried for me. He wasn't at all acting like the closed-off Darrow I knew.

"You chose to confide your plans in Lord Raivan," he went on. "Lord Raivan is known to be lazy and cowardly."

I tipped back my glass, the sweet taste of wine filling my mouth. "He's the head of ambassadors between humans and Sidhe, and he knows Lord Niall personally. If you're offended that I didn't ask you instead, you're better at standing in the corner glaring at people than organising parties."

The words came out harsher than I intended, tinged with disbelief that my near-death had apparently bothered him so much that he'd got himself inebriated in the same place where we'd ended up... closer than intended, last time. Thank the gods the spelled forest lay on the opposite side of the room.

A moment passed. "You want me to leave?"

"No." Wait, I did, didn't I? Was the magic from that

grove drifting over here, or was it the elf wine? "That's not what I meant. I spoke without thinking."

Not for the first time. In ordinary circumstances, this would be the last place I'd want rational thoughts to intervene, but not with Lord Daival somewhere out there, prepared to walk right into our trap.

"I thought so," he said. "You tend to do that when you're uncomfortable."

"Not uncomfortable. Confused." Okay, this was getting too weird. "Darrow, you're working for another Court. *My* Court is in the middle of a crisis, and the talisman you're looking for isn't here. You're wasting your time."

"The talisman isn't the reason I'm here," he said. "The Summer Court's situation has the potential to affect far more than your own Court, and while the Aes Sidhe might not be part of the Seelie Court any longer, we are still Summer fae."

"Then why does Etaina not come in person to offer her help?" He wasn't working behind her back, was he? Surely not, after his honest statement that he believed Etaina was undoubtedly the best person to take care of the Erlking's talisman. His motives might be incomprehensible to me, but he was as consistent as it was possible for one of the notoriously mercurial fae to be.

"Because she wishes to retain our secrecy." He didn't quite meet my eyes. "Our survival depends on it."

Really? Because from what I've seen, Etaina is more than a match for most other Sidhe. That glamour of hers…

"Interesting," I said. "Why, then, does she still want the Summer Court to think of your people as extinct when most of us weren't even born when you split from Summer?"

And why did I keep needling him? Was it because I wanted to keep digging myself into a hole, or was I searching, against all the odds, for proof that he wasn't Etaina's lackey after all? That he'd had a change of heart?

"She's never told me," he said, "but I broke your trust when I took you with me to my Court, and I'm sorry for that."

"I imagine your vow gave you no choice."

"No…" His gaze turned downwards, as if ashamed. "I did have a choice. I wasn't ordered to bring you to her."

No, you were ordered to find the talisman. Too bad the two are one and the same. "Not being bound by a vow doesn't mean you had a choice in the matter. Is she going to come after my family?"

His mouth parted. "She said that?"

A frustrated noise escaped. "How much glamour did she hit you with? Don't tell me you're so far under her influence you can't see the truth. Even I can see it, and I'm human."

"I would prefer not to discuss that in the presence of others," he said, the words measured. "But let me assure you I am here because I wish to be and not because I was ordered to do so, and I will ensure that nobody brings harm to your family."

"I take it your vow to her doesn't stop you from forming friendships with other Court members?" I said. "I'm assuming not, considering what nearly happened by the forest last time."

Almost involuntarily, my gaze darted towards the curtain of vines concealing the entrance to the spelled grove. His did, too, as though remembering the last time the faeries' magic had slid out and drawn us to one another like two opposing forces colliding.

"You told me you enjoyed it."

"Uh-huh." My heartbeat kicked into gear. "I never said otherwise. That's not the same as trusting your leader not to order you to slit my throat on a whim."

His breath rushed in sharply. "She would never order me to harm you, and if she did, I would refuse to do so."

My feet teetered at the edge of a cliff. "Would you, though?"

Even if he turns on her, we'll know how it'll turn out when he finds out what you did with the talisman.

Go away, I told the mental voice. It was really starting to tick me off. Darrow's behaviour had knocked me off-kilter, made me doubt myself where I'd have otherwise ploughed on without a second's thought. Because he *did* have feelings for me, and the warmth I felt when he held my gaze made it hard to look away.

An inexplicable smile stirred on his face. "Is there any way to be certain with one of the fae? You aren't like other humans. You know the risks of associating with one of us, and there are no guarantees. Even your own freedom hangs by a tenuous thread."

"I should be offended on behalf of my species," I said. "Yes. I know the risks. That's why this isn't going to go anywhere, Darrow. There's nothing between us."

"Are you sure?" His hand slid down my face to my chin, and my pulse fluttered, my body stirring to life. Not from the forest's magic, but the tingle of his skin against mine, awakening my senses and making me acutely aware that my knives were stashed in *really* inconvenient places.

Darrow brought his mouth down on mine. His scent

of oak and ash wrapped around me, while my arms encircled his shoulders. He tasted of elf wine, like me, and his intoxicated state sent my blood roaring in response.

My freedom hangs by a thread, does it?

I kissed him recklessly, driven by a need that refused to be sated and a wild urge to quell the string of questions drifting through my mind.

Would you kill me if you knew I claimed the talisman?

Is it bad that I want to screw you anyway?

The sound of someone calling my name cut through my dazed state. I dropped my hand and looked around for Lord Daival, but instead, Lady Aiten marched towards us. Bright green magic shone from her eyes, a sure sign she was pissed as hell at me.

"What is the meaning of this?" she said.

"Of what?" I stepped back from Darrow. "Lord Niall doesn't need to ask your permission before hosting a revel. Talk to him, not me."

"Do you think I'm unaware this is your handiwork, Gatekeeper?"

"It's all the same to me, to be honest." My annoyance spiked, not least because of the timing of her interruption. "I'm here to catch Lord Daival. If this doesn't work, then feel free to chastise me, but not before."

"That's not what it looks like to me." Her gaze went to Darrow. "You look like you have other things on your mind."

"I can multitask." Maybe I should dive into the fountain to cool down. Or just throw Lady Aiten in there. "As I said, talk to—"

The sound of sobbing drifted over from the back of the hall, and Lady Aiten's gaze fell on a couple of young women sitting by the tangled tree roots. One of them bent her head, a wine glass dangling from her hand and spilling crimson droplets onto her cape. *Coral.* Willow had an arm around her, murmuring condolences, and Coral's head pillowed on the other half-Sidhe's chest.

Lady Aiten made to walk towards them, but I stepped in her way. "What are you doing?"

"Willow is my daughter." Disapproval laced her tone. She and Willow looked alike enough that I'd suspected they must be related, but clearly, she hadn't known who her daughter had been spending her time with.

"Look, Coral's brother is going to be executed tomorrow," I reminded her. "Maybe leave her alone?"

"My daughter should not associate with another Court's heir," she said. "It's unbecoming of a Summer high-born."

"She's half-blood, right? That means she's not a full Court member." Come to think of it, her existence meant Lady Aiten had once had an affair with a human.

"She swore to uphold our family's honour," she insisted.

"Lady Aiten, might I remind you we're trying to catch a criminal here?" I said through clenched teeth. "You were just lecturing *me* for getting distracted. Talk to Willow later, if you must, but we have more important things to—"

The sound of a harp's strings cut through the surrounding clamour: the signal I'd agreed on with the half-faeries to indicate Lord Daival had been spotted.

He's here.

I turned my back on Lady Aiten and whipped the knife from my cleavage, heading for the source of the noise. Darrow shouted my name, but I kept my attention on the crowd gathering in front of the doors.

"Move aside!" I shouted to the Sidhe. "Cover all the exits. Do not let any of them escape."

Pandemonium broke out in a flurry of bloodthirsty cries and weapons being drawn. Clumsy troll feet kicked over tables, sluaghs drifted over the vats of elf wine, and all manner of Vale beasts fell on the guards' blades. From the sound of swords clashing outside, my half-Sidhe guards had been ready. *Told you we were prepared, Lady Aiten.*

Lord Raivan led a group of Sidhe on the attack, his hat lopsided and his hair in disarray. Together, they brought an armoured troll crashing down into the dirt with well-timed strikes to its bulky legs, avoiding the iron chains that dangled from its bloody wrists.

I stabbed a sluagh with my knife, and the beast evaporated into thin air the instant the iron made contact. "Some of them might be illusions!" I shouted in warning, but the Sidhe didn't give any indication they'd heard me. The ruckus near the door continued, but whirling swords and rampaging Vale beasts blocked my view.

Losing patience, I leapt onto a table and ran through the middle of the hall. My feet kicked at fancy dishes, upended plates, and slipped in spilt drinks. With a flying leap, I landed in a mass of tangled bushes. An ogre lifted its head to intercept me, but I skewered it through the neck with a single thrust. Kicking the ogre's body aside, I made for the mass of bodies near the door, and the silver-haired figure pinned beneath the blade of another Sidhe.

Lord Daival.

I raised my knife, and saw a group of Sidhe circling

Lord Daival. He raised his hands in defence, and the flinch in his movement made me pause. "Wait—he doesn't have thorns. It's not him. Stop!"

The Sidhe didn't hear me. A blade opened his throat, the illusion unravelling at the seams and falling to the ground in a shower of crimson blood.

"Murder!" someone shouted. "Lord Garin is dead!"

The Sidhe who'd killed the false Lord Daival backed away from the corpse, revealing the sightless eyes of the Sidhe I recognised as the wolf shifter who'd declared himself the Erlking's heir.

"He killed Lord Garin!" Accusing fingers pointed at the male Sidhe, who had a curtain of ink-black hair and furred ears.

The Sidhe shook his head violently. "I thought he was with the enemy. By my family's blood, I swear he looked like Lord Daival when I stabbed him."

My stomach lurched. Had the enemy projected illusions so the Sidhe would stab their own people? *Was Lord Garin the heir all along?* Perhaps Lord Daival had heard talk of his declaration and had targeted him for that reason, but either way, he'd kept his word to kill one Sidhe per day without even showing his face.

More than one, in fact. I spotted several other bloodied bodies scattered throughout Lord Niall's house, surrounded by stunned guests and the bodies of fallen ogres, trolls and other beasts.

"Did anyone see the real Lord Daival?" I walked over to the half-faeries. "Who gave the signal?"

Nobody answered. My gaze sought out Mum, whose blade dripped with troll blood, and I ran to her side. "The gate—"

"Safe," she said. "He's not there. Ilsa told me."

Then where is he? Who among the shell-shocked Sidhe was the heir to the Erlking's throne?

I edged over to Coral, who stood wrapping a bandage around another half-Sidhe's arm. "Are you okay?"

She nodded. "I got an update from the jail. He's not there. Lord Daival never came to the Court, Hazel."

"He didn't need to." I swallowed, tasting anger like bile in my throat. "He tricked the Sidhe into slaughtering their own people."

I would have thought Lord Daival would have gone for a more personal kill, but this way, he didn't have to risk showing his face in person. The Sidhe would see him as a faceless, terrifying killer. Once again, he was one step ahead of me.

But someone among the guests had helped him lay his trap. I left Coral and Willow and made my way to the door, spotting a flash of light glinting on silver hair. Darrow held Aila in his grip, his knife pressed to her throat. A whimper escaped as she tried to struggle free, but he held her fast.

"She's the one who raised the signal so the Sidhe would slaughter one another," he told the others, breathing hard.

"I didn't!" she squeaked, a sob in her voice. "I saw the illusion and panicked. I thought it was him."

Darrow glared down at Aila. "Who put her in charge of raising the signal?"

"Nobody did," said Coral. "In fact, I thought you said you didn't want to get involved in this ridiculous plan at all. Who did you bribe to let you in?"

Aila's cheeks reddened. "I—"

Darrow's eyes narrowed. "Search the room for other spies and see to it that this one gets what she deserves."

Aila shot me a furious glare as though I'd forced her to betray the Sidhe myself. Anger rose in my throat, thick and potent. "What did they promise you? That you'd get to serve alongside Lord Daival himself, or carry the Seelie Queen's bags for her? Maybe act as a footstool? You make me sick."

Aila spun around and ran, but she didn't make it a metre before the Sidhe had her surrounded. As they closed in on her, the anger faded from Darrow's face, replaced with an expression I couldn't read. Damn, he'd sobered up fast.

"I'm sorry," Coral murmured. "I should have known she was eavesdropping on our plans. I made the mistake of thinking she was harmless."

"It's not your fault," I said. "I bet that's precisely why Lord Daival picked her out. Should have figured he'd have his own spies among the Court."

"Seven people are dead," Lord Niall said. "Seven Sidhe slaughtered in my own house. There will be justice for this."

The moon rose over the forest, blood-red tinged with dark shadows, like an omen from the gods themselves.

15

"You're sure the heir wasn't one of the Sidhe who was killed?" asked Mum.

"No." I rubbed my tired eyes. "I'm pretty sure he said 'potential heirs', which means the sprite hasn't cracked yet, but that's not much of a consolation. Can I please go and get some sleep now?"

I'd stayed behind for ages, searching for any signs of the real Lord Daival within Lord Niall's estate, but once again he'd been one step ahead of us. Seven Sidhe lay dead, slaughtered at the hands of their own, but none bore the mark of Lord Daival's thorns. By now, blood soaked my ruined dress and I ached down to my bones, and while my mind was far from satisfied, my body cried out for rest.

Mum called me into the kitchen. "Hazel, I know you're tired, but I need to talk to you for a moment. Alone."

I walked into the kitchen and began removing my weapons, dropping them onto the table one by one. "What is it?"

She pursed her lips. "I saw you with Darrow earlier. Before Lady Aiten accosted you."

"Ah." Awkward. My mother had seen me making out with my ex-mentor. "Yeah. That was a thing. The guy's a lightweight, apparently."

"It's none of my business who you spend your time with," she said, "but if you decide to take your relationship to the next level, you need to be prepared for the consequences."

"Mum, you can't seriously be giving me the sex talk right now," I said, wishing I could glamour myself invisible so we could both avoid the rest of this conversation. "You didn't even give us a proper talk when we were kids. I had to ask Agnes of all people."

"Yes, well," said Mum. "You need to remember that now you're Gatekeeper, there is no heir. If you have children of your own, they'll be the next in line."

Absolutely fucking not. It was bad enough being involved myself, let alone my hypothetical offspring. "Mum, I became Gatekeeper five minutes ago. Give me time to adjust to that first. Besides, do you think I could ever raise a child in this mess? The Sidhe are like toddlers and I sure as hell can't wrangle *them* into obedience."

Mum had raised three of us, but not while fending off a potential coup and a leadership changeover. I didn't even know if I wanted kids in the future, but I'd make that decision on my own terms. Not the Courts'.

"I was just telling you," she said. "Your ex-mentor likely doesn't know all the potential consequences of sleeping with the Gatekeeper."

"I'm not pregnant," I said. "And I'm not sleeping with

Darrow. Even if I was, I know fifteen different kinds of contraceptive potions and spells."

"How do you know… I don't want to ask, do I," said Mum. "Just remember that the rule against romantic involvement with faeries was put into place because a half-faerie cannot be chosen as Gatekeeper."

"Because they'd be more powerful than the average Gatekeeper and the Winter Court would see it as unfair, I know. I haven't screwed Darrow, and I'm careful." As far as I'd heard, no Lynn had ever had a child with a faerie or half-faerie, but I shuddered to think what the Sidhe might do to them if they did.

"I hope so." Mum gave me a long look. "You can go to bed now, Hazel."

She left the kitchen, while I stood there in the dark, a pile of knives next to me on the table. *I can't believe she actually thinks I'd consider bringing a child into the world with all hell breaking loose.*

It was bad enough still living in the same house as my mother at twenty-four years old, but working for the Sidhe had put the final nail in the coffin on my chances of ever having a normal relationship. Mum and Dad had stayed together until he hadn't been able to stand living in a house where piskies nested in the ceiling and his hay fever acted up all year round. None of the Lynns could leave the Ley Line, so anyone I entered a serious relationship with would be tied to this house for life. Add in my penchant for attracting faerie-related trouble whenever I went into the human world, too, and my options were depressingly limited.

Ilsa entered the room, and the ceiling lights snapped on. "Hazel, why are you standing in the dark?"

"Mum just sprang the sex talk on me. I'm mildly traumatised."

Her brows shot up. "Seriously?"

"I wish I was joking." I pulled out my last knife and dropped it on the table, then went to the sink and washed the blood from my hands. "She saw me with Darrow at the party and drew her own conclusions. Did she do the same when you met River?"

"No, of course not. Are you and Darrow—?"

"No!" I scowled. "I can't believe she didn't lecture you, too. You lost your virginity before I did."

Ilsa went scarlet. "Thanks for that, Hazel. You're technically the younger sibling, so maybe she's overprotective of you."

"Overprotective? She always let me do whatever the hell I liked when we were kids." It wasn't like she could watch us while she was in Faerie. "No, she's going on about my responsibilities for raising the next Gatekeeper. Since if I have any kids, they'll be potential heirs."

Nausea swirled in my stomach. I knew enough of our family history to be aware that every Gatekeeper had tried evading their responsibilities at some point or other, but all had succumbed to said duties in the end. Including the child-bearing part.

A plate of cookies appeared on the table. As usual, the house had picked up on my mood and tried to comfort me in its own way. Forgetting my nausea, I picked one up, and Ilsa did the same.

"I'm not dealing with this now," I added. "Not with the Court falling apart."

"But you do like Darrow." She tilted her head. "Right? You talk about him often enough."

"Etaina sent him to bring the Erlking's talisman to her, and you know how it'll turn out when he realises I have it," I said. "Even if I did like him—which I don't—it'll all go up in flames soon enough. Better to pick out a normal human like Mum did. I'm not sure how she convinced Dad, to be honest. Did she ever tell you?"

"Nope," said Ilsa. "You know what she's like. She probably told him the bare minimum, so he kind of knew what he was getting himself into."

"That, or she took out an ad in the local paper saying, *Wanted: potential father for my offspring. Pros: hot sex and no responsibilities. Cons: said offspring are liable to be dragged off to Faerie.*"

Ilsa choked on her cookie. "Hazel, please never say that in front of Mum. Ever."

"I don't have a death wish." Though at this rate, I'd never live long enough to have a first date with a human, let alone procreate. "I also wouldn't know the first thing about dating humans. At least with River, you have common ground."

"Mm." She turned the remainder of her cookie over in her hand. "You still want to break the curse? After it's over, I mean?"

"If this crap ever gets sorted out?" I said. "The instant another heir takes the throne and the staff is taken care of —however that works out—then yes."

Ilsa chewed on her cookie. "Mum spent ages looking for a way to undo it, too. She told me. So did Grandma. Not that I don't want to give it a try, I'm just reminding you what we're up against."

"But the Sidhe aren't immortal anymore," I said, undeterred. "Okay, they're still long-lived, but we aren't playing by the same rules as Thomas Lynn did. The Courts are changing. Fast."

Too fast. Given the Sidhe's shock and horror at Lord Niall's house, the tide of change might well sweep them all away, and whether we won or lost this conflict, I'd lose the title of Gatekeeper one way or another. I was already struggling to remember what it felt like not to have the Erlking's talisman weighing on my mind, like a constant nagging in the back of my head.

"I was thinking future Gatekeepers can opt in," I added. "It's not like having contacts between Faerie and the mortal realm is a bad idea, I'm just a little leery of my future offspring being volunteered to deal with them. Hell, *I'd* like the option to drop out without my body being torn to shreds by a curse. Choice is a good thing. The Sidhe could use more flexibility."

I collected up my knives and took them through into the storeroom under the stairs where Mum kept her weapons, spells and other junk. The ping of a message on someone's phone drew me into the living room, where my mobile phone lay discarded among the notes on the Erlking's family tree. Morgan had sprawled on the sofa, the faerie dog curled up against his side on top of a pile of Ilsa's notes. The phone pinged again, and I picked it up. A message from Dad. *How's life?*

His texts rarely varied—always *how's life* or *how're things.* I generally sent him a generic response, the best I could do without giving information that might make the faeries target him. The less he knew of the current drama in the Courts, the better.

Sometimes I wondered what he thought my life as Gatekeeper was really like. When he'd lived here, he must have seen hints of the world beyond the Summer gate, but after the faerie invasion, he didn't need the Sight to see piskies flitting around, half-faeries dancing on the hills, Vale beasts hiding in the shadows waiting to snack on unsuspecting humans. The horrors of the real world sometimes made it hard to remember why the faeries managed to entrance so many people, but the horror was part of the attraction, and the longing they evoked had no rational basis.

The faeries and the talisman had that much in common, at least.

The faerie dog whined in his sleep, knocking a stack of notes off the sofa. I scrambled to pick them up before Ilsa noticed and got mad at Morgan for making a mess of things, and my gaze snagged on a name on the topmost page.

"No fucking way," I murmured.

"What?" Ilsa entered the room behind me. "Oh, Dad texted you again."

"Never mind that." I showed her the page. "Look."

She blinked. "At what?"

"That." I pointed at the line connecting the Erlking's name with his wife's at the top of the family tree. On the other side, the Seelie Queen's name was connected to one other: *the Lady of Light.*

Ilsa's brow furrowed. "The Seelie Queen's sister?"

"Etaina's people called her that. The Lady of Light." I looked up as Mum entered the room. "Does that give her a claim on the throne?"

"No," said Mum. "She isn't related to the Erlking, only his wife."

That didn't reassure me, but it explained how Etaina

had known the Erlking. Did the Seelie Queen know her sister was alive? If the entire Court believed the Aes Sidhe extinct, maybe she didn't.

"What're you all yelling about?" Morgan looked up blearily from the sofa.

"You fell asleep on my notes," Ilsa said accusingly.

I tuned out their argument and looked more closely at the page. On the list of heirs, the name *Lord Garin* leapt out at me. "Lord Garin was one of the Sidhe who died."

Ilsa looked sharply at the page. "He was the heir?"

"One of the potential heirs." A wave of nausea rose in my throat. "He's the guy who got into a brawl with the bear shifter at my party when he claimed he was the Erlking's successor. Guess he wasn't that far off the mark after all."

"So he *was* on the list?"

"Unless this is a different guy." Half the Court might be related to the Erlking. It didn't mean they were all suitable heirs, and it sounded as though the Erlking had handpicked someone based on trust, not status.

But it seemed Lord Daival had kept his word, and now we had a list of the next potential murder victims right in front of us.

16

What with the chaos of the day before, I'd forgotten all about the executions scheduled for the following morning. When I entered the ambassadors' palace, I found Coral sitting on a bench inside the hall, her gaze downcast and her eyes dull. The other half-faeries gathered in groups, milling around, but Willow was notably absent and so was Aila. Last I'd seen, the latter had been hauled off by armed guards for an extended prison sentence.

"Shit, Coral." I walked over to her side and hugged her. "I'm sorry."

She looked at me through red-rimmed eyes. "Don't be. I should have known the Sidhe would go ahead with the executions despite what happened at Lord Niall's party yesterday."

"They have to feel like they're in control somehow." The Sidhe's grief and anger yesterday would come to a head sooner or later, and it was probably for the best that they had an outlet rather than blaming one another for the deaths. Still, it seemed unfair that after Coral's brother had been the one who'd chosen to kill the Erlking and conspire with the Seelie Queen, it was his sister who'd suffer the most for his crimes. "Is Aila being executed today, too?"

Coral dipped her head. "Yeah. Small consolation, huh."

I'd never liked Aila—her bitter hatred towards me made that difficult—but it seemed tragic for her life to come to such a brutal end, even if she'd brought it on herself.

"Where's Willow?" I asked. "Lady Aiten didn't give you a hard time yesterday, did she?"

"No…" Her forehead crumpled. "Why?"

"She's Willow's mother," I said. "I worried she'd give you grief. She told me she disapproved of her daughter associating with another Court's heir, and I had to stop her from interrupting you at the party yesterday. Just giving you a head's up."

"Oh." She blinked, tears trembling on her lashes. "I didn't see. But thank you for stopping her."

"What are friends for?" Not that I'd been a great one lately. "I really am sorry. Forget Lady Aiten. You don't have to stand on bodyguard duty or anything, either. I can put someone else in charge."

She shook her head. "I still have a responsibility as your bodyguard. Some of the Sidhe seem to think Lord Daival might target the executions."

My heart sank. "What, and use them as a diversion to free the Seelie Queen?"

His own escape proved the jail's magic could be fooled, and since the executions were the first time any Sidhe had been put to death in Summer for a long while, there'd be quite a gathering. Perhaps I should go and keep an eye on things, but there was no telling who'd be the next potential heir to suffer death on his orders.

The door opened and Darrow entered the hall. My cheeks seared with heat at the memory of our kiss at the revel—and Mum's lecture, too—but one look at his stern face told me he was back to his usual, distant self. He met my eyes without humour as he walked over to us.

"He looks pissed," said Coral in an undertone.

"Uh, yeah, he was kinda drunk yesterday," I muttered. "Not my doing, but I'll talk to him."

If he planned to pin the blame on me for how he'd acted, I would not be amused. I'd been more sober than he had.

I halted in front of him. "Hey. Need a hangover cure?"

"No." He did look tired, his eyes shadowed and his glamour not quite as glossy as usual. His gaze flicked to Coral and the others. "Are you going to the executions?"

"Depends if Lord Daival's more likely to target the jail or sneak around the Court and find the other potential heirs while everyone's distracted. Who the hell knows."

"He's unlikely to try a direct assault," he said. "With the list of heirs… is he following a specific pattern, or picking them at random?"

"Depends if he has a copy of the…" I trailed off. "What list are you talking about, exactly?"

"Your mother told me the names on the family tree matched last night's victim," he said.

"You talked to my mother? When?" *Please tell me she didn't give him the sex talk, too.* That was all I needed.

"When she caught me watching the gate this morning."

"You mean *our* gate? In *our* garden?" He'd been

watching the Lynn house while I'd been sleeping? Had he seen the Inner Garden? Surely not—he'd have brought it up right away if he had—but a rush of panic and anger seized hold of me.

"Lord Daival attacked your family before," he said.

"That's none of your business." Couldn't he leave well enough alone? The Erlking's talisman was the last piece of leverage I had left against the Seelie Queen, and if he and Etaina kept intervening, Lord Daival would be able to get away with taking more lives. "My family can take care of ourselves. You're lucky Mum didn't skewer you on the spot."

He shook his head. "You can't watch your family while you're here in Faerie. If you had faith that I'm not out to harm you—"

"Don't make this about you, Darrow." Anger and guilt churned inside me. He wasn't to know the odds of Lord Daival targeting my house again were slim now he'd seen the talisman move of its own accord and devour his pet wraith. "Look, I appreciate the effort, and I'm grateful for the help, but you're Etaina's..."

"Etaina's what?"

Don't say servant, Hazel. "The point is, you're reporting my every move to her. Can you blame me for feeling edgy about you watching my house at night?"

"I wasn't doing it for her." His voice was quiet, but each word was precise. "If she found out, she'd be incredibly displeased with me for wasting my time rather than doing my job."

You were *doing your job. You just didn't know you were a breath away from the Erlking's talisman.*

"Can we not do this now?" I said. "Coral's brother is

set to be executed today, and Lord Daival will be back to claim another victim. I doubt the Sidhe will be up for another party to bait him, but he's coming here one way or another."

The palace doors flew open, and Lord Niall stormed into the hall, his peacock-blue cloak swirling and his eyes ablaze. What was the master of revels doing here? He looked, if possible, more pissed off than he had when he'd seen several of his people slaughtered yesterday.

Lord Niall stalked towards me, his mouth pulled taut with rage. "Today, I received a note informing me that one potential heir will die each day the Summer Gatekeeper refuses to cooperate with Lord Daival. You set me up to host that party to lure him into a trap, and when it failed, he slaughtered us. You have our blood on your hands, Gatekeeper."

Crap. Had Lord Raivan ratted me out? Or Lady Aiten, to get me back for not confiding in her?

"It was my idea," I admitted, "but I didn't want to cause a panic, especially as nobody knew the heir's identity. I thought he'd show up in person—"

"You lied to all of us," he spat, his eyes sparkling dangerously. "Thanks to you, seven fine warriors are dead."

I took a step back. "I told Lord Raivan, and it was his decision whether to share my plan or not. Lord Daival didn't give me the name of the person he was going to target, and if the entire Court knew he was going after the potential heirs of Summer, there'd have been a riot."

"You have no authority over us, human," he said. "I will see to it that you have your Gatekeeper's title removed, and you'll never set foot in this realm again."

Whoa. "Hang on, there. I'm sorry for those who died, but Lord Daival is the enemy here. He's coming back—"

"To kill the heir," said Lord Niall. "Our next monarch."

"A *potential* heir," I said. "That might be any of you. Nobody knows who the heir is, like I told you."

"Lord Daival does," Lord Niall said. "He bragged of it."

Several gasps came from behind him. A number of other Sidhe had entered the hall, silently, and fanned out behind the master of revels.

Fuck you, Lord Daival. He'd let the Sidhe know exactly what he was doing, and the Sidhe, predictably, had skipped all the way to full-scale panic.

A light-skinned male Sidhe with fair hair stepped to Lord Niall's side, wielding a sword that rippled with Summer magic. "Do you think your foul human blood makes you superior to us? Let's spill it and see."

I called on my Gatekeeper's magic, forming a shield in front of me. "Lord Daival is coming back for another victim today. Focus on him, not me."

"I will not allow you to deceive us any longer, Gatekeeper," said Lord Niall. "You will give up your title, or you will die."

"Yeah, there's a slight problem with that," I said. "This pesky curse in my family name makes it impossible for me to step down."

"Then we'll lock you up," said the fair-haired Sidhe. "For the rest of your pathetic mortal existence."

"The traitors are being executed today," said a female Sidhe with thorns growing from her head in place of hair. "She should join them."

"Did you not hear the part about the curse?" Magic sizzled off my shield, bouncing right back at the Sidhe who'd thrown it at me. He darted to the side, his eyes sparkling with rage. "If you try to use magic on me, it'll only backfire. Don't do anything you'll regret."

If I drew a weapon, I'd land myself in even deeper shit, but like hell was I going to let them attack me without defending myself.

Coral hurried to my side. "I think you should consult with the higher Sidhe before making rash decisions, Lord Niall. If you want to make a complaint against the Gate-keeper, Lord Raivan and Lady Aiten are the people to talk to."

"Why should that be so?" said Lord Niall. "None of us elected to have a human running around our Court, leaving a trail of lies everywhere she walks."

"Tell that to my ancestor, not me," I said. "I'm trying to *help* you. Lord Daival wants to turn us against one another, and it's working. Lady Aiten tasked me with catching him, so if you don't like my methods, you're welcome to take your complaints straight to her."

"You have no respect for us, mortal," said the blond Sidhe. "Perhaps you'll change your mind when I carve you up."

A jet of blue-green magic slammed into the Sidhe's weapon, freezing it in his grip. *Thanks, Darrow.* Coral tugged on my arm, indicating a tapestry which concealed a hidden passage. There was a time to fight and a time to run—and now was definitely the latter. Darrow stepped between me and the Sidhe, while I ducked behind the tapestry and into the stone-walled passageway.

"Thanks," I whispered to Coral, stepping into the dark.

"C'mon." Coral grabbed my arm and pulled me after

her. "Stay out of range until they calm down. I sent some of the others to find Lady Aiten."

"Assuming she doesn't join the mob herself." We emerged from the passage into another corridor, where a door near the end led into the palace grounds. "What the hell do I do now? Lord Daival did this on purpose. He's going to kill one of them while everyone's distracted, and they'll probably blame me for that, too."

"I know, Hazel, but they won't listen to reason at the moment." Coral indicated the woods at the back of the house. "Run into the forest—anywhere will do—and leave a false trail. I can help, but Darrow is better at creating illusions than I am."

"Illusions. Good idea." An uneasy pang hit me at the image of Darrow fighting the Sidhe alone in order to help me escape, but it wouldn't do us any good if I turned back now. He'd be fine: he had his glamour magic.

I ran for the maze where Darrow and I had once trained together, and its hedges rose above my head, soft leaves cushioning my footsteps. Taking aim, I conjured up a couple of glamoured Hazels and sent them around the corner of the palace. My clones weren't as detailed or convincing as Darrow's, but they should be enough to lead my pursuers astray and allow me to make my escape.

As I emerged from the maze into the mass of shadowy trees beyond, I spotted a group of Sidhe crossing the lawn in pursuit of one of my illusions. Giving myself a mental high-five, I wandered deeper into the woods. I needed to go somewhere the Sidhe wouldn't follow me, or at least somewhere they wouldn't expect me to go. The Gatekeeper's training grounds were deserted, but they might be too obvious a choice. The Erlking's territory might work, but Lord Daival wouldn't find any of his potential murder victims there, and despite the Sidhe's ingratitude, I had a job to do.

The jail. If nothing else, I'd be able to ensure Lord Daival wasn't lying in wait to intervene at the executions. The guards wouldn't allow Lord Niall and his cronies to start a brawl outside the jail—I hoped.

Lord Raivan's meadow lay somewhere nearby, so I turned in that direction, hoping the Sidhe wouldn't expect me to linger so close to the palace. With Faerie's tendency to rearrange the world at will, I hadn't the faintest clue how to get to the jail from here without someone to give me directions, and besides, I had words to say to Lord Raivan about letting Lord Niall attack me in the one supposed safe zone for humans. Then again, Darrow had one thing right—the guy was an unreliable coward who was out for himself alone.

A steady breeze swept towards me, carrying the fragrant scents of Summer's forest—and beneath, the bitter tang of decay.

I halted at the edge of a clearing, flanked with trees. Their trunks rotted, heaving with dead leaves, and the skeletal remains of human-like faces were visible in the bark, etched in expressions of despair and misery. Dryads. Dead—very dead. The rotting trees bore an eerie resemblance to the Erlking's territory when his talisman's magic had run amok, but the dying dryad I'd met in Half-Blood Territory was the closest comparison.

Past the trees lay wilted flowers, their enticing scents turned sour, and dead piskies sprawled in the beds of roses, steeped in the sickly smell of rot. Above all, the green glow that pervaded Summer territory was eerily absent. The magic sustaining all life had seeped out of this area as though someone had left a doorway into the Vale open, with an effect like blood leaking from an open wound.

The only magic I could sense at all was my own, pulsing from the circlet and bringing a glow to my hands. Healing the damage to the forest would require more magic than I was willing to expend, and the destruction didn't end here. I trod further, finding more dead trees, their trunks buried in a bed of rotting leaves.

I scanned the undergrowth for a doorway into the Vale, a life-eating monster—anything to explain the decay, the lack of magic, the despair and death. How had nobody noticed part of their Court rotting from the inside out?

"Wonderful, isn't it?" said a familiar voice. "The darkness festers, and the Court will soon rot from within."

I stiffened, raising my iron blade when a Sidhe glided out from behind a tree onto the path in front of me.

Lord Daival.

17

The sight of Lord Daival—or something that looked like him, anyway—brought a groan to my lips. "I don't have time for more bullshit, Lord Daival. Unless you're going to tell me you were responsible for this, so I can add it to my reasons to turn you into an iron pincushion. Then by all means, go ahead."

"This?" He indicated the rotting trees and beds of wilting flowers. "This decay is the result of the darkness that festers in the absence of a ruler of Summer. With nobody wearing the crown, the Court's magic is weakening, and soon enough, the Sidhe will begin to feel it, too. Their strength will wane, and they will be ill-equipped to handle the threats to come."

Chills gripped me, not just at his eager tone, but because he didn't talk like an illusion created by magic. Most didn't have Darrow's skills to make glamours who acted exactly like the person they imitated.

He wasn't an illusion this time. He was real.

"You bastard," I said. "What did you do, send Lord Niall a letter telling him your plans?"

"The Sidhe deserve to know their fate," he said. "I've never met a Gatekeeper as devious as you, Hazel Lynn. Scheming behind the Sidhe's backs, deceiving them with every minute you spend in their realm..."

"Your point?" I reached for the blade strapped to my waist. "At least tell me my plan gave you some trouble. Forced you to change things up a little. Did you tell your people which potential heirs to trick the Sidhe into killing?"

"It didn't matter either way," he said, straight-faced. "There is no heir, only the rightful Queen."

He doesn't know who the heir is. The sprite hasn't given in yet.

"I beg to differ," I said. "If you aren't interested in who the heir is, why don't you do us all a favour and hand the Erlking's sprite over? There's no sense in continuing to torture a harmless creature when you don't care about the information he has."

Lord Daival gave me a pitying look. "His torture is over. The sprite claimed he would rather die than reveal the truth."

Bile burned my throat. "You *killed* him?"

I should have known Lord Daival wouldn't have the patience to wait for answers, not when the truth didn't matter. Nobody else in the Court knew who the heir was, and now... nobody ever would.

I raised my iron blade and pointed it at the exposed skin of his neck. "If you hand yourself in, the Sidhe will show you more mercy than I will."

Thorns wrapped around the blades in his hands. "You

should have died of those wounds, Gatekeeper. That talisman you stole can only destroy, not heal."

"You know nothing about my talisman." My blade clashed with his, jarring my wrist. Thorny vines lashed at my skin, and I sliced down, severing them. "Or the Gatekeepers. Would your queen be happy if you strike me dead and force her to face the backlash of your choice?"

Dodging whirling thorns, I launched into another attack, dealing a glancing blow to his arm. His armoured sleeve repelled the iron. He'd left no skin exposed except for his face, and the thorny magic wrapping around his hands formed sharp-edged gloves trailing threads of magic that snagged the edge of my blade. Dodging the thorns and deflecting his sword at the same time used all my energy, and despite my best efforts, I found myself losing ground. As long as those blasted thorns got in my way, I'd be at a disadvantage.

Lure him through the gates into the talisman's path. It'll eat the flesh from his bones.

Quiet, I told the sinister voice in my head. I wouldn't put my family in danger just to be in with a shot at using the talisman on him. Besides, he'd never let me lure him willingly within range of the talisman's magic.

"You're weak, Gatekeeper," he said softly. "You have a mere slither of the Court's magic to call your own, while I have far more than Summer magic on my side. I have the power of the Lord of Thorns."

"Did you come up with that title or did you steal it along with your talisman?" I cut and hacked, severing more vines, but they kept growing, fuelled by the magic in his hands. He had an unlimited supply, while the dead trees and rotting leaves wouldn't respond to my own

Summer magic. Each strike jarred the blade in my palm, while every lash of thorn snagged my clothes or skin. A sharp sting lashed my cheek, and I bit back a wince.

"I think I've toyed with you enough, Gatekeeper."

A wave of thorns shot from his hands like a flurry of arrows. With a curse, I flung myself behind a rotting tree. The thorns struck the tree, hammering into it like steel bullets. Footsteps set me on the move again, and I ducked out from the tree to see the back of Lord Daival's head as he departed. *Running away?*

No… moving onto his next target. Either the heir or the jail—where dozens of Sidhe gathered to wait for the executions.

I broke into a sprint after him, cursing the Sidhe for their ability to run for miles without tiring. He was too damned fast and agile, leaping clear of the fallen branches with a swiftness I'd never achieve no matter how I tried. My lungs burned and my legs ached from the effort to keep him within sight, but I refused to let him escape this time. I pushed on past the rotting trees and into the sun-drenched forest of evergreens which formed the main part of the Summer Court. My circlet's light brightened in response to the return of Summer's magic, and I raised my hand and imbued the trees with a torrent of power. The trees parted before me, revealing Lord Daival up ahead. *You won't get away that easily.*

I fed more power into the trees, whose branches grew, forming a net that blocked his path. Lord Daival blasted them aside without breaking his stride. Undeterred, I drove my magic at a branch overhead, sending it crashing into his path, but he simply leapt over it with inhuman swiftness.

"You still seek to undo me with your Gatekeeper's magic alone?" he said. "My queen will put that talisman to better use."

"It'll never be hers." A fresh burst of speed took me, fuelled by rage, my knives rattling against my legs. Taking aim, I conjured an illusory troll into his path. He kept running, breaking the illusion the instant he caught it up, but the reminder of another trick Darrow had pulled during my Trials gave me an idea.

Raising my hand, I fired off a jet of magic at a tree on my right, urging it to grow, branches extending to brush its neighbours. Then I leapt for a low-hanging branch and climbed into the canopy. Using magic to steady the trees beneath me, I began leaping from one branch to the next in a zigzagging trail that brought me closer to him with every tree. I conjured more illusions at every opportunity to block his path, and while he broke them with ease, each distraction closed the distance between us.

When I was less than ten feet away, I hurled an iron dagger at him from behind. The hilt smacked him in the back of the head, sending him staggering to a brief halt. I jumped to the neighbouring tree, riding its growing branches to a tree just across from Lord Daival, and threw a second dagger. This one hit his jaw with a satisfying ringing noise.

Lord Daival spun on me with a snarl, an ugly red mark on his jaw. "You should have run while you could, Gatekeeper."

Thorny vines shot from his hands into the tree I hung from like bladed whips. I dropped to a lower branch to avoid them, took aim, and pushed all the magic I had into the tree directly behind him.

The tree's roots shot out of the earth beneath Lord Daival's feet. He leapt back, closer to my tree, and I let go and dropped onto him. My knees clashed with his armoured shoulders, my knife sinking through his armour into the nearest bit of flesh I could find. Warm blood gushed over my hands. I'd hit his arm, not his neck, but it did the job. The thorns began to flicker and fade out, deprived of the magic that fed their power.

I yanked the knife out of his arm in a gush of blood, then I drove it towards his heart. The blade bounced off his armour, and he slid out from underneath me, flipping me onto my back. He bared his teeth in a snarl. "You will be your own ending, Gatekeeper."

"Try again when you aren't bleeding to death." I tried to stab him from underneath, but his heavy armour weighed me down.

"Tell me," he snarled. "How did you trick the staff into giving you its power? What deceit did you use?"

"I didn't trick it." I gave another shove, feeling his blood soak into my clothes. "I claimed it as my own, and if you strike me dead, its magic will infect and destroy you."

"You are not the talisman's master, mortal," he said. "Even the Sidhe know we are slaves to their magic, for the alternative is having no power at all. If it is truly yours, then you will feel its pull even now, a constant urge to feel its magic slide through your very being and offer you everything you'll ever need."

"You sound like you're the one who's enslaved, not me." My gaze darted to the thorny knife in his hand. *Talismans.* Might the power he'd stolen have come from the gods, too?

"If any traces of your talisman's magic remain within

you, I could remove them now, with the right words," he said. "Yes, don't think I'm unaware that your sister has the power of an Ancient, and she used an Invocation to free you of the talisman's magic so you could continue to deceive the Courts about its location."

"Do you want a medal?" Whether it was my rebellious streak, the memory of my troublemaking grandmother, or just pure Lynn stubbornness, I didn't know, but I would not bend my head and let an inanimate object make decisions for me. My Gatekeeper's magic might not be as strong, but it was eternal.

And there always had to be a Gatekeeper.

I tapped into my circlet's magic, drawing on every ounce of power I could conjure. The glow brightened, and Lord Daival's eyes squinted against the dazzling light.

That was all the distraction I needed. I rolled to the side, locking my legs around his and sending him crashing onto his back. The Gatekeeper's magic broke free from my hands and directed the tree roots to wrap around Lord Daival from behind. Thorns burst from his hands, but the effects of the iron had begun to kick in. His face greyed, the green light in his eyes dimming, his body weakening along with his magic. Blood soaked his arm, and his feral expression promised pain.

"You will die, Hazel," he said. "You can't fight that talisman's magic, no more than you can fight a rising tide or a setting sun on your mortal plain. The power will consume you, along with your Gatekeeper's magic, and you will wish for death's touch for the remainder of your existence."

"That's a pretty speech." I'd dropped my knife somewhere in the undergrowth, but I had plenty to spare. A blade slid into my hand, and I pointed it at his throat. "Where do you want me to stick this one?"

The sound of hooves beating on the path rang through the trees. Then came a shout, followed by more hoofbeats, and two armoured Sidhe rode into view. Whether they were Lord Niall's people or not, I didn't know, but I had no patience for their bullshit.

"I found your escaped criminal." I gestured with my knife. "You're welcome."

Lord Daival spat out a curse. "My lady will make you pay for this. The Courts will collapse from within as the Sidhe destroy one another. This, I promise you."

"If anything, I'm doing you a favour by handing you over to them rather than finishing you off myself.," I said to him. "As luck would have it, there's a mass execution scheduled for this morning. Maybe the Sidhe will be nice enough to give you an invitation, too."

The Sidhe drew their horses to a halt in front of me.

"It's him!" one of them said, pointing to Lord Daival's silver head pinned beneath the web of tree roots.

"Watch out for those thorns," I warned. "If you want me to stick another iron knife in him, I'd be more than happy to. And please put his talismans somewhere he *can't* steal them back this time."

"You have no right to give us orders," said a fox-eared female Sidhe with auburn hair. "You broke the law when you fled to escape justice and asked your fellow half-Sidhe to turn on Summer's soldiers."

Crap. I hope they didn't arrest Darrow. He'd been a royal pain in my arse yesterday, but he'd stepped in to defend me at the risk of his own freedom when he didn't even belong to my Court.

"I came here to look for Lord Raivan, because Lord Niall and his band of merry men were set on stringing me up and using me for target practise," I said. "The half-Sidhe were defending me, that's all. You must know that killing or arresting me will only work in the enemy's favour."

"My Lord, she claims to have been looking for you," the fox-eared Sidhe called over her shoulder.

Lord Raivan strode into view. I never thought I'd be so glad to see his grumpy face again. "Hazel Lynn, what have you done?"

"I caught Lord Daival," I told him. "I completed my mission. That ought to cancel out my transgressions, right?"

He gave me a look tinged with frost. "Come with me, Gatekeeper."

18

The Sidhe wouldn't even let me retrieve my weapons from the bushes. Instead, Lord Raivan marched me back to the ambassador's palace, while his fellow Sidhe hauled the limp and bleeding Lord Daival off to jail. The one upside was that he continued to call me 'Gatekeeper'. Maybe not all the Sidhe thought I deserved to lose my title after all.

"Lord Raivan," I said when we reached the doors to the palace. "I would like to see Lord Daival taken into the jail in person. Feel free to do whatever you like with me afterwards, but you might have gathered by now that I don't have all that much faith in your ability to keep hold of your prisoners."

Lord Raivan merely gave me a prod in the spine, urging me towards the palace doors. My hands itched to punch him in the nose, but the sight of Lady Aiten inside the hall stopped me in my tracks. *About damned time.*

Across the hall, Coral gave me an encouraging smile. I nodded back at her and approached Lady Aiten.

"Where have you been?" I asked. "Lord Niall brought a mob to kill me. He's gone way off the rails."

"The Gatekeeper betrayed us all," said the fox-eared female Sidhe, slinking behind me into the hall. "Lord Raivan thinks we should grant her leniency because she caught that criminal, but her actions still cost lives."

"Yes," said Lady Aiten. "They did."

My heart gave a sickening dive. After I'd pissed her off yesterday, I could expect no mercy from her, and if she wanted, she could seal my fate and cast me out, leaving everyone to suffer the consequences.

"You gave me the task of catching Lord Daival," I reminded her. "You didn't give me any instructions on how to go about doing that, and I had the Court's safety in mind when I decided not to share his threats to murder the potential heirs with every Sidhe in Summer. You yourself were the first to agree that the rest of the Court shouldn't know all the details of his escape. Also, Lord Raivan supported my plan to arrange a revel at Lord Niall's. If I'm to blame, then so are the two of you."

"Is that true?" asked the fox-eared Sidhe, addressing Lady Aiten. "Did you know he planned to target the heir?"

"I suspected," she said. "Hazel is… correct, in assuming that certain members of Court would react hastily to that knowledge becoming widespread. We have no evidence the true heir, whoever they are, is his intended target."

"Is it true or isn't it?" she demanded. "He cannot lie, can he? If he said he planned to murder the Erlking's successor then we will take him at his word."

"He promised to murder the *potential* heirs," I corrected. "But he just told me the whole thing was a bluff. He doesn't know who the heir is, and he only made that threat because he wanted to cause everyone to panic. Ask him if you don't believe me. He might start talking now you've cornered him."

"I will speak with Lord Daival to verify his words myself," said Lady Aiten. "If it's true, then as far as we know, the true heir has not been harmed."

The sprite has, though. "Can I talk to you alone first?"

"No," she said bluntly. "I must speak with Lord Daival at once. In the meantime, you will remain here in isolation for your own safety, until our newest prisoner has been dealt with."

"I don't think so." I stepped forward, but Lord Raivan barred my path.

"You will stay here, Gatekeeper." He indicated the tapestried room. "Until the executions begin."

I hope Lord Daival is among them. If he didn't perish from iron poisoning before then. "Fine, whatever. Don't get your tail in a twist."

Coral slipped into the room to join me. "They shouldn't be punishing you for helping them."

"Nah, it's probably to stop Lord Niall coming into the palace and stabbing me before Lady Aiten gets back," I said. "But I wanted to see Lord Daival jailed myself. I wouldn't put it past the bastard to try to wriggle away at the last second."

"I know." Coral peered through the gap in the door, noting two stony-faced Sidhe had moved to stand on guard. "That blood isn't yours, is it?"

I glanced down at my blood-streaked shirt. "It's Lord Daival's. I stuck an iron knife in him. Missed anything vital, but the Sidhe ought to finish him off once they'd verified that his threats were utter bullshit."

Coral leaned against the wall next to me. "But he *did* trick the Sidhe into slaughtering their own, didn't he? Might one of them have been the heir?"

"It's anyone's guess at this point." Guilt lanced through me, but the poor sprite had been doomed the instant Lord Daival had found him. I'd never have reached him in time. "Considering how often I've fucked up lately, maybe losing my Gatekeeper status would be the best-case scenario, though Summer doesn't need to bring down even more bad luck on their Court."

I sank into a sitting position on the polished floor, wishing the Sidhe had locked me in a room with a sink so I could wash Lord Daival's blood off me.

Coral sat next to me. "They can't fire you, can they?"

"Nope." My hands folded in my lap, marked with cuts from Lord Daival's thorns. "My siblings are too old to take my place and my cousin Holly is the only survivor on the Winter Gatekeeper's side of the family. If I have kids, one of them will be chosen as the next Summer Gatekeeper, and the whole cycle will repeat."

She swore under her breath. "They can force your kids into this?"

"If you're wondering how Mum turned out the way she did... that's how." I heaved a sigh. "Every Gatekeeper has tried to find a way to undo the curse. Even the Sidhe don't know how it started. Most of the ones who were around in the early days when my ancestor was first bound either didn't witness the curse being cast or don't remember it."

She lifted her head. "Your ancestor?"

"Thomas Lynn." I studied my blood-encrusted fingernails. "He made a promise to come to the Sidhe's aid whenever they needed him, and they took him at his word. There's one Gatekeeper in each Court because he had twin daughters. One went to Summer…"

"And the other went to Winter," she said. "What does the Winter Gatekeeper think about all this?"

"You saw her, at the party. Holly Lynn." I raised my head. "None of us knows what happens if the last Gatekeeper dies. If *I* die, in other words. The curse might pick out another human, or it might backfire on the whole Court. I've survived up until now because nobody wants to risk breaking a centuries-old curse, but Lord Niall and his pals seem to have stopped giving a damn."

"Oh." She went quiet for a moment. "So the Sidhe are obligated to keep you in their good graces to protect themselves from the potential effects of breaking the vow?"

"Pretty much," I said. "Even the Seelie Queen fears it. That's why she wants me on her team. And Lord Daival promised both Holly and me a place at his side when his people invited us to that party. Not sure whether he planned to betray one or both of us, to be honest."

Raised voices came from outside the room. I rose to my feet and trod to the door to eavesdrop. "Dammit. Lord Niall. Hasn't he got another revel to plan?"

"I'll go and distract him." Coral inched the doors open and walked through. "Oh… hey, Darrow."

"Hazel." Darrow stood in the doorway. "May I come in?"

"You know I'm a prisoner, right?" I had no idea what to say to him, but with Lord Niall in the hall, leaving the door open was a bad idea. "All right, but the master of revels is still out for my blood."

"I'll make sure he doesn't try anything," said Coral.

"He seems to have calmed down somewhat." Darrow let Coral pass him then stepped into the room, closing the door behind him.

"You mean he's not trying to stick a knife in me," I said. "Thanks for helping distract him earlier."

"Of course," he said. "You told me not to follow you, so I did the next best thing."

Well, this is awkward. He'd taken my shock at his keeping an eye on the gate to my house as a rejection, and who could blame him? Silence spread between us, thick as mud.

"What I said earlier," I began. "I meant 'don't come to my family's property while I'm sleeping or otherwise absent'. Helping me fight egotistical thieving Sidhe who want to destroy the Court is fine. Encouraged, even.'

He raised a brow. "I thought you wanted to take out Lord Daival alone, you said."

"I wouldn't have minded if you'd helped."

Not when we were in Faerie, away from the staff. *You can't fight that talisman's magic, no more than you can fight a rising tide or a setting sun on your mortal plain. The power will consume you, along with your Gatekeeper's magic...* what total bollocks. What did Lord Daival know? He'd never held its magic in his grasp.

Oh, who was I kidding? Even when the talisman had helped me, it'd always had its own agenda, and at the moment, my staying alive served its own purpose. Given how it'd exposed itself to Lord Daival, it *wanted* the Courts to know someone had claimed its power, and with every passing moment, the talisman wore down the Inner

Garden's defences with no trustworthy individual to take it off my hands.

Darrow cleared his throat. "I should tell you… I know Lord Daival took the Erlking's sprite captive in order to learn who the heir to the Summer Court is."

My heart missed a beat. "You do?"

"I heard Lord Raivan and Lady Aiten talking," he said. "I understand why you didn't share that information publicly, considering how the Sidhe reacted when Lord Daival told them."

"Then I guess you know Lord Daival killed the sprite before he could give anything away." I looked down at the swirling patterns on the carpet. "We were too late. That's on top of his sending Lord Niall a note outlining his plans and emphasising that it's all my fault for scheming against the Court. That's why he told his followers to hunt me down. If you haven't guessed."

Darrow swore under his breath. "Lord Niall has no influence over the higher Sidhe's decisions, and it should be easy to prove Lord Daival lied about his intentions to manipulate the other Sidhe."

"I doubt it," I said. "Lord Daival didn't even want to know who the heir was; he just wanted to make sure nobody else did. Maybe they'll surprise us all and make *me* pick the heir next, assuming Lord Niall doesn't convince them to cast me out into the Vale."

With the sprite's death, the identity of the heir was lost forever, so our half-assembled family tree was the closest the Courts had to any sense of direction on who to choose as their next leader. Even if everyone on it did have code names and one of them happened to be Etaina. Did Darrow know she was the Seelie Queen's sister?

Does it matter? The Sidhe needed to pick someone, and fast. While they delayed, there'd be other parts of the forest going the same way as those unfortunate dryads, rotting from the inside out as the magic sustaining their existence melted away.

"Lord Niall has no authority," Darrow said. "He's popular with the other Sidhe, but his name won't be anywhere near the list of potential heirs, and at this rate, he won't even remain in control over his own estate for much longer. He's already in debt to another Sidhe for fixing the damage to his house after the recent attacks."

"Debt? Really?" I should have guessed throwing that many parties cost money, but the Sidhe seemed to have gold falling out of their fingertips.

"You forget I'm here as an outside observer," he said. "Lord Niall has little magic of his own, so he's forced to rely on others. It sounds like he hired someone to fix the damage to his house who charged rather more than he could afford."

Right. Darrow's a spy. A fact I seemed to forget all too often these days. "I really don't give a shit about Lord Niall, to be honest. I'm surprised you noticed him yesterday, considering…"

Considering he'd been off his tits and endearingly so. The day might have ended in bloodshed, yet it'd had some highlights. Mum's bizarre sex talk skirted through my mind, and I wondered if he knew about the reasoning behind the *no dating faeries rule.* He did know it existed—I'd told him—and yet he'd kissed me anyway.

He looked down into my eyes, his own aquamarine irises brighter than usual. "When I guarded your house last night, it was not my intention to make you uncomfortable. I was concerned for you, nothing more."

My mouth parted. He thought I'd meant to end my sentence with *considering you were too busy spying on me.* "I meant because you were drunk. Are you still drunk now?"

"No." He took a step closer to me. "Why?"

He stood closer than I'd thought, and my heart started beating faster as though my body remembered how he'd touched me, how his magic had slid along my skin and brought tingles to the surface. "Because you're not usually so… open."

He drew in a breath. "No, you're right. I've been a fool, but after yesterday—after Lord Daival left you for dead—I realised there's something much more important to me than my mission."

I licked my dry lips. "You said something similar before, yet you then abused my trust and brought me to Etaina against my will. You're here for her sake, Darrow. Whatever you think you feel for me—"

"I don't think," he said. "I know. And I also know you feel the same for me."

I couldn't bring myself to step away, even though I knew we had no future together. We barely had a present, and it would only last until someone opened the door.

His hand cupped my chin. "You're covered in blood."

"Not mine. I stabbed Lord Daival with an iron knife."

"Of course you did." His lips swept over mine, and my heart stuttered to a halt. "Are you sure he didn't hurt you?"

"Not as badly as last time." I stiffened beneath his touch. "Come to think of it, he wasn't trying that hard. He only fought me because I chased him down when he tried to run."

Darrow released me, his expression darkening. "It did surprise me to hear he showed his face in the Courts at all."

"He was on his way to the jail." Unease slithered down my spine. "Which is where he's going right now. He might be in handcuffs and bleeding from an iron wound, but it's where he wants to be."

I shouldn't have let Lady Aiten leave me behind. The Sidhe had handed Lord Daival exactly what he wanted… access to his queen.

19

The instant I exited the tapestried room, the two Sidhe guarding the doors stepped in to bar my way. "We have orders not to let the Gatekeeper leave this room."

Oh, for crying out loud. "I'm positive Lord Daival got himself arrested on purpose so he could bring down the jail from the inside, because you're more focused on me than your own criminals."

Behind the guards, Lord Niall and a few of his cronies stood arguing with Lord Raivan, while Coral stood at the side with some of the other half-Sidhe. From the expression on Lord Raivan's face, he was not thrilled with the master of revels.

"She's right," added Darrow. "You must send word to Lady Aiten and warn her at once. Tell Lord Raivan, too."

Magic tingled in his words, and the guards' expressions grew slack. Then they spoke in unison: "We will send word to Lady Aiten."

The two guards walked away, somehow picking up

Lord Raivan on the way out the doors and leaving Lord Niall and his companions behind.

"You again?" Lord Niall glided across the room and halted before Darrow and me. "You shouldn't be allowed to stay in our Court after the lies you told. You should be locked up with the other traitors, including this one." He jerked his head at Darrow, whose eyes narrowed right back at him. The bite of magic in the air warned me to avert my eyes, and Lord Niall took the full blast of it in the face. His jaw slackened, his eyes glazing over.

"You have no authority here," said Darrow, his voice low, dangerous. "Step aside, or I won't hold back this time."

Lord Niall did so without a word of protest. *Damn, Darrow.* Lord Niall's adoring gaze was fixed on him as though nothing else existed in the world.

"What is the meaning of this?" The female Sidhe with thorny hair stepped up behind him, followed by the blond male who bore more than a passing resemblance to Lord Raivan. "What did you do—?"

Darrow's magic locked the two of them to the spot, rendering them speechless.

"How long will that hold them?" I looked between the Sidhe, marvelling at how efficiently Darrow had shut them down. *He's definitely been holding back. Then again, that ability of his is about as subtle as a hurricane.*

"Not long enough," said Darrow, his hands alighting with green Summer magic.

Lord Niall's gaze cleared. "What devil are you?"

Coral appeared behind him, swinging a vase. The blow connected with Lord Niall's skull, and he crumpled into a heap. Quickly, I directed my magic at the thorny plants against the wall and ordered them to bind Lord Niall's legs and arms together. Then I did the same to his companions.

"That'll hold him." I ran for the doors, Darrow and Coral close on my heels.

Lady Aiten had left the path to the jail open outside the palace gates, but the absence of any Sidhe outside the sprawling building made my gut clench.

"Where are the guards?" Coral whispered. "My brother…"

"Stay safe," I warned. "I think Lord Daival has made his move."

I led the way up the short path leading up to the jail entrance. Outside, two guards' bodies lay unmoving on the ground, the branches and roots that formed the door severed as though by a sharp instrument. Their faces had turned grey, their eyes bleached of colour.

Iron poisoning. For an instant, horror rooted me to the spot. Lord Daival hadn't been carrying iron—but I had, and I'd lost several knives in the forest when I'd thrown them at him. The Sidhe had hauled me away before I could retrieve them, and while Lord Daival had been bleeding badly, he'd had enough strength left to grab a knife. And if the whole structure was made of magic… *We're too late.*

"Hazel!" Coral grabbed my arm and yanked me back as the building trembled to its foundations. The great oak trees flanking the jail quaked from their roots, and a tremendous crash sounded as part of the ceiling fell in. A cascade of similar crashes followed, while other sections of the jail sagged, no longer able to support the weight of their roofs and walls.

Dammit. There's got to be something I can do to stop it from falling apart.

I ducked into the doorway, calling on my Gatekeeper's powers. Magic lit my hands with a green glow, and I transferred it to the branches, but I couldn't make them grow fast enough to counter the effects of the iron poison.

Backing out the doorway, I ran for the trees around the sides of the jail, the ones from which its branches and roots originated. My hands found one of the trembling trunks and a jet of magic shot from my palms, urging the tree to repair itself.

"Hazel!" Darrow shouted.

A horrible cracking sounded, and I conjured a shield in defence as the tree's neighbour toppled, sending its companion crashing down. Elsewhere, another section of the jail fell into dust and ashes and broken branches. My Gatekeeper's magic wasn't enough to keep the place from falling apart. Lord Daival was still in there, and until I got the iron away from him, it'd be impossible to repair the damage.

"Where—" I whipped my head around to face Darrow. "Where is Lady Aiten? And the other guards?"

"They must still be inside." He lifted his hands, which glowed with blue-green magic. "If I try to get in, it'll cause more damage."

"I don't think it matters at this point," I said. "We have to get them out before Lord Daival murders them all."

I ran back to Coral's side, where she stood frozen to the spot, her gaze fixed on the west side of the collapsed building. I followed her line of sight and saw figures crawling from the ruins of the jail, feeling blindly through the dirt.

"He freed them," she whispered. "He used them as bait."

"Get them!" A cry came from the surrounding forest, and a group of Sidhe guards ran at the prisoners, weapons in their hands and bloodlust gleaming in their eyes. One transformed into a wolf and seized a prisoner by the throat, flinging her body into the bushes.

Coral pressed her hands to her mouth. "My brother—I don't see him."

"Save yourself first," I ordered her. "Don't let the Sidhe run you down along with the prisoners. I'm going in."

Despite the jail's collapsed state, no signs of Lord Daival were to be seen. He'd have stayed behind to help the Seelie Queen, and when I found him, I'd cut his throat with the iron he'd taken from me.

I climbed over piles of shattered branches, stilling each time they shifted under my feet, following my memories of the corridors. When I found a gap large enough to climb through, I conjured a shield around myself before ducking under a low-hanging branch and into the corridor within.

Devastation greeted me. Guards lay dead or injured beneath boughs the size of cars, and whole corridors were blocked with piles of debris. I drew my spare iron blade and began hacking my way through the ruins. The iron would hasten its collapse, but the Sidhe would have to rebuild the jail from the ground up whatever I did.

Prisoners crawled past or huddled in their cells, unable to move or crushed by the falling debris. Some would have been starved of daylight for years, left to rot in the darkness. Lord Daival had freed them as a diversion, nothing more, and those who survived would all face death at the Sidhe's hands.

As I hacked through the branches, I made out the shadow of a person, their head bowed over the open door to a cell.

Lord Daival.

I lunged at him from behind. He spun around, our twin iron knives colliding in a jarring crash. The thorny gloves on his hands protected him from the iron's touch, though his face remained grey and his eyes dull. That must be why it was taking him so long to get the Seelie Queen out—the stab wound I'd dealt had weakened him.

"I *knew* you stole from me, you scumbag," I spat.

"You have written your own demise, Gatekeeper," he said, in a raspy voice. "If you hadn't stabbed me, I'd never have been able to hold the iron long enough to get it in here. I suppose it's like that talisman you stole… you grow used to the pain."

"It's nothing like the talisman, you sadomasochistic weirdo." I blocked his attack with ease, cursing those blasted thorns for protecting him against my strikes. "But hey, if you're asking me to poke more holes in you with my knives, I'm happy to do you the favour."

Lord Daival laughed. The sound rattled in his chest, but the grey cast began to vanish from his face, his body straightening, the wounds sealing closed.

Oh… shit.

I threw up a shield as the cell behind him exploded, walls flying open and sending me crashing into the ruins of a collapsed cell. I landed on my back, breathless, buried under a shower of tree roots. Lifting my head, I shielded my eyes against a surge of blinding light.

The Seelie Queen walked out of the ruins of her cell, her ragged clothes turning into a gold dress that hugged her willowy figure. Her tangled hair became a waterfall of stunning curls, a crown materialised on her head, and radiance shone from every inch of her.

"Ah, Gatekeeper," she said. "So kind of you to come and watch my return. I do wish you hadn't stabbed my assistant, though."

Lord Daival dipped his head. "My Queen."

"Get back," I growled at her. "Get back into that cell, or so help me."

I sprang to my feet, directing my magic at the cell walls and willing them to grow once more. *Stop her. Cage her back in.*

If she walked free, the Court would fall, and every one of us would crumble along with it.

The Seelie Queen gave me a smile. "Admirable effort, Hazel, but I see you don't have that talisman you wrongly claimed in your hands."

Magic sparked into her palm, blindingly bright, and the walls of the jail crumbled around us. I squeezed my eyes shut and waited for the end.

20

My eyes flickered open to vibrant sky and warm sunlight. The remainder of the jail roof had gone, ripped clean away by the force of the Seelie Queen's power. The Sidhe, if any survived, had fallen into silence, stunned by the force of the blast. Piles of shattered tree branches and roots lay in place of the once sturdy jail, most reduced to a cloud of dust that caught in my lungs and made me cough uncontrollably.

Beneath the dust, Lord Daival crawled out of a pile of debris. His Queen had left him to be crushed by the collapsing building, it seemed, but she was nowhere in sight. Bodies lay throughout the jail, Sidhe guards and prisoners alike. Dread brewed in my chest. Outside the jail, some of the bodies stirred. My heart contracted at the sight of Coral crouching over her brother's limp form, her head bowed.

A pair of thorny vines wrapped around my wrists,

swinging me around to face Lord Daival. "You won't escape this time, Gatekeeper."

I bared my teeth at him. "Did your Queen seriously leave you behind? That's cold."

"I had some business to take care of." The Seelie Queen approached, her statuesque form glowing with health and magic. Not so much as a speck of dirt had touched her perfect visage, and she looked none the worse for her imprisonment. "We will reclaim my old estate first, I think. Bring the Gatekeeper with you, Daival, won't you?"

"Like *hell*." I fought against the thorny bonds, drawing blood. "You won't set one foot on the Erlking's territory."

Lord Daival snapped his fingers, and the vines yanked me forward as though I was nothing more than an animal to be herded. Ahead of him, a path appeared, leading away from the jail to a familiar set of gates. The Seelie Queen led the way, not needing a security talisman to urge the gates to open at her touch.

By now, the forest inside the Erlking's territory had grown thickly enough that the path was no longer visible. Earthy smells, crushed leaves and fragrant flowers replaced the decay which had once drenched the Erlking's home.

"You do remember you're the one who destroyed your old estate, don't you?" I gritted my teeth against a jab of pain as Lord Daival yanked me after him through the gates. "I suppose it's a waste of time to ask if you care that you probably killed your own allies when you blew up the jail back there, including those loyal cultists Lord Daival took the time to recruit."

"They were marked for death anyway," she said dismissively. "Come, Lord Daival."

The Seelie Queen took the lead. While she strode through the woods, the trees moved aside as though in response to an unheard command. Lord Daival walked one step behind her, a dutiful servant, tightening the vines until my hands were slick with blood. I knew he'd let me bleed out without a thought, but I lifted my head and glared at him, refusing to give ground.

The ruins of the Seelie Queen's estate peeked out from beneath a canopy of trees. One wave of her hand cleared the undergrowth blocking the entrance and freed the way into the main hall. As before, vines and weeds choked the hole in the floor where Lord Veren had used the Erlking's staff to murder Lord Kerien, and the ceiling had collapsed beneath moss-laden boughs.

Lord Daival dragged me to a halt behind him, waiting for instructions from his Queen. While his attention was on the manor house, I tugged at the vines on my arms, pushing the thorns towards the iron wristband on my arm. It wouldn't be as effective as hacking away with a knife, but inch by inch, the iron would wear away at the vines until they snapped.

The Seelie Queen waved a hand and cleared another wave of undergrowth from the doorway. "Pity the crown has gone... have you heard any whispers of its location?"

"I have not," said Lord Daival. "But I will find you another one, my queen. We will cure the sickness that has this realm in its grip. Whatever it is you desire, I promise that I will make it so."

I made gagging noises, my hands behind my back as I worked on freeing myself from the thorns. The vine on my left arm uncoiled when it came into contact with the iron, and I wriggled one hand free. Now we were getting somewhere.

Lord Daival twisted around to scowl at me. "I should cut out that deceitful tongue of yours."

"You must know she's glamoured the crap out of you," I said, hoping to keep his eyes on my face and not my hands. "She's the one who killed the Erlking and caused the realm to start rotting away. She's the sickness in this realm, Lord Daival, and she's corrupted you, too."

The Seelie Queen cleared more debris from the house with a snap of her fingers. "My late husband is the one who caused this when he took what was rightfully mine."

"The talisman?" I continued recklessly. She hadn't killed me, which meant she must still fear the backlash of my family's curse if she struck me dead. That, or she needed me alive for some other reason. "You must have agreed to the union with him. A vow goes both ways."

She was too clever to be manipulated, so she must have married him for a reason. It wasn't clear to me what she'd got out of the arrangement, except power she'd been unable to exercise. What had I heard once? That she had no magic of her own. The Sidhe had whispered that they must have married for love alone, for he had nothing to gain from their union and she had no talisman. Granted, the ability to heal from any injury was one hell of a useful power no matter how you looked at it, and whatever the Erlking's motives were, they'd remain as much a mystery as the true identity of the heir. Small comfort that the crown was elsewhere, in a hidden location that even I didn't know. After all, the Seelie Queen could easily make a crown of her own and rewrite the laws to fit her own agenda.

The stinging pain in my wrists lessened as the vines snapped. I shook them off, then conjured an illusion of the same thorns in their place. Lord Daival continued to gaze up at the Seelie Queen like a love-struck puppy, so I needn't have bothered. I took a step back, debating whether to attack or run. I could only stall them, but damn if I didn't wish the Erlking had left a weapon behind by which I could rid myself of both of them at once.

The Seelie Queen turned to Lord Daival. "Before I settle in here, I have a few matters to attend to," she said. "My late husband's talisman, for one. I think I can guess where you hid it, Hazel… the one place with magic that comes close to mine. But not close enough. Lock her away, Lord Daival, wouldn't you?"

"Of course, my Queen."

No.

My family didn't know she'd escaped and would be unprepared for her to enter the Lynn house and take the talisman. Worse, with her healing magic, even if the talisman didn't accept her, it would cause her no harm, and she'd be able to use its magic to destroy the Courts and rebuild her own from the ruins.

An image entered my mind, of the Seelie Queen sitting atop her throne with the staff in her hand. The last true immortal, able to destroy her enemies at a touch with the talisman I'd claimed.

Raw anger seared my veins. I shook the vines free from my wrists, yanked a knife from the sheath on my thigh and hurled it at the Seelie Queen.

I didn't expect to hit her, but for all her glamour, she didn't wear armour. The blade sank into her neck to the hilt, and her mouth parted in surprise, a thin trail of blood trickling down her ivory-white skin.

Lord Daival released a hoarse cry, as though he was the one who'd been stabbed, and I ran for my life, hurtling through the undergrowth and out of the forest. Wild panic drove me onward, and I skidded to a halt in front of the gates, which didn't yield when I pushed on them. *Dammit, Lord Daival must have locked them.*

A wave of thorns flew at me from behind. I ducked and rolled behind an exposed tree root, grabbing another iron knife.

"How *dare* you strike my queen?" Lord Daival's face was white with rage, thorns gleaming on his hands. "Your blood will feed the forest and our territory will grow strong from your flesh."

"Lord Daival," said the Seelie Queen. Her voice was no longer melodic, but low and raspy. Yet despite the crimson blood soaking her neck, the wound had sealed closed, and she held a pointed blade in her hand. "Please do not kill the Gatekeeper. I plan to deal with her later... after I take care of her family, that is. Restrain her."

Thorns pierced my arms, the bonds reforming, and the gates sprang open to allow the Seelie Queen through. I threw myself after her with a snarl of fury, but Lord Daival kicked me viciously in the back of the leg, pointing his blade at my throat.

"Go on." My leg throbbed, blood dampening my wrists. "I dare you to kill the Gatekeeper and see what the aftermath of my family's curse does to you. This curse outlasted the Erlking's death, Lord Daival, and there's a good reason the Seelie Queen hasn't ordered you to kill me. She knows it would destroy you both. Would you risk the life of your queen to see me dead at your hands?"

Fury glinted in his eyes, but a hint of doubt crept in. Nobody knew the contents of the Gatekeeper's vow—the vow I'd loathed all my life, yet the only thing that might save me.

"The Queen wishes you to live," he growled. "You might be an effective weapon if this curse of yours can be utilised effectively against our enemies."

No thanks. "Nah, I think I'll pass."

As far as I knew, nobody in the Court knew the truth of how the curse had ensnared my family—but Etaina did. It'd be nice to imagine Darrow's Court would show up to help me out, but they'd forsaken the Summer Court long ago, and Etaina would shed no tears when it was gone.

"You have no choice, Hazel Lynn," said Lord Daival. "We will build a new Court from the ashes of this one, a single one uniting Summer and Winter. The mortal realms will bow before us, and the lesser Courts will crumble at our feet."

"Yeah, that's not gonna go the way you think, mate." But who was left in Summer to challenge him? As for the lesser Courts like the Sea Kingdom, they hadn't the armies to stand up to Summer. Winter might be able to fight back, but did they have an equivalent to the Erlking's talisman? Even if they did, the Sidhe weren't known to care about collateral damage. Earth would suffer no matter the outcome.

Dammit, I need to get the fuck out of here and back to my family. My gaze skimmed over Lord Daival. He must have the key to the gates somewhere on him, and he hadn't noticed how I'd broken the vines the first time he'd used them on me.

"I guess she hasn't fixed up the torture rooms or prison cells yet," I said to him. "So we'll have to stand here until she gets back. Do you have anywhere I can sit down? My leg hurts."

"Stop talking."

I twitched my hands. "Your Queen told you to keep me alive, so if I bleed out, she'll be pissed at you, you know. Even if you ignore the whole *backfiring curse* issue. I heard one person who tried to flee the curse was ripped in two, one half on each side of the Ley Line."

He gave me a flinty look. "You don't look like you're on the verge of death."

"Aww. That was almost sweet of you." I moved my wrists up and down to bring the vines closer to the iron band. "I never asked—did you ever tell your followers the truth in the end? I mean, that you had no intention of putting the Erlking back on the throne?"

"I never lied to them," he said. "They heard what they wanted to believe, no more."

I bet they did. After all, the Seelie Queen had done the same to him. Over the years he'd worked for her, she'd poisoned his mind and turned him against the Court. Lord Daival's confidence in her abilities was absolute, but as for his confidence in himself? To place his faith in her suggested he craved a strong leader to tell him what to do. Just like the Erlking's worshippers had absolute faith in their leader to do the impossible and return from death.

"Lord of Thorns?" One arm broke free of the vines. "Was it you who started that one, or did someone else give you the nickname?"

He said nothing, but his hands twitched at his sides as though he longed to strangle me. My gaze lingered on the sword at his waist which he hadn't unsheathed yet. That one had to be the security talisman.

"Did you two used to hang out here all the time?" I went on. "Back when you were lovers? Was that how you entertained yourselves over the long years? It must have been excruciating to go back into the Court and pretend to worship the Erlking instead."

"Be *quiet.*"

"I bet she uses the talisman on you as soon as it's in her hand," I added. "You know what the Erlking did after she betrayed him? He started from scratch. Fired all his advisors and hired new ones. The two of them are more alike than she'd ever admit, and she doesn't trust anyone. The difference is that she won't just fire her advisors. She'll kill you to ensure you tell nobody her secrets."

"She trusts me above all others," he said. "I'm the one who set her free."

"Wait and see," I continued. "As soon as she has her throne, she'll start seeing enemies everywhere, especially among those who saw her at her weakest. Look at how she let the jail collapse on top of you and left you to drag yourself out of the ruins. Trust me, she wouldn't care if you died."

A muscle ticked in his jaw. "I am her trusted assistant."

"That's a fancy word for 'expendable'."

"She healed me." His voice rose louder, yet the slightest tremor remained underneath. "She used her magic to heal the wound you dealt me."

"Like a master healing their servant, that's all," I said. "She'll have her army waiting in the Vale, and she'll replace you soon enough. She doesn't care for anyone but herself, Lord Daival. You're nothing more than a puppet, easily discarded and cast aside as soon as she finds someone better."

He snarled, advancing on me, and I hurled my knife at him. The blade sank deep into his chest, and he toppled backwards, his mouth gaping open.

"You should have realised how I broke the thorns the first time." I waved the wristband engraved with the name *Lynn* as I reached down and plucked the security talisman from his belt. "Amateur move there, Lord Daival."

I hadn't quite hit his heart—that armour was a bloody nuisance—but I didn't care about Lord Daival anymore. Stopping the Seelie Queen from reaching my family was more important.

Then I'd take that talisman from her or die trying.

21

*P*lease, please don't let me be too late.

I broke into a sprint, ignoring the sting of the thorns' scratches on my hands and arms and the throbbing pain in my leg where Lord Daival had kicked me. Reaching the end of the path, I veered past the jail's ruins, where more Sidhe gathered to fetch their wounded and dead, and continued on towards the ambassadors' palace.

As I reached the doors, Darrow stepped into my path. *Shit. Not now.*

"Hazel." He hurried to intercept me. "You escaped?"

"I know." I kept walking, heading for the Summer gates. "The Seelie Queen has gone after my family."

"She hasn't." He caught my arm. "Lady Aiten and some of the other Sidhe who survived the blast chased her down and set up an ambush for her. She didn't reach your family, Hazel."

My shoulders sagged with relief. "The jail is gone, though. What will they do with her?"

"Leave it to the Sidhe," he insisted. "Get your family away from the Courts. I'll come with you."

Damn. He just had to offer to do the impossible. "You should go back to Etaina and warn her in case the Seelie Queen goes after her next."

"She won't," he said, continuing to walk alongside me. "I meant what I said—my mission isn't the important thing anymore, Hazel. I wish I'd seen it earlier."

My heart stuttered. "Please—don't."

Don't care too much. Don't make me do this.

We both knew the Seelie Queen's healing magic would make it all but impossible for the Sidhe to ensnare her, with or without the jail intact. Only the talisman would suffice, and the emotion shining in his eyes was proof enough that I'd have to shatter both our hearts if I wanted him to live.

Darrow's hand reached for mine. "I'm not asking you to come with you out of manipulation, or because Etaina asked me to. I'm asking you because the thought of losing you is more than I could bear."

My throat closed up. "Can't you just trust that I have a plan? I have to do this alone."

I pulled my hand out of his and covered the short distance to the Summer gates. Shadows flowed from the edges into the surrounding forest, eating away at the moss on the gates and turning the vibrant Summer leaves to ashes.

Darrow swore. "The Erlking's talisman—"

"My talisman." The shadows nudged the gate open, tingling against my skin. The grass beyond lay shrivelled and dead, and darkness blanketed the hedges. "It's mine,

Darrow, and I'm going to use it to defeat the Seelie Queen."

I didn't close the gates behind me, but I heard no footsteps on my heels as I hurried into my family's garden. Silence lay thickly over the lawn, while shadowy magic extended long limbs over the hedges from the Inner Garden, seeking life to feed on.

Seeking their master.

"Mum?" I shouted. "Ilsa?"

No reply came. A dark patch near the door to the house drew my eye, and dread pooled inside me. I skidded to a halt at the back door, my heart plummeting into the earth.

A doorway into the Vale lay in mid-air, gaping like the open mouth of some great beast. The Seelie Queen hadn't gone after the talisman at all. She'd taken my family and left the talisman as bait so I'd have no choice but to claim it if I wanted to get them back.

My heart pounded in my ears, the cuts on my arms trickling with blood. Shadows lapped at the blood, drawing closer, hugging my limbs. A whisper rang through my head… *mine. This is mine.*

I ran to the Inner Garden, or what was left of it. The pool was more of a puddle now, its surface grey and shadowy, while the staff lay propped against the bank. My hands sank into the water and the cuts from the thorns closed up, the pain in my leg vanishing at the touch of the healing magic.

"I've come to take you back," I whispered to the talisman.

My hand closed around the hilt, and pain rippled through my arm, breaking my grip. Shadows pulsed out from the talisman, knocking me clean off my feet. My back slammed into the cracked earth, leaving me winded. "What the—?"

Climbing upright, I reached for the talisman again. Shadows lashed at me, sending me flying back into the hedge. Sharp leafless branches speared my arms.

"Stop that!" I snapped. "Stop it. I'm here to claim you. I'm not going to abandon you this time—"

The shadows wrapped around my extended arms, but rather than a pleasant tingling sensation, they brought an uncomfortable itch that felt like sharp nails were scratching at my skin. Like those thorns were back, tightening their grip. *Is it feeding on my life force?*

I fought hard, unable to move, even with my instincts screaming at me to flee. "If you kill me, the Seelie Queen will claim you. She'll use you to destroy everything... she'll destroy us all."

I knew the talisman could understand me on some level, but if I'd truly left it too late, it'd devour my fragile human flesh from my bones as it had done to the others who'd tried to hold it without claiming its power.

"Hazel!" shouted a voice from behind me.

Dammit. Darrow had followed me after all.

"Stay back!" I shouted, without turning around. "If you come any closer, it'll kill you, too."

I didn't need to look at him to know the stubborn fool hadn't moved an inch. A fresh wave of emotion gripped me. Not just fear—but anger, too. *Don't you dare attack him, talisman. Don't you dare.*

With a roar of fury, I broke free of the shadows and lunged at the pool, grabbing the talisman with both hands. "You won't break me, talisman. You're mine."

The itching sensation ceased. Instead, an odd vibration travelled beneath my skin, almost like the murmur of a voice I couldn't quite hear. The implication was clear: *do not abandon me again, or you will die at my touch.*

A rush of dizzying magic spread from the shadows under my skin, into my bones and blood. Shadows threaded through my fingertips, no longer feeding on me but sustaining me. Like a breath taken after submersion underwater, like the first glimpse of sunlight after days of darkness, the talisman awakened a part of me that had been sleeping ever since I'd given it up.

This is mine.

Darrow's sharp intake of breath made me wheel around. He stared at me, as though I'd punched him so hard in the chest that I'd knocked all the fight out of him. "Hazel."

"Don't come any closer." I backed up a step, gripping the staff with both hands. "I can't control it. It *wants* to feed on anything living, and it won't stop now I've claimed it. I need to use it to destroy the Seelie Queen. It's the only way."

He took a step across the lawn, indicating the house. "There's an opening to the Vale over there, Hazel."

"I know." I stepped out of the grove, mentally calculating the distance between us. "You need to go further away from me. If you don't, the shadows will reach you, and I won't be able to stop them from hurting you."

He didn't move. Neither did the shadows. "You gave the talisman up, didn't you? That's why you managed to hide it."

"I did," I said, "but I need it now. I'm going to the Vale to save my family, and then I'm coming for the Seelie

Queen. You should leave. I don't think it's going to let me go so easily next time."

"You can't go back into the Court with that," he said. "The Sidhe will destroy you."

A grim smile stirred on my face. "Do you really think it'll let them?"

I let the words hang between us like Lord Daival's thorns given voice. Loathing ate at me from the inside, even as part of me revelled in the flow of shadowy magic roaring in my veins. The grass shrivelled under my feet, and in the house, the lights flickered and died as I ran for the entrance into the Vale.

Tears stung my eyes, tears I refused to let fall. Darrow would be fine. He'd live. That's all that mattered. Etaina wouldn't punish him for leaving the talisman in the hands of its new wielder in order to preserve his own life. There was nothing more to do for him.

My family needed me. They needed my talisman's power.

On the other side of the doorway, silver-lit paths greeted me, and this time, I felt an odd kinship with them. The Vale was the talisman's natural habitat, and a long time ago, the gods had once walked along these winding paths, driven out of their home by the wrathful Sidhe.

"Give me my family back," I told the path. "Take me to them."

The staff in my hands vibrated, shadows flickering around the edges. I needed to do this fast. Then I'd go after the Seelie Queen, using the talisman to subdue her long enough for the Sidhe to find a way to cage her again. And then...

They won't let you back into the Court, Hazel.

My shoulders stiffened. The voice in my head sounded like me, but not quite. The shadows moved as it spoke, their cold caress brushing against my skin.

You will be exiled. They will strip my magic from you and leave you to die.

They will kill you.

You'll be a human again, weak, insignificant.

"Stop it," I muttered, quickening my pace. "I need to save my family. You can gripe at me later."

There will be no later. Let the Court handle their wayward Queen. If you go back to them, you will die.

The voice quietened as a dark shape moved across my path. Its body was like an unnaturally tall, emaciated humanoid with saucer-like eyes. A sluagh. I let go of the staff to grab my weapon, but the shadows lashed out of their own accord, disintegrating the beast into wisps of smoke.

"You're efficient, I'll give you that," I told the talisman. "Thanks."

I do not do this as a favour. I am yours, and you are mine.

"That makes it sound like we're married," I said. "I guess the Gatekeeper's rule says, 'no dating faeries', not 'no eternal bindings to dodgy ancient artefacts which contain the magic of a dead god', so you're probably safe from the backlash there. Can you sense my sister's talisman?"

Silence came from the staff. If all else failed, I could always employ my best weapon against it—annoying chatter.

"Come on," I told the path. "Take me there. I know you know where my family is."

You are wasting your time, Hazel. Your family would be

better off here than in the Courts. The Sidhe will kill them along with you.

"You can't know that," I said. "I won't abandon them. They deserve to be allowed to live their own lives."

And you don't? I know your heart, Hazel Lynn. I know you think of yourself as the one who must make the sacrifice. You could be more than this. This realm could be your kingdom. You could rule.

The shadows formed a cloak around my shoulders, and I shivered. "I don't want to rule."

How do you know? You've never allowed yourself to imagine. Your entire family have been slaves to this curse of yours for generations.

"I told you, I don't want a crown." I'd never dreamt of sitting on a throne, and not just because that would never be an option for my family. As I'd since seen in Faerie, a crown was just another kind of cage. "I want freedom. That's all."

Freedom is an illusion. You're mine, Hazel Lynn. I know your heart.

"You're not the only one, considering I wear it on my sleeve." My steps halted when the path abruptly cut out. A pit lay below, a yawning chasm of darkness, and above it, a cage hung suspended in the air.

Ilsa, Morgan and Mum sat inside the cage, surrounded by darkness that mingled with the shadows of my own talisman's magic.

The shadows' voice whispered in my ear, *I am death and life all in one. I destroy, in order to be. I am the Devourer.*

2 2

I halted on the edge of the cliff, staring into the abyss. "What the hell?"

The shadowy cage hung suspended from nothingness, and a void of darkness filled the space around it. Within, shapes stirred, their shadowy forms flickering with remnants of their magic. Wraiths. The gleam of Ilsa's talisman shone from inside the cage, and while it would have been enough to get rid of the wraiths under normal circumstances, it was all but impossible here in the Vale where there was nowhere to banish the dead.

"Hazel!" Ilsa yelled at me from the cage. "It'd be nice if you gave us a hand."

"I'm working on it." Dammit, how was I supposed to get them out of there? Shadows swirled around my hands, further darkening my vision and smothering the ground beneath my feet. The staff wasn't any use in this situation, not when it prevented me from seeing how to get through the shadows to my family. The wraiths didn't help either, all but invisible in the darkness.

But the talisman fed on magic, and the wraiths were nothing *but* magic.

"Hang tight," I gritted out.

I gave a wild swing with the talisman, directing a volley of shadows at the nearest wraith. The shadowy creature recoiled away from the darkness, and its brethren backed off, fearing the talisman's bite.

A blaze of blue light appeared as Ilsa held up her own talisman, sending a wave of magic at the wraith I'd pushed back. The beast flew sideways into the shadowy assault of my talisman, evaporating into nothingness.

"Nice job," she breathed out. "They're scared of both of us. We can take them."

"You bet." Shadows spread from my hands, extending like tentacles over the abyss to chase the dead away from my family. A wild laugh brewed in my throat. *Even death fears the talisman.*

"I banish you, dickhead," Morgan yelled from inside the cage. His hands glowed with blue light, pushing one of the wraiths back into the path of my talisman. He must have really upped his necromancy game since joining the guild, and if he'd tried it on Earth, the banishment would have worked. But here, death did not exist. Only oblivion.

And my shadows were thirsty for magic to feed on.

Wraiths fled the shadows, but there was nowhere for them to run. I snagged them one at a time, the staff directing my hand. I hardly felt like myself, lost in the haze of shadows, caught between darkness and deeper dark. Shock jolted through me when I looked down to see oblivion beneath my feet. The darkness held me upright, sustained me.

"Hey!" Ilsa said. "Not to kill your game, Hazel, but I

can't see how to get out of this cage when you keep throwing shadows everywhere. Can you turn down the darkness, please?"

Reeling, I came to myself, backing away from the cage. My heart thundered like the hoofbeats of the Wild Hunt; sweat slicked my hands beneath the cover of darkness. I'd killed the wraiths, but the darkness remained absolute, and the talisman's laughter echoed in the back of my mind. *You're human, Hazel. You cannot fight the dark. I will devour you, too.*

"Hazel." Mum's voice came from the gloom. "You're still Gatekeeper."

"I know." What did that matter? Even my circlet's light didn't penetrate the gloom.

Or did it?

With difficulty, I retracted the shadows and tapped into my Gatekeeper's powers. The sudden shock of green light temporarily blinded me, before illuminating the thin bars of the cage hovering above utter darkness.

"I don't think I can get you out without you falling into the abyss," I admitted. "I can't *move* the cage."

Morgan groaned. "You've gotta be kidding me."

"Yeah, I'd rather that didn't happen." Ilsa tugged at the cage bars, and shadows began to creep up my hands as though trying to dispel the remnants of my Gatekeeper's magic. I'd almost become the Devourer then, in the heat of battle, and the talisman had all but swamped the human in me.

But underneath, I was still the Gatekeeper. I was still a Lynn, and I would see to it that my family got out of this in one piece.

The image of the Lynn house appeared in my mind's

eye. "Guys, I think I know how to get you out, but it's risky."

"I'm all ears," said Ilsa.

I drew in a breath. "I have no idea if I can open a doorway back home over the abyss, but I can try. I need to be on top of the cage, though."

Please, please don't let the shadows hurt my family.

Destruction wasn't the only consequence of my talisman's magic. The Devourer might claim otherwise, but the talisman came with another side effect… the ability to cross realms at will.

Ilsa leaned forward, her face glowing in the blue light of her talisman. "You can do that?"

I hope so. I leapt at the cage, gripping the bars with my free hand. The cage swung above nothingness, and for a terrifying instant, it wavered beneath my grip. *An illusion.* Glamour or not, if it vanished, my family would fall into an oblivion darker than the shadows in my hands.

Holding the shadows back, I willed a doorway into the Court to open below the cage. The shadows flickered, and then grey light filtered through, a window-sized doorway appearing behind the others.

"Oh, thank fuck." Morgan peered through the doorway. "Is it safe over there?"

"The Lynn house is fine," I told them. "It's still standing. The Court might not be, but if you run for the Summer gate, you should be okay. Don't let anything in Faerie distract you, that clear?"

Morgan grabbed Mum's arm and helped her climb through the doorway, but Ilsa hesitated. "Aren't you coming with us?"

I shook my head, hanging onto the cage and trying not

to think of the nothingness beneath us. "Not yet. I can't risk doing any more damage to the house's magic or hurting any of you. I'm not in control." To say the least. The talisman and I had a reckoning to face, one way or another.

Ilsa made an exasperated noise. "You know I'm not gonna leave you alone here, Hazel."

What was with people risking their necks on my behalf? Maybe I should have done what Darrow did and intentionally alienated everyone I met so nobody would attempt any heroic sacrifices. "I'll be okay, Ilsa. I have the talisman."

"You—" Ilsa broke off, recoiling from the darkness behind the open doorway. "You missed one."

Shadowy magic coalesced into the form of another wraith, larger than the others, more *present*. Raw fear filled me like ice in my lungs at the sight of the transparent, skeletal shape before me.

You think I died? The talisman's laugh vibrated in my bones. *My body may have expired, but part of me lived, Hazel Lynn. I survive thanks to you. You woke me.*

It wasn't the ghost of a Sidhe, but something much, much worse. The ghostly form of whatever had once owned the magic that lived inside my talisman hovered in the air, eyes like dark pits, body cloaked with shadows.

An Ancient.

"That's... not a regular wraith," I said through numb lips. "It's... the Devourer."

Ilsa's eyes widened. "That's its name?"

"So it tells me." The tilting cage reminded me of the insubstantial surface beneath my feet. "Ilsa, please go through the doorway. I won't let it follow you."

"Like hell am I leaving you alone." Ilsa held up her own talisman, which gleamed blue around the edges as though sensing the presence of another god. On the cover, the image of the raven stirred, and the wraith moved closer, extending a skeletal hand.

The cage's illusion broke, and Ilsa and I fell into the abyss. Biting back a scream, I waved the talisman, demanding the shadows break our fall.

Ilsa yelled in alarm, clutching at me. Then my feet touched solid ground, and the shadows cleared to reveal the winding path of the Vale. I reeled, holding onto the staff with everything I had.

"It was an illusion." Ilsa stood at my side, her face chalk-white. "Even the creature which brought us here."

"You did this," I told the wraith. "You put my family in danger to force me to claim you back. Don't deny it."

Even the initial rejection was a ruse, a ploy to make me desperate enough to promise to never give up the talisman's magic this time around.

"Why did you ever think a mere human like yourself could control me?" whispered the shadows.

"Because we Lynns aren't normal humans." Ilsa held up her own talisman, and the image of the raven on the cover brandished its claws at the wraith. "Sorry to disappoint you, but you aren't the first Ancient to choose to serve a Lynn. We understand how you operate."

"That one is nothing to me," whispered the wraith. "I have sensed your power, Gatekeeper of Death, and I find it lacking."

"Then you just weren't looking hard enough." Ilsa didn't flinch when the wraith's shadows folded back like a cloak and its skeletal hand reached for her. Bile burned the back of my throat at the sight of its foul, rotting form. Was this what Ilsa saw with her spirit sight whenever she set eyes on a wraith?

"Don't you dare touch my sister," I told the shadows.

"It's not alive." Ilsa gave the wraith a calm look. "I know it seems like it is, but the gods died out. What's left in there is barely a fragment of its power. I will stay here and help you master the talisman, Hazel. I won't leave you alone in the Vale. You own the staff. You can control it."

Oh, god, Ilsa. I'd have done the same if our positions had been reversed and would never have condemned her to die alone in the Vale even with a life-destroying talisman in her hands, but that same blasted Lynn stubbornness might be the death of us all.

"Fragment, am I?" whispered the shadows. "I think not."

As the wraith moved in, I threw myself over Ilsa's body, shielding her from its touch. The wraith's magic engulfed me, and waves of coldness drove prickling needles under my skin, seeking the warmth beneath. Striving to rip the talisman's power out of me and take it back to feed its rotting soul.

"You can't destroy me," I told the wraith. "I'm Gatekeeper. I belong to the Court of Summer."

"You belong to me, human," whispered the wraith. "You will yield your freedom or surrender your power and let me devour your soul."

"Like hell." I tightened my grip on the talisman, but the shadows smothering me were no more under my control than Faerie itself. The wraith might be a mere fragment, but its magic came from a vast abyss even the Sidhe had feared.

Ilsa stirred, pinned somewhere beneath me. The sharp blue glow of her own talisman mingled with a faint green light somewhere in the gloom. Not grey, but Summer green. My circlet. Somehow, it was still glowing, even though the wraith's magic should have devoured it. There was no power to draw on in this realm, nothing but the circlet itself, and yet it endured.

Lord Daival might have dismissed my Gatekeeper's powers, but they'd remained intact even when Ilsa had stripped the talisman's magic from me. I hadn't thought anything of it at the time, but the power that ran through my family's bloodline along with the curse our name carried went deeper than the staff's power. It must be older than—or at least as potent as—the talisman itself.

I tapped into my circlet's magic, and the light grew brighter, pushing the shadows back. The circlet's magic was like the pool in the Inner Garden—it fuelled itself, restoring its magic as quickly as it disappeared. The shadows folded back, freeing Ilsa and me, until nothing remained but the staff in my hand and the wraith hovering on the path.

"You will not defy me, Gatekeeper," whispered the shadows. "You are mine."

"No, I'm not." I lifted my head, directing the bright green glow at the wraith. It recoiled, hissing, but there was nowhere to go. I'd banished the darkness from the path, revealing its pitiful, vulnerable form.

And the staff is still mine.

"Hazel." Ilsa nudged me. "I can banish it, but I need the name."

"The...?" Shit. Of course. If you spoke an Ancient's name, it could be summoned or banished in a manner similar to blood magic or necromancy. Names were power, and the Ancients' language carried such potency that no human could speak the words aloud… except one who had the protection of an Ancient's magic.

In other words, like Ilsa or me.

I flipped the staff over. Runes covered its length, but the dark coating was too dark to see through. I willed the remaining shadows to retreat into the staff until the merest flicker remained on the surface. The symbols grew clearer, readable. Their meanings slipped through my mind, but I understood every symbol, every word. The magic gave me the knowledge, and I whispered the word, the name.

"Stop," hissed the wraith. "Stop it."

I said the name again, louder, and the wraith recoiled, hissing. Power welled beneath my skin, and a grin curled my lip. "I know your name, which gives me mastery over you. You should have thought twice before yielding one fragment of your power to a human, because right now? I have more power than you do. You're nothing."

Ilsa raised her voice. "On three, Hazel. I banish you—"

We both raised our talismans and spoke the name, and the piece of the Devourer's consciousness shattered.

All that remained was the staff in my hand, the winding path of the Vale—and a tall figure approaching Ilsa and me.

The Seelie Queen.

23

"You." I gripped the staff with both hands. "Those wraiths were yours, weren't they? What other monsters have you enslaved?"

"I didn't need to enslave them," she said. "They flocked to me. Yes, even the Devourer."

She was one of the Sidhe who banished the gods and stole their magic. She'd even known the god whose power was in the staff. Which meant the Erlking had, too.

Ilsa stepped to my side, holding her own talisman tight to her chest. "We killed him. He was already dead, thanks to you. You're one of the Sidhe who killed the gods or kicked them out of Faerie, aren't you?"

The Seelie Queen's gaze flicked to the Gatekeeper's book. "They would not bend to our will, so we forced them to. A fair exchange, one you mortals wouldn't understand."

"My Queen!" Lord Daival walked to her side, his silvery hair gleaming in the Vale's eerie light. "I will not allow you to harm her again, mortals."

"Oh, you're still top of my hit list, don't worry." I sent a wave of shadows at him, but the Seelie Queen stepped in the way, the talisman's magic dissipating the instant it touched her.

"See, mortal?" Lord Daival's voice brimmed with triumph. "My Queen wants nothing more than for me to rule at her side."

I snorted. "She's not defending you out of the goodness of her heart. Look what she did to the Erlking."

"She never loved him," spat Lord Daival. "She cares for me above everyone else."

The expression on the Seelie Queen's face could hardly be called loving. More like the look of an indifferent monarch regarding an expendable subject.

"You know, I kind of feel sorry for you," said Ilsa.

Lord Daival advanced on her, and I barred his path, my staff outstretched. "If you set one foot near my family, I will flay your queen before your eyes while you watch."

"You cannot destroy me, Hazel," said the Seelie Queen. "No matter what you do, I will endure. I was there at the creation of the Courts themselves, and you will beg for death at my hands when that talisman takes your soul."

"As a matter of fact—" I raised the talisman—"The Devourer and I have come to an understanding."

The Seelie Queen's brows arched. "Is that so?"

"You lie." Lord Daival's face pinched with rage, and he hurled a handful of thorns at me.

With the talisman in my hand, it was easy to block his attacks and send handfuls of shadow to feast on the magic coursing through his blades. Yet I was tired, and while he wasn't the most skilled fighter I'd faced, his Sidhe speed coupled with the thorns made it hard to gain ground.

Time to fight dirty.

I spun behind the Seelie Queen to avoid his attack. The thorns dropped harmlessly to the floor, but he exclaimed in rage. "How dare you use my lady as a shield?"

Thorns rose into the air, aimed at me. Ilsa blasted him with her own talisman, sending the thorns scattering into the shadows. My sister and I stood back to back, fighting the wave of thorns. Her talisman hummed, its magic resonating with mine. A smile formed on my mouth. *We both fight with the power of the gods. Not as its pawns, but as its masters.*

The Seelie Queen made an impatient noise. "Stop toying with them, Lord Daival. Destroy the spare and subdue the Gatekeeper."

"If you call my sister a *spare* once again, I'll see if your healing power can grow you a new head." Shadows arced from my hands, forcing Lord Daival to back away, the thorns wilting in his hands. He conjured a fresh wave of vines, only for them to be swallowed up in the shadows. He gritted his teeth, sending vine after vine at Ilsa and me—so intent on his goal, he didn't see the human figure slip up behind him.

Then, Lord Daival staggered, an iron blade protruding from his neck. Behind him, Mum withdrew the blade, and the shadows came to life in my hands. The former Gatekeeper nodded to me. She'd done what she came for.

The talisman's magic surged over Lord Daival's body, the flesh disintegrating, bones turning to ashes. When there was nothing left, the talisman's shadows retracted, satisfied.

For an instant, the Seelie Queen and I looked at one

another, and there was something like respect in her eyes when she regarded the talisman in my hands. *I was right. She didn't love Lord Daival. Poor bastard.* "It's not too late for you to join me. I would have you rule at my side, Hazel, an ally if not a queen."

"No thanks." I raised the staff, and she sidestepped with dizzying speed, vanishing into the woods of the Vale. "Get *back* here."

Mum shouted my name, but I was already running after her. The Vale's path changed, hiding the Seelie Queen from view. I focused hard, willing the Vale to take me to her. The Seelie Queen appeared, and an instant later, she vanished once more. It was a battle of wills, and she had infinitely more willpower than I did. Her healing power was relentless, while my energy levels had plunged below zero long ago. I was running on adrenaline and magic and little else.

"Damn you!" I called the shadows again, which unfurled around me, cloaking my body. "You will obey me, Vale, like you obeyed the gods who used to walk your paths."

The Seelie Queen flickered into view. "Do you truly think you have the power to harness the gods, and I have none of my own? This is my domain, Hazel Lynn, not Summer, and I have an army waiting for me."

Ghostly forms appeared behind her, and a wall of the dead rose to surround me on all sides. Wraiths... hundreds of them, bringing a chill to my skin and masking even the talisman's shadows.

My hand froze to the staff. I couldn't move an inch. I'd given too much of the shadows when I'd destroyed the

Devourer, and I didn't have enough power left to beat them.

Then Darrow appeared in my peripheral vision, his hand alight with magic.

"Stay back," I whispered through numb lips. "You can't fight the dead. Get out while you can."

The cold sensation disappeared. The ghosts recoiled, while the Seelie Queen's eyes widened. "You're… you're supposed to be dead."

Unable to stop myself, I turned around. Darrow's body floated in a halo of light against a starless backdrop—a dark void that drew me in, and the ghosts, too, drawn to him like a planet orbiting a star.

Nothing else existed. He spoke, but the words ran together, blurring to meaninglessness. I fought oblivion, and oblivion won.

———

"Hazel?" Darrow leaned over me. He was within range of the talisman's shadowy magic, yet it didn't harm him.

"Where…?" I waved a hand vaguely at the spot where the Seelie Queen had been.

"She's gone," he said. "She took her army and ran."

"She was afraid of you." *She knew where your magic came from. She knew the Aes Sidhe when they lived in Summer, because their leader is her sister.* "I mean, the glamour."

"It happens." The hitch in his breath tugged at something deep inside me. I became aware of my hands clenched around the staff, and him kneeling beside me. If he'd wanted to, he might have taken the talisman to his queen at any point while I'd been enthralled by his glamour… but he hadn't.

As though he'd heard my thoughts, his gaze dropped to the staff, and my death grip on the hilt.

I swallowed hard. "Will the vow kill you if you fail to take the talisman?"

"No," he said. "I was ordered to find it and bring it to her. Not claim it."

"You did find it." I pushed my body into a sitting position. "If you don't bring it to her…"

"She didn't specify a time frame." Jaw clenched, he looked away. "I will not betray you, Hazel."

"Hazel!" shouted Ilsa. "Get through here—quickly. They're coming."

"Who—?" I used the staff to push myself to my feet, and a flash of light sent a wave of dread rushing through me. *Sidhe. They're here.* I leaned on the staff for balance and looked directly at Darrow. "Get out while you can. They might spare my life, but they'll kill you if they catch you with me. I'm not rejecting you, I'm saving your life."

This time, thank the gods, he listened to me. Darrow took off with swift faerie steps, past Mum and Ilsa, and out of sight around the Vale's path.

Even if I hadn't been incapacitated, I'd never have outrun the Sidhe. The instant Darrow disappeared, Lady Aiten and her fellow Sidhe entered my line of sight, their eyes fixed on the talisman in my hands.

I'm so screwed.

"Watch out," I bluffed. "Don't come any closer. I can't control it. the Seelie Queen is loose in the Vale, and she's the one you want to find."

Short of handing over the staff and letting them tear

the magic out of me, there was nothing I could do. I'd betrayed them from the instant the talisman chose me.

It was over.

"Go and find the former Queen," Lady Aiten ordered her companions. "Hazel Lynn, come with me."

Light folded around us, and an instant later, we stood in the hall of the ambassadors' palace, which was much more crowded than earlier. Most of the Sidhe recoiled the moment they saw the talisman, backing to the edges of the room.

"You traitor," whispered Lady Aiten. "You claimed the Erlking's talisman, yet you told us it was lost in the Vale. You lied to the entire Court. Do you seek to rule over us?"

"No, of course not," I said. "I want the Seelie Queen gone and the Erlking's heir on the throne. That's all. I'm not going to challenge the new monarch, and I'm not looking to rule anyone."

Lady Aiten's flinty gaze pierced me. "Many would say the talisman proves your worth to take the throne yourself. Others would kill you for it.

"It's not Summer's talisman," I corrected. "The Erlking took it because he knew it would destroy the Courts if he didn't, not because he was the king. He kept himself isolated from the Court because it tried to destroy everything it touched. The talisman has a mind of its own. It's not your ally, but it's not mine, either."

"It is merely a tool," she said. "Not an ally, but a tool you have chosen to use."

"It's conscious." But I knew it was no use speaking to her. The lies I'd told had erased every truth I might speak. "It chose me, not the other way around."

"You will give it to us, then." She extended a hand. "Let

us take the talisman back and return it to where it belongs."

Dammit. "I can't do that. Not yet. I sort of… promised to keep it a bit, in exchange for it helping me defeat Lord Daival and the Seelie Queen."

Her cold gaze stripped the flesh from my bones. "Then there is nothing more to say to you. There will be no peace for you here, or anywhere else, Hazel Lynn."

The finality of her words sent chills through my blood. I turned my back and left the palace, my heart thudding in tandem with my footsteps.

My family stood outside, waiting for me, and I went to join them, heading for home—and exile.

24

Shadows coiled in my palm. Sweat gathered on my forehead as I sought to keep it under control, and the shadows withdrew into the talisman without touching the grass.

"Better," said Ilsa.

I wiped sweat from my face on my sleeve. "You're a ruthless teacher, you know."

"Blame the person who taught both of us." She jerked her head in the direction of the house.

In the week I'd been recuperating, the garden at the Lynn house had returned to normal, despite all the times my shadows had accidentally killed all the plants and cut out the house's electrical supply. Even the waters of the grove had returned to their usual blue sheen. If not for the thin trail of shadows wrapping around the talisman's hilt, it looked much like an ordinary wooden staff most of the time.

"Not sure I'm ready to try my luck in Faerie, though," I added. "Even the borderlands."

"Is that where Darrow went?" asked Ilsa.

"No, he went home first."

I'd seen no signs of Darrow since he'd gone to report to Etaina, which worried me a little. Okay, a lot. I'd expected the Aes Sidhe to show up on my doorstep any day now and insist I hand over the talisman. There was no reason for Etaina to fear me if she had an ample supply of those stones which countered the talisman's magic.

While Darrow might remain absent, most of the other half-faeries had relocated to the borderlands, including Coral. She'd made sure to stop by the house once or twice a week, since her own Queen had yet to call her back to the Sea Kingdom, and she'd been the only person aside from Darrow and my family who wasn't totally freaked out by the talisman.

How the Sea Queen would react when she found out I wielded the talisman was anyone's guess. Raine and Cedar, too. Raine's own talisman was similar enough that I was sure she'd guessed there was something up with me when we'd met, but she hadn't set eyes on the talisman, and I wasn't legally allowed to enter Faerie anymore.

"Try again," said Ilsa. "The flowerbeds this time."

I twirled the staff in my hands, directing the shadows to move and stopping short before they made contact with the flowering plants.

"Nice," said Ilsa. "See, you'll be fine in Faerie. If they ever let you back in. I kinda expected the Sidhe to kick us out of the house, to be honest."

"That would require them to come near the talisman again," I reminded her. "Pity it doesn't work on the one person we need it to."

No sign of the Seelie Queen had been seen since the

battle, but the lack of news meant little except that she'd continued to evade the Sidhe's attempts to recapture her. The Court wasn't supposed to be any of my business any longer, but damn if I didn't regret leaving it in such a state. It was bitterly ironic that my position as Gatekeeper had saved me from the talisman's wrath, yet the Sidhe had still kicked me out.

"No kidding." Ilsa picked up her own talisman. "Let's go and check up on Mum. She's spending way too much time indoors lately."

We found Mum in the living room of the house, sitting in her usual spot with stacks of papers all around her.

I prodded the top of the nearest pile with my staff. "Why are you still making that family tree? I thought Lady Aiten retracted all responsibilities from us."

Mum looked up from the topmost document. "To see who we might be dealing with when the Sidhe select their next leader. For all we know, they might be open-minded enough to accept a Gatekeeper who wields the staff."

"Open-minded?" I snorted. "The Sidhe wouldn't know the meaning of the word. Including whoever they pick as their next ruler."

"That's not it," Ilsa said. "There's another reason you're set on solving the puzzle."

Mum paused for a long moment before answering. "No new monarch has been named in the history of the Gatekeepers. We don't know how the curse will react."

"What—you mean if a new heir is named, they might gain power over our family?" I frowned. "The Erlking didn't have any power over me, though. No more than any other Sidhe, at any rate."

If even the talisman's magic couldn't fight against the

circlet's power... *who* had been the person to curse us? Who'd managed to circumvent the magic of the gods? Now I'd outright burned all bridges with Etaina, I might never know the truth, but that voice in the vision I'd seen from the memory-eater revisited my dreams more often than I'd care to admit.

The doorbell rang, and we all jumped.

"Ilsa, what you said about the Sidhe kicking us out of the house..." I lifted the staff, just in case.

"They wouldn't." She looked at Mum. "Would they?"

"That, or Etaina has come to duel me for the talisman." I walked to the door, bracing myself, and peered through the spyhole. Not Etaina, but close. Darrow stood on the doorstep. *Here we go.*

I opened the door. His gaze went to the staff in my hands, then back to my face.

"So you chose to keep it," he said.

"It was that or let the Sidhe kill me," I said. "And then leave the talisman in the Courts, where it would have left a trail of destruction behind it."

"I suppose that was your reasoning when you took it in the first place," he said. "When you led me to believe it was lost, along with everyone else."

Ouch. "I really am sorry, Darrow," I said. "I didn't mean to claim it, but once I did, I couldn't let anyone else know. You know why."

Despite the shadows swirling around the hilt, he didn't back away. "Where did you hide it?"

"The magic inside my family's grove has healing properties," I said. "The Seelie Queen told me it's the only thing close to her own healing magic, and it was the only way to avoid the talisman's magic damaging the Court. It feeds on any living thing it touches, and anything magical, too. I've got it under control for now, but that's always a risk."

Darrow said nothing. That was worse than a reprimand, if possible.

"Stop looking at me like that," I said, my voice brittle. "Wouldn't you have done the same? I trusted my family a damn sight more than any of the power-hungry dickheads in Faerie. Yes, including Etaina. If I'd given the talisman up, the Seelie Queen might have destroyed the Court. The Erlking was barely able to keep her in check, and she got through his defences in the end."

He remained quiet throughout my outburst. "It's not too late for you to give it up. Many Sidhe have given up their talismans without any ill effects."

I shook my head. "I know how to get rid of talisman's magic, but I don't trust anyone else to wield it. It's insidious and will corrupt anyone with even the noblest intentions. Only my Gatekeeper's magic stopped it from destroying me or turning me into a weapon. Not so sure anyone else has an equivalent."

"Perhaps Etaina knows."

"Nice try." I gave a sad smile. "Sorry, Darrow. You know, I do like you. I just have a complete shit show of a life. You should go back to your queen and tell her I threatened to kill you. She'll forgive you."

"She won't forgive me," he said. "This is the second time I've let down my Court, and she gave me one last chance, that's all."

"One last chance?" I echoed.

Was I about to learn the truth he'd killed the memory-eater to hide?

Darrow's mouth pinched. "The Aes Sidhe have lived underground for centuries. For that reason, the Sidhe rarely take in outsiders, but I was abandoned by my human family and left on their doorstep by my father, who was half-Aes Sidhe. As one of the few half-Sidhe with both Summer and Winter magic, I was lucky enough to fall under Etaina's attention."

He gave a measured pause, his gaze fixed at a point somewhere in the distance, while I waited for him to continue.

"Reyna was my friend from childhood," he went on. "She was also the daughter of a prominent Aes Sidhe, their first child in generations, and half-Sidhe, like me. We were close, and both of us wanted the respect of the other Aes Sidhe. As a result, we made a pact, and talked ourselves into signing up for a dangerous mission to hunt down a group of redcaps. If I succeeded, I'd gain a spot at Etaina's side."

Another pause. My heartbeat sped up, and I waited once again for him to speak.

Darrow closed his eyes. "Reyna wasn't ready for a mission on that scale, but I convinced them to let her come with me. I believed I could protect her if necessary, but I was wrong."

"I'm sorry," I whispered.

"She died," he said, the words soft, final. "And the redcaps made it into our Court. We chased them out, but the Court turned on me when they learned I'd compromised our safety. Her family knew Reyna had declared herself to me and saw to it that I found no friendship among my fellow Aes Sidhe. If not for Etaina's protection, they would have killed me."

A lump grew in my throat. "Of course it wasn't your fault."

"You should know that one mistake can change the course of your life, Hazel," he said quietly. "Etaina kept the other Sidhe from casting me out. She employed me as her personal guard, and when it became unbearable to stay in the land of the Aes Sidhe, I travelled all over the mortal realm and into the Courts.

Seven years have passed since that day, but the Aes Sidhe do not easily forgive. Despite that, I had Etaina's support and respect. She saved my life a dozen times over the years. I know you don't trust her, Hazel, but she is the reason I'm still alive. Perhaps that doesn't give me the place to judge whether she is worthy to hold the Erlking's talisman, but you are the second person I would trust to keep it from harming others."

She'd supported him when the rest of the Aes Sidhe had turned their backs on him. No wonder he wouldn't hear a word against her.

"So you're doing what?" I asked. "Staying in Summer? If they find out you're supporting me, they'll probably send their people to hunt you down as well. The only reason they haven't sentenced me to death is because of the talisman."

"They won't," he said. "Not while I'm here."

"You mean, not if you use your glamour," I said. "Can you talk them into letting me back in?"

He shook his head. "I can't reverse big decisions like that, not without applying a level of glamour that would draw attention to my Court."

"Because they'd start worshipping the air you tread on

and make you the next king?" I said. "Pity. I'd like to see Lady Aiten bow down to you."

"No, you wouldn't,' he said. "I may stay in Half-Blood Territory instead, but I won't use my glamour any more than I have to."

"Aren't you worried I'll turn the talisman against you?"

"No." He unfurled his palm, revealing the cool, round stone Etaina had given me. "I trust you not to, but just in case it decides to act of its own accord, I have this."

My heart stuttered in my chest. "You really want…?"

Did he seriously want to find a way to make it work between us? Even after everything I'd screwed up?

In answer, his mouth met mine, and he kissed me so hard I forgot all about the shadows coiling around my hands.

Ilsa cleared her throat behind me. "You have another visitor."

I looked up to find Holly Lynn hovering awkwardly by the gate, looking between Darrow and me in confusion.

"Until next time." Darrow dipped his head to me, then he was gone.

Holly stopped short at the sight of the staff in my hand. "I… heard you claimed a talisman. Is it true?"

I dragged my gaze from the spot where Darrow had vanished. "I guess I shouldn't be surprised the Unseelie Queen heard the rumours."

Holly eyed the shadows curling around the hilt. "Did that talisman once belong to the Erlking?"

"It did." There was no point in denying it—no doubt the Unseelie Queen already knew, and she'd be making her own plans as we spoke. "I claimed it by accident, though the Sidhe don't believe me."

"I heard they kicked you out," she said. "So why are you still in this house?"

"They never revoked my title as Gatekeeper," I told her. "They're a little busy dealing with the aftermath of the Seelie Queen's coup."

I knew better than to think she'd leave well enough alone now she had her freedom. For her, freedom wasn't enough. She wanted to rule Summer, and she wanted revenge on my family. What she'd do now she knew the Aes Sidhe survived—and her sister was still alive— remained to be seen.

"All right," said Holly. "So if you're still Gatekeeper, the curse is still active?"

"Yes…" I said, unsure what she was getting at. She'd all but said she wanted to keep the title of Gatekeeper for life the last time we'd seen one another. "Nothing will have changed for you. I'm the one who got kicked out of Faerie. Unless Winter's plotting to start a war, in which case they might invite me back. Or pick someone else to act in my place."

The Summer Court was weakened. There was no heir, which left them vulnerable not just to the outcasts but to the Winter Court. Despite that, I didn't believe Holly had come here for malicious reasons. In her place, I'd be curious, too.

"Winter has no plans to start a war with Summer," said Holly. "That's not why I'm here."

"Then why?" Shadows wrapped around my hand when my grip tightened. At some point, the power I'd gained over the talisman might weaken and it would start pushing its boundaries, but not yet. I still had time.

Holly hesitated. "This is going to sound kind of weird,

but a package showed up on my doorstep the other day. I think it might be yours."

"Mine?" Nobody delivered me snail mail. If the Sidhe wanted me, they showed up in person.

She held out a small box. "I found it on the doorstep. You see the emblem? It's Summer's."

The image of a unicorn's head stood out on the jewelled lid, while green light shone from its edges. There didn't appear to be a keyhole, but the instant I took the box from her, my circlet ignited. Light spread from my hands to the box, and the lid sprang open.

Inside sat a small creature, semi-transparent, with wings and pointed ears. I damn near dropped the box. "Hummingbird?"

No. it wasn't Darrow's sprite, but another, one who was supposed to be dead.

The Erlking's sprite opened his beady eyes, looked up at me, and flew around my head, settling on my shoulder. "My Queen."

ABOUT THE AUTHOR

Emma is the New York Times and USA Today Bestselling author of the Changeling Chronicles urban fantasy series.

Emma spent her childhood creating imaginary worlds to compensate for a disappointingly average reality, so it was probably inevitable that she ended up writing fantasy novels. When she's not immersed in her own fictional universes, Emma can be found with her head in a book or wandering around the world in search of adventure.

Find out more about Emma's books at www.emmaladams.com.

9 781915 250766